LOVE
IN
COLOUR

BOLU BABALOLA

HEADLINE

First published in 2020
by HEADLINE PUBLISHING GROUP

First published in paperback in 2021 by
HEADLINE PUBLISHING GROUP

13

Cataloguing in Publication Data is available from the British Library

Paperback ISBN 978 1 4722 6888 4

Typeset in Dante MT by CC Book Production
Printed and bound in Great Britain by Clays Ltd, Elcograf S.p.A.

Inside cover images © Shutterstock

Headline's policy is to use papers that are natural, renewable and recyclable products
and made from wood grown in sustainable forests. The logging and manufacturing
processes are expected to conform to the environmental regulations
of the country of origin.

HEADLINE PUBLISHING GROUP
An Hachette UK Company
Carmelite House
50 Victoria Embankment
London
EC4Y 0DZ

www.headline.co.uk
www.hachette.co.uk

To my parents, who taught me love,
To my God, who is love,
To my love.

Contents

New Tales

Introduction

To say that i love 'love' would probably be akin to me saying that I am quite fond of inhaling oxygen. Love is the prism through which I view the world. I truly believe it binds and propels us. This isn't a naive denial of the darkness that we know exists in the world, rather it is a refusal to allow the devastation, the horror or the heartache to consume us. It is affirming the knowledge that there is light. Love is that light. Romance sweetens the casual bitterness we can encounter; it heightens the mundane and makes the terrestrial supernatural. The time it takes for two pairs of lips to meet could be milliseconds, but it can feel as if time has stretched indefinitely; you are transposed into a different world, your *own* world; just for you and the one who holds your affection. It makes you uniquely aware of both your body and spirit, it grounds you and it raises you up. Love enriches the world we inhabit.

In this book, I have had the honour and privilege of exploring how the power of love has been expressed within a variety of cultures from around the world. I pay homage to the textures of each original tale while also adapting them to fit a new, modern age. In doing this, I hoped to draw out and excavate what these stories can teach us about ourselves and love itself. My personal mission was to highlight how love and affection is magnificently multi-dimensional, both universal and deeply personal, its expression as nuanced, diverse and complicated as humanity itself.

Love is tender, tentative, brutal and bold. It's messy and magic! It can be the most frightening thing in the world, purely because it feels like safety, and that safety is reliant on total trust in another, with whom we share our hearts, expose ourselves and allow ourselves to be seen for exactly who we are. But when we allow ourselves to trust like this, there is a freedom that we can attain – a *glory*.

This book is about being seen in all your iterations, in every dynamic, brightly and in colour. It's about the joy and hope that accompanies the celebration of that phenomenon. I hope that this book brings you joy.

Yours, lovingly,

Bolu Babalola

Ọṣun

Ọṣun WAS USED TO BEING LOOKED AT. In awe, lasciviously, curiously. Instinctively, she knew when eyes were drawing across her, trying to figure out what they could from her figure. Chin slightly raised, arms and legs lean and athletic, and wide hips that swayed and exuded a femininity so innate it refused to be contained; to some it was a call they felt they had to respond to, to others, a declarative statement of power, something to fear, revere. As a competitive swimmer at Ifá Academy, she had an intrinsic allure that followed her as she flew into the air before diving into the pool. Prize-winning, majestic, her limbs flew through chemicalised water as if it was the sea and she was the current itself. The energy itself. The gravity from the moon itself. She transformed the pool into a sun-dappled lake. Though she moved with incisive swiftness, she made her preternatural ability look breezy. It was casual magnificence. She pushed and pulled as if she was conjuring power from the water. Those who watched often mused that it seemed as if the water only existed to propel her.

Ọṣun was accustomed to being a spectacle, people observing her in wonder, trying to surmise what they could from what they saw. Which was why she hid as much as she could, and kept as much of herself to herself as she could. Swimming was her sanctuary, it was just a shame that it necessitated an audience. During swim-meets she paid no attention to the roar from the bleachers or the superfluous commands from her coach (the coach was decorative, a symbol that represented the school's power over Ọṣun's triumphs, as if Ọṣun hadn't made a dry basin bloom into a lake by dancing in it at three years old). In those swim-meets, she focused on the sound of the water smacking against her skin like a hand against the taut hide of a talking drum. Her swimming became a dance to a rhythm she was creating with the water. With each hip switch a hand sliced through the water till she was no longer just a body among bodies within a false aquatic body – tiled and sterile. No, she was the body, the only body, vibrant and heavy breathing. By the time the music stopped, she was over the finish line, alone. All they saw was an excellent athlete; only she knew that she was a dancer.

Ọṣun was used to being looked at and ignoring it. Most people would say that, when they looked in the water, they saw themselves, but what they really saw was their reflection, light bounced back. A reflection was just the water rejecting an unwelcome intrusion. Water was generous, but mostly it wanted to be left alone. Come in if you want, drink if you want, but don't peer in without engaging. However, when Ọṣun's gaze met the waves, she really saw herself.

Her hair was soft, dark and roiling, with thick coils swelling around her face like a towering tide. Her face held deep, striking eyes that tilted inwards slightly, as if too heavy to stay steady. They carried too much, they carried the whole universe, and were fathomless like the ocean. Her skin was as deep and smooth as a vast lake, its sparkling surface harbouring an unfathomable depth beneath, a whole world, beneath. The water beckoned her in as kin. She was a high-born; unknowable, untouchable and unable to be contained. One could enjoy but never possess. Experience but not capture.

But Ọṣun felt captured by the gaze on her now. It was all-consuming and sank through her skin. She detected the most tucked away parts of her stirring, being drawn to the surface. She didn't know the source of it but she felt it. She was sitting on a large hide-skin mat at the academy's celebration of the iteration of the Ojude Oba Festival with a loose smattering of people who liked to call themselves her friends, drinking palm wine from coconut cups, her lips glistening with fried sweetbread oil, observing the festivities. The air swelled with laughter, music, the scent of fried plantain, roasted meat and spiced rice. Ebony horses in colourful leather swayed, their manes entwined with red, yellow and green ribbons, and were led into the parade by the academy's jockeys, who matched their steeds' majesty with brightly dyed, flowing agbadas and fila. They directed their horses through elaborate routines with elegance and expertise, despite their heavy cumbersome outfits. Talking drums were having loud conversations, orchestrated by The Tellers, the elite drumming league of the academy, who learnt and recorded history through music. They spread news, provided entertainment and bantered through verse. Their chests were bare, gleaming, and their arms were tense as they slapped and tapped the hide-skin with both palm and stick, alternating in notes and somehow gleaning harmony from each strike. Students were dancing to the tale of their town's origin, to love stories told through cadence, laughing, waists rotating and feet blowing up red dust as they pounded. They celebrated the gods and goddesses who comprised their alumni, those who had ascended to the highest of heights. All throughout the merriment, Ọṣun felt that look searing across her skin, making her heartbeat quicken so it syncopated with the sound of the drums.

Part of the reason Ọṣun didn't know who was looking at her was practicality. She couldn't turn to see. Her neck was secured under the firm, sinewy arm of Ṣàngó, Student Chief Elect of Ifá Academy, Captain Sportsplayer (of all the sports), Captain Girlplayer (of all the girls), with a charm as ferocious as his temper and grey eyes that lightened and darkened according to his mood. It was a known fact within the academy and within the county that Ọṣun was the only one who could calm him when he thundered over some perceived disrespect or when someone dared to question his innate authority.

Ọṣun was the only person who saw Ṣàngó's eyes slide from slate to silver close up. She would walk into the midst of a brewing fight, the crowd parting way for her, and lay a hand across his tense jaw and look up at him. Murderous fire would turn to amorous flame, angry gusts of air into soft billowing breath. She would take his hand and lead him out of his own chaos. All of Ṣàngó's girls didn't matter, because Ọṣun knew she was all of them put together, and more. They were just iterations of her, splintered into lesser forms. There was a smiley girl who lived a few compounds away from Ṣàngó that he liked to spend time with. Ọṣun didn't mind this. Ọṣun knew that, when she smiled – rare, but it happened – it was as bright and as intense as the sun at noon. It could intoxicate those around her into such euphoria that, when the high ebbed, they felt like they were plummeting into the depth of all the despairs of the world, compounded. Ọṣun didn't know what would happen if she laughed. She never did. Then there was the girl that Ọṣun had Constellation Observation class with. Ṣàngó often visited her after festivities, loosened with palm wine. She was a girl who acted as if she hadn't drunk since the moment she was born, and whose thirst could only be satiated by Ṣàngó's sweat on her tongue. Ọṣun didn't mind that either. Ọṣun knew that, when they were together, Ṣàngó drowned in her, died and came back to life in her, and that when their hips rolled together, it was stormy waves; almighty, thrilling, terrifying. She knew she tasted like honey and liquor and that she left him both satiated and insatiable, tipsy, and all at her whim. Ọṣun knew that she was all Ṣàngó ever wanted and more. She knew it was the More that terrified him. The surplus taunted him. She knew that sometimes having everything you desire can make you question your own worthiness. Ṣàngó didn't like the taste of his own insecurities. He never liked to wonder whether he was Enough to match her Too Much, so he had to seek balance with diluted derivations of her. She was fine with all of this until the week before, six days before the Ojude Oba Festival, at her sister Yemọja's Earth Journey celebration.

The party was thrown at their compound, and Ọṣun had ventured out into the surrounding forest for a break. She admired her sister, who'd ascended from the school a year ago, but she often found her presence overbearing. When Yemọja laughed, it sounded like waves crashing against the shore, and often Ọṣun felt like the craggy cliff walls the waves cuffed against and eroded. The two sisters had the same face poured into different forms. Ọṣun felt her sister was a more sophisticated version of her. Yemọja was taller and lither, whereas Ọṣun was shorter and curvier, defying the prototypical mould for athleticism. Yemọja was an expert sailor, often leading teams of forty or fifty vessels on voyages of exploration. She had mastered the waters so that she needn't ever submerge. Ọṣun felt weak for needing to feel the ebbs against her skin. Yemọja highlighted what Ọṣun lacked, and though Ọṣun loved her sister and her sister loved her back, she couldn't help but feel lesser around her. People hung on to Yemọja's every word and Ọṣun watched them do it, saw them use those words to hoist themselves up spiritually, charmed and bolstered by Yemọja's presence. Seeing this, Ọṣun had tried to strike up conversation at that party, in a valiant attempt to emulate her sister's charisma, but she found that, when she spoke to people, they watched intently as her lips moved, their eyes following how her mouth shaped words, rather than listening. So Ọṣun left the teeming party and went for a walk through the forest, aiming for the river, a place where she felt peace. It was a surprise when, through the thicket by the riverbed, she saw the broad, muscular shoulder of Ṣàngó, who, a mere thirty minutes earlier, had wrapped a thick arm around Ọṣun's waist, pulled her to him and whispered that she was his love and that it pained him that he had to socialise when all **he wanted was to be with her,** but that he needed to collect more ale from the seller with a few of his men. Now that arm was around someone else. Through branches that seemed to cower in embarrassment, Ọṣun saw that Ṣàngó's neck was bent as he whispered something into that Someone Else's ear before kissing it.

He then said, louder, 'Ọṣun doesn't like to dance. I miss dancing. Dance with me.'

He moved slightly to reveal Ọba; Ṣàngó's former lover-friend, pre-Ọṣun, her baby-round eyes soft and stupid, small pretty flower mouth, waist moving with smooth respectful reverence as Ṣàngó called to her with his hips, jutting in response to the beat of the faraway drums. The way her waist moved was polite and coy, technically rhythmic but with no fire of its own. Even in dancing, she was bowing for Ṣàngó. Ọṣun rolled her eyes. This, Ọṣun hadn't been fine with. Ọba was meek and irritatingly sweet, a sweetness that Ọṣun found cloying. Even after Ọṣun had successfully captured Ṣàngó's attention, Ọba had been kind to Ọṣun, insisting she held no ill-feeling, that all she ever wished was for Ṣàngó to be happy. Ọṣun had found this exceedingly pathetic and would have had more respect for the girl if she had sworn a vendetta, if she had told her to her face – like a warrior – that she would not be letting him go. However, Ọba's involvement was not what struck Ọṣun so hard in her chest that she almost stumbled back. It was Ṣàngó's words. It was a lie. Ọṣun loved to dance. She and Yemọja danced by the seashore every night at sunset, drumbeats rising from the ocean for them, their laughter melding with the roar of the tide. Ọṣun danced every time she was in the water. She thought that Ṣàngó, at least, saw that. Through everything, the one thing that kept her tethered to Ṣàngó was that he *saw* her. They saw each other. Sometimes, not often, but sometimes, when she was with Ṣàngó, she felt close to how she felt when she was in the water. She realised now that this was an illusion. Sometimes, when you are hungry enough, you can will the ghost-taste of sweet-bread in your mouth. It will make you hungrier, though, and emptier. And sometimes you won't know how truly bereft of food you are until it's too late.

After a few moments, Ọba saw Ọṣun through the branches and froze. Ṣàngó followed Ọba's gaze, saw Ọṣun too, his eyes flashing in alarm, a bolt across his face. Ọṣun observed his eyes slide from silver to slate. He stepped forward, Ọṣun raised a hand. Ọba looked sorry for Ọṣun, which made Ọṣun feel sick to her stomach. So Ọṣun smiled, wide and beautiful, dazzling and terrible. It made Ṣàngó call on the rain clouds for anchor, and the sky turned grey. It made Ọba feel like she was submerged in the river behind her, unable to breathe, to see, to speak. Then, Ọṣun turned around and returned to the party as if nothing had happened. After that day, Ọba found that the ear that Ṣàngó had whispered in felt like water had plugged it. Try as she might, nothing would pour out. Herbalists couldn't fix it, priests feared it. It forever felt as if she was half submerged in the river. From that day on, Ṣàngó was too terrified to speak to Ọba ever again and didn't dare visit his other girls. For reasons Ọṣun could not confess to anyone, not even herself, she stayed. Ṣàngó still never asked Ọṣun to dance.

He was talking to his boys now, palm wine sloshing out of his cup. Ọṣun rolled her eyes. Ṣàngó loved an audience, adored holding court, regaling them all with stories from sports tournaments, from the places he visited and sought to conquer when he ascended the academy. His people laughed on cue, a chorus in a call and response tale, unable to display anything but sycophantic joy as Ṣàngó told of how, once, a market man refused to sell a lion-skin cape to him. The man had told him the cape was for men with honour, and that he hadn't seen enough in Ṣàngó to sell it to him.

'I told him I would rule over him one day. Old fool said that he knew. He said that he hoped that I would accrue enough honour for the lion-skin, that my back would become broad enough for it. Can you imagine? A whole me. A whole me who can carry an ox on his back? Two oxen! I thought he must have surely been joking.' Ṣàngó spat into the earth as his eyes melted into something darker than slate at the memory. 'So I laughed in his face.'

With Ṣàngó's angry laughter came thunder, and with thunder came lightning.

'The only problem was that now the lion-skin was stained with ash. Dyed with idiot.'

His court roared with jest. Ọṣun felt ill.

She shrugged Ṣàngó's arm off her neck, feigning that she was readjusting the multicoloured beads that hung around her throat. The feeling of being watched grew more intense. She turned around, and through the heated dancing bodies, she saw a tall, lithe, muscular figure, leaning against a tree. His arms looked like branches twined to make a trunk, and so it almost seemed as if he was mocking the fever tree's strength. He was eating a rose apple, white teeth sinking into membrane and then flesh, playful eyes never leaving Ọṣun's. His left ear glinted with a silver crescent cuffed into his lobe and it matched the flash in his eyes. It was different to the light she saw in Şàngó's eyes, which was entirely indicative of himself, his whims. Şàngó's eyes flashed lightning when he was in the mood to drown in her, but he never asked her if he ever made her catch fire. This man's eyes were calling her, pressing through her. He was seeing into her and he wasn't bowing. He had three striking scars across his muscular chest, on the left side, welts she immediately wanted to run her fingers across. He smiled at her as if he knew.

She turned back around, alarmed. She pinched her sister next to her and drew her away from the conversation she was engaged in. Yemoja was Oşun's closest friend, in that she was her only friend, bound by blood and bonded through water.

'Turn around slowly, like you're looking for someone. Do you know who the tall new boy is?'

Oşun said 'boy' to calm herself, to allow herself to feel some semblance of control over this man whose gaze was making carefully compacted parts of her stretch and bloom into their fullness.

Yemoja blinked twice, thrice, startled that Oşun was talking to her casually about things that regular sisters talked about casually. Yemoja's baby sister was extraordinary beautiful, and extraordinarily, beautifully *strange*. Once, when they were on the benches in the school field, watching Şàngó and his boys defeat another county, Oşun's eyes had glazed over and she'd said, 'Did you know that thunderstorms don't always produce rain? It's a shame, because the rivers hear the thunder and see the lightning and expect to be filled up, only to end up disappointed. Dry thunderstorms are just show offs. Scaring birds and burning trees while the river pants. Forgetting that the river helps feed the clouds that thunderstorms are created from.' Her eyes never left the sports field as she spoke. Soon after, Ṣàngó scored the winning goal.

Yemọja rarely knew what Ọṣun was talking about. She often nodded and smiled when Ọṣun uttered things like this, knowing that anything she replied would only ever make Ọṣun's eyes shadow in impatience, would cause her to retreat quickly again, when her cerebral soulfulness wasn't matched. Yemọja was of the ocean as Ọṣun was of the river, but Yemọja was earthy, practical, tethered to the things of this world, tied to the non-anointed peoples, so she could relate to them, mother them. Her younger sister had the freedom to stay connected to the heavens, to allow her psyche to dwell outside this realm. Yemọja was the root and Ọṣun was blossom, forever reaching for the sky. And so, Yemọja pretended to understand what Ọṣun was saying and Ọṣun pretended that she was understood. It was a sweet kindness they shared that benefitted them both. But Yemọja understood Ọṣun clearly now and was pleased. Ọṣun needed more than Ṣàngó. Ṣàngó would rather make himself feel bigger with women less powerful than Ọṣun instead of elevating himself. Yemọja did as she was told – turned around casually – and when she turned back to Ọṣun, her smile was gleeful.

'Ah. That's Erinlẹ. He is joining the academy next season. He won the country-wide competition for a spot and was invited to this festival as an early introduction.' They had shifted away from Ṣàngó and his boys – not that it mattered. They wouldn't have been able to hear the sisters speaking over the sound of their own voices and the giggling girls surrounding them anyway.

11

Ọṣun nodded and sipped at her palm wine. Yemọja smiled wider. Ọṣun barely drank. 'What won him a place here?' Their academy was selective, a training campus for the gifted. One was either born into it, being of celestial heritage, high-blood (Ọṣun, Yemọja and Ṣàngó), while others were scouted for their particular skill, sourced through tales of power and often mysticism throughout the counties. They were known as the earth-born; of the rooted realm.

'Hunting, my heart,' Yemọja said, allowing herself the indulgence of using an intimate term of endearment. To Yemọja's pleasure, Ọṣun didn't flinch.

Ọṣun nodded and poured more wine into both their bronze cups from a gourd.

'So he's an earth-born.'

Yemọja shrugged. 'Aburo mi, it means nothing. We are all equal here. Those who are supposedly high-born often act like they were born beneath ground.' Yemọja sidled her eyes to where Ṣàngó was sat, tipsily jeering, and Ọṣun bit into her smile.

Yemọja continued, shuffling closer to Ọṣun, so their shoulders were touching. If strangers saw them, they might have presumed that they'd always been this way, companions, confidantes, sisters by blood and friends by choice, that they sat between each other's knees and braided each other's hair while gossiping as ritual.

'He is a master bowman. Farmer too. It's said he can bring crops to life with a touch. Good with his hands.' She shot a knowing, playful look at Ọṣun, and to Yemọja's surprise, Ọṣun allowed herself a tiny, fraction of a smile. It made Yemọja feel like she'd won something and she felt bolstered to continue. 'It's said that the scars on his chest are from when he fought a lion. They say the lion wanted to eat his heart for his strength.'

Ọṣun took a sip of her wine. 'Or the lion wanted to eat his heart because it was a lion.'

To Ọṣun's surprise, Yemọja released her ocean roar of a laugh; it bubbled out of her. People didn't often laugh around her. Did she say something funny? She wasn't aware, but she found she liked the feeling of being enjoyed for what she freely gave.

'Well, Erinlẹ won. Clearly. As you can see.' Ọṣun looked up and saw that Erinlẹ was now in front of her, in the middle of the courtyard, a talking drum leaning against his taut torso and his arm, joining in with the music. Her eyes dropped and she realised that, around his waist, was a wide strip of tanned, sandy hide over his deep rust-hued woven cloth. Lion-skin.

Erinlẹ was smiling as he made the talking drum sing, joining in easily with The Tellers. The Tellers were notoriously unwelcoming to newcomers, an elite band of expert musicians who came from expert musicians. But here they were, folding him in, and Erinlẹ not only matched them, he made them better. Now that he was closer, she could examine him more. His skin was a deep reddish brown; the exact tone of the earth by the riverbed at her favourite place to swim.

'May I speak with you?'

She heard a low, cool voice that she somehow knew belonged to Erinlẹ, and yet his mouth didn't open. His eyes were trained on her intently. She held still. Ọṣun was very sure that he had spoken without speaking.

13

'It seems that you've already allowed yourself that honour,' Ọṣun dared to think, playing with the notion that he might hear her. From the broadening of his smile and the light in his eye, it was clear that he had.

'No. I was just knocking. Testing. Seeing. We both know that, if you didn't want me to speak with you, I wouldn't be here.'

Ọṣun could see now that time had stopped – or at least it had been suspended. The red earth and deep green of the forest melted into a thick smog. Ṣàngó's laughter sounded as if it had been submerged in water, and her sister's warmth had ebbed away. Everybody was a blur. The festival was occurring in slow-motion, as if it were a dream. She found that she was now standing opposite Erinlẹ, inches away from him, close enough to reach out and touch the ridges of his scars if she were so inclined.

Ọṣun forced her eyes away from his chest and directed them plainly into his. 'Why would I want you in my mind? I don't know you.'

Erinlẹ's gaze made Ọṣun's blood blaze beneath her skin.

'I don't know you, but you've been in my mind. I guess just not in the same way. Not in this literal sense.'

Ọṣun tried to swallow her curiosity (she wasn't used to the taste, as she rarely found what men said to be interesting), but it rose back up to push a question from her lips. 'In which sense, then?'

'In the sense of a young man wondering about the woman who would one day hold his heart.'

Ọṣun found it in her to roll her eyes, to conjure the semblance of dismissal, despite the fact that every cell in her body thrummed with the knowledge that this man wasn't speaking with regular flat flattery – this was not an attraction tethered to how her being in his possession would make him feel. He spoke plainly of her power over him, and he didn't cower, didn't puff up his chest to over-compensate.

'And how do you know that's me?'

Erinlẹ shrugged in a matter-of-fact manner. 'How do crows know when an earthquake is about to happen?'

Ọṣun raised a brow. 'So you sensed your destruction?'

Erinlẹ laughed, eyes glinting. 'I sensed my world about to shift.'

Ọṣun's heartbeat was steady at all times, but now it was frantic, hectic, at odds with the stillness surrounding them.

Ọṣun cleared her already clear throat. 'So is this your power? Summoning people out of the world and meeting them in their own?'

Erinlẹ stepped closer to her. 'It's your power. You called me here. I am earth-born – my gifts were blessed to me. But I read that sometimes this can happen when two energies find something in one another that compels them to each other.'

'And what about you should compel me?' Aside from his smile, his warmth, and the fact that she felt herself unfurling around him. 'I don't need anybody.'

Erinlẹ laughed, and nodded, 'I am aware. It's not about need, but desire.'

Ọṣun swallowed. 'What I desire is to know why a strange boy was staring at me from afar. I want to know what made him lose himself to be so bold as to look at Ṣàngó's beloved so openly.'

Erinlẹ shrugged. 'I didn't lose myself, I found myself. Whether or not you are Ṣàngó's beloved is of no consequence to me. You are not his possession. It's a lie he believes to make himself feel better about himself. I wasn't looking at Ṣàngó's beloved, I was looking at you.'

Oṣun held still for a moment and regarded him, feeling something swell within her. Something visceral, that pushed her to carry through with her inclination to allow a finger to sweep against the lines across his skin, transgressing the lines she drew for herself, rules that disallowed anyone to see her innermost desires. As she touched the scars left by a jealous beast, the long-healed and sealed gashes shimmered beneath her touch, glowing bright and amber.

Erinlẹ watched her, his eyes veered from playful to serious as he reached to tilt her chin so that her gaze met his, unabashedly, nakedly.

'What do you want, Oṣun?'

Oṣun opened her mouth but found that her words got stuck. *Want*. Oṣun hadn't wanted in a long time. She was obliged to hone her gifts. Obliged to represent the academy. In many ways, she felt obliged to be with Ṣàngó, representing the highest of the high-born, but Oṣun couldn't remember the last time someone asked her what she actually wanted. People sought to touch without acknowledging her desire to be caressed, to consume without realising her craving to just be held. They looked but never saw.

Erinlẹ looked at her intently, as if he was seeing her More. He smiled and it rippled sunlight through her.

'*Oṣun, oh, Oṣun . . .*'

Oṣun froze. Was he singing? His mouth was moving, and he seemed to be starting a chorus with her name, beating the drum, looking her in the eye. The world rushed back into sharp focus, the sound flooding back into Ọṣun's ears with almost painful clarity, just in time for her to hear Ṣàngó's conversation draw to a complete halt.

'Did he just say your name?' Ṣàngó's voice was incredulous.

'Yes. He did.' Yemọja responded smugly, on the opposite side of Ọṣun, as Ọṣun forced herself to quickly acclimatise to the world around her. Her conversation with Erinlẹ hadn't been more than a split-second in the temporal sphere, but her whole body felt more alive than it ever had, everything around her seemed more vivid, clearer. Ọṣun felt more of herself brought forth to the rooted realm. She felt more of herself in general.

Erinlẹ's singing was a bold move. Nobody sang but The Tellers. To sing you had to be elected by them or appeal to them in front of an audience. Nobody sang directly to others unless they were friends teasing each other, friends congratulating each other, or if they were initiating courtship. It was more than being able to hold a note: one had to be able to draw song on the spot, it could not be pre-composed. It's how you knew it was from the heart, and it had to be from the heart. Ṣàngó had never sung to her. Ṣàngó had never sung to anyone. He prided himself on never having to.

Ọṣun could hear Ṣàngó beginning to thunder next to her and she turned to him, allowed her eyes to be as fathomless as possible. 'Be still.'

Ṣàngó's jaw tightened, but she felt the rolling of his thunder subside immediately. Whether he liked it or not, Ọṣun had his heart in her palm. She scared him. The whole festival had now turned to pay attention to the spectacle, Erinlẹ's small hooked cane beating an intricate, delicate tune that seemed to conjure up the image of Ọṣun. It rolled like the gentle ebbs of a river, it sounded sweet and fierce and plush. Erinlẹ was walking slowly up to her, drum slung across his torso, gripped under his arm as tightly as his eyes gripped on to hers.

'Ọṣun, may I borrow you,
I will kill a thousand lions for your dowry,
Scale mountains to pluck the stars for your wedding jewels,
Slap the clouds to make them cry so your rivers will always overflow.'

Ọṣun laughed. That was what she wanted to do. She wanted to laugh. To allow all the parts of her she tucked away to flow freely. To escape the trappings of expectation. To *be*. People gawped. No one had ever heard her laugh before. Ṣàngó had never heard her laugh before. It sounded like birdsong and the laps of a river. Erinlẹ was beckoning her, looking directly into her eyes. The timbre of his voice made her blood thrum and the hairs on her skin stand up. Ọṣun suddenly felt lifted, as if she was swimming. The drumbeats felt like waves crashing against her skin, beckoning her as kin.

'Stand tall, my queen. I would give you the universe but how
Can I gift you to you? So I will give you my heart, strong and true,
I cannot conjure thunder, but
I will plant a forest for you, sow flowers that bloom
In your presence, fruit that tastes like your essence.'

It was supposed to be bawdy, these songs usually were. However, the way he sang caused electrical currents to course through Ọṣun's body in a different way to when she was with Ṣàngó. These currents depended on her; it was as if his energy caught fire through contact with her. She had to agree to it for it to blaze.

Erinlẹ was now in front of her.

'Ọṣun, oh, Ọṣun,
My beat is calling your waist,
Won't you answer?
Won't you answer?
You look like a woman who loves to dance.'

Ọṣun got up, legs unfolding easily beneath her as the clouds above rolled. She paid no attention to Ṣàngó. She followed Erinlẹ to the middle of the courtyard and allowed her hips to switch with the beat, her arms to sway through the air, laughing as she did so, as Erinlẹ bent low with his drum and dipped and rose as she moved, responding when she called with her waist. There was thunder, but Erinlẹ's drum rose above it, interlaced with Ọṣun's laugh. There was lightning, but Ọṣun's smile outshone it. Ọṣun was used to being looked at, but, from this moment, she would become used to being seen.

Scheherazade

I SUPPOSE, IF I TELL OUR STORY, I should start at the beginning. That's the convention, right?

Once upon a time. Except you and I don't feel bound by the temporal. Not in a pretentious mystical way, because I'm not into all of that, but very basically: we were not a 'once' and we were never pinned to a 'time'.

I felt this even when I told myself we were just a transient fling. I don't think I ever fathomed a time when I wouldn't know him – not fully, not comprehensively. At first, I'd assumed I would move on, because that's what I usually did, and I was good at it. I like to do things I am good at, as a general rule. I thought that we would end as a matter of course. All things end, and so I always sought to deal with romance by making the experience shorter, by controlling the length. By limiting the length, you can make the experience sweeter, like a six-episode season of your favourite TV show. It's less able to

21

disappoint you, less able to mess up character development and leave threads hanging. My character development was finite, and I liked to keep my threads taut. I thought there was beauty in the ephemeral and that I was being an aesthetician by hastening the death of a relationship. But, if I'm honest – and I figure that I have nothing to lose by being honest here – I never really sat down and considered what it would mean for my life to not have him in it. I must have been scared to. I'm not usually scared of anything. I should have known then what this love was.

So, what was our beginning? When we first met? When we first fell in love? But falling in love is continuous and perpetual, an activity that continues under the aegis of capital letter Love. Perhaps it was when we first *made* love, as he called it . . . I called it our First Fuck, which he hated. He said it corrupted it, I said it was whimsical. It was gorgeous, euphoric, primal and preternatural all at once. Our First Fuck definitely had the power to ignite a beginning. It was the kind of lovemaking that has you feeling more beautiful the next day; walking smugly with a sway, hips swishing, with a nimbus of power and joy around you, as if you were a goddess among mortals because, the other night, you inhabited heaven. You were the only thing a person could see, could taste, could hear, could feel.

I texted my best friends the morning after:

Me: *'God. What have I done?'*

Them: *'That bad?!!'*

Me: *'That good. Too good. I have made a terrible mistake.'*

The first time we met did not feel like an introduction nor did it feel like a reunion; we were just two spirits meant to be in communion. I could maybe start with the initial flirtation, the flicker of fire that occurred with our first knee brush, but even that was us formally learning the grammar to a language that our bodies and souls already knew. The closest thing I can think of to a beginning for us, or perhaps the first time we both saw and acknowledged we *were* an us, was our first fight.

'Say something,' I said.

I watched him sitting across from me at my kitchen island. He took a sip of his wine. We'd picked the bottle up together; he'd read out the description, '*dark and sweet flavours, full bodied*', and shot me a wicked look with a raised brow before he put it in the basket. 'My taste.' He smiled.

It was so corny, and he knew it and I knew it, and I mimicked retching sounds, and he grabbed me up in the wine aisle, in front of the auditorium of sauvignons and pinots, and he kissed me; because it was in public, it was quick, but quick did not mean passionless. He kissed me and I felt like I'd drunk a whole row of the supermarket's finest wines. My knees were weak. He kissed me and my second favourite pair of jeans automatically fit me better, curved around me better when his hand filled the back pocket. He kissed me, slipped a little tongue into my mouth, just a little promise, enough flavour to make me ravenous, before he whispered into my ear again, 'my taste.'

He took a sip of that wine while sat at my kitchen island that evening. The look on his face was expertly impassive. The aroma of layered herbs and stewed meat rose into the air, mingled with the scent of my rose-and-peony candle and his cologne. Low murmuring R&B filled the dim of the room, humming at us sultrily, mockingly, almost hauntingly, *'nobody else but you . . .'*

He shrugged. 'What do you want me to say, Scheherazade?'

I rolled my eyes. He was so dramatic, no *Scher*, no familiarity. He needed the full length of my name to maintain his distance. He was talking to me as if I was one of his students trying to flirt with him. He might as well have called me Ms Shirvani.

He worked in a university as a professor and researcher, the youngest in the faculty, and the most eligible in his faculty. He taught Iranian politics and history (the right amount of grit and softness). He looked (too) storybook, (too) fairytale; he looked like a prince who had maidens swooning in the market. He had an auric nobility, with his crown of thick wavy hair, a sunrise smile and caramel skin that almost gleamed gold. He looked so pure and perfect that it was uniquely satisfying to watch his sweet eyes darken with passion when he was about to kiss me, to rumple his hair as I ran my fingers through it, to make his calm voice lower into an uncontrolled growl as my teeth nipped at his neck.

Right then, however, his tone remained even. It was highly irritating. 'You're being really passive aggressive right now, Shahryār.'

He smiled and genially speared a forkful of saffron rice and herby stew into his mouth. His eyes were bright.

'I'm being passive aggressive? You don't think confessing you hooked up with your ex-boyfriend at a mutual friend's birthday party over ghormeh sabzi is a little more passive aggressive? You know it's my favourite meal . . .'

Oh, he was good. Better than I'd anticipated.

I shook my head and took a sip of my wine. 'I wasn't confessing. Confessing implies that I think I did something wrong. I just thought you would like to know. But sorry. Would you have preferred I told you over pizza?'

Shahryār nodded. 'Yes. I would, actually. I would prefer it if I didn't think about you fucking your pestiferous ex-boyfriend whenever I ate ghormeh sabzi. Pizza, though? Pizza, I could do without. I think I'm lactose intolerant anyway.'

'*Pestiferous*? Pestiferous! Who says pestiferous? Also, we didn't fuck. We just made out. With tongue. There was like two, or maybe three boob grabs, tops.'

I'd almost lost it with my questioning of his use of such a pretentious word, but I was proud of how I'd brought it back and gained ground. That 'pestiferous' really pissed me off. How did he have the presence of mind to use the word *pestiferous* when I'd just told him I'd got with my trash ex-boyfriend, who I'd once referred to as a budget Wolf of Wall Street (Coyote of Canary Wharf, Shahryār had laughed)? Did he just not care? How was his brain so relaxed that words such as pestiferous were so easily accessible? He was maddening.

Shahryār looked at me for three long seconds, before he nodded, the corner of his mouth flicking up. He scooped another forkful of food into his mouth and chewed slowly, his gaze fastened on to mine, leaden with something that slowed down time and quickened my heartbeat. It shot a spark through me, and I took a large gulp of wine in an attempt to drown it, but all it did was fan the spark into a flame.

I forgot that he knew me. I was so used to being with men who didn't. I was so used to making sure it was a certain way that I'd taken Shah for granted. I'd made the mistake of taking my unknowability as an immutable fact. I'd become too reliant on it for protection.

Shahryār and I had been seeing each other for three months at the point of our first fight. We'd met at a political luncheon; him as a researcher and community organiser and me as a strategist, sent to control and quell people like him. I'd spotted him while my client – a promising middle statesmen with ambition and drive – was giving a speech. I was sitting in the crowd as I always did and perusing who was sitting around me when our eyes caught. He released a small smile. An angular, sharp and knowing smile. It was at odds with how he looked; sweet, handsome, charmingly affable in his plaid shirt, soft sweater and chino combo, with chic tortoise-shell glasses. You would assume the most threatening thing he could do to you was check your references in a last-minute paper. That smile during the speech had a texture I found appealing, a taste I couldn't quite place: it had an umami to it. It whet an appetite I didn't know I had. During this stage, I'd thought that my curiosity was purely professional: locate a potential problem and deactivate it before it detonated.

After the speech I'd approached him where he was sitting in the coffee shop of the conference centre with a laptop. My leather, finely crafted bag was a statement, and so I placed it firmly on the table to make one. He slowly raised his gaze to mine.

'Fine. I'm going to let you buy me a coffee.'

His brows hitched. 'That sounds like a command.'

I smiled. 'Only sounds like it? Let me try that again . . .'

Shahryār leant back in his seat and ran his eyes across me, taking me in. I was in my formal gear: pencil skirt, blouse, court shoes, dark hair up in an intricately tied ochre scarf. And I wore a deep autumn-brown lipstick, despite it being summer. But that was not why he was looking at me.

'Scheherazade Shirvani.'

I held still. He knew who I was. My job was hinged on the fact that near nobody knew my job unless they needed to know who I was. I was in the business of discretion. I was a storyteller and a world shaper. I was behind the scenes of the great cultural and political performances. I cleaned up messes, I anticipated messes, and, if needed, I manufactured messes. At thirty-two, I was one of the greatest strategists in the city, going toe to toe with the biggest predators. My story was rather pathetic: motherless, would-have-rather-been fatherless, unloved, unwanted, and so I wrote my own and conjured myself up from nothing. I stayed in libraries till closing time and put myself through school. I spun gold from dirt. Soon I discovered that the dirtiest places were the gleaming glass towers of the city, and so I made them my business. Those in the glass towers needed their narrator to be invisible for their new stories to work.

I pulled up a chair. 'Who are you and what do you do?'

'Shahryār Javid. Professor at The City University. Politics and history.'

I nodded. 'Right. And let me guess, as well as this you are the leader of the pressure group? Holding the powers-that-be to account? Well, you call yourself a pressure group, but what you actually do is spy and sabotage.'

Shahryār smiled breezily. 'Not at all. I'm just here to learn and do my civic duty. Get locked into the thrilling world of municipal politics.' He shrugged. 'I'm on the side of peace.'

Well that was bullshit. This man was a quiet warrior and, now that I was close enough, I could smell it on him. I found I quite liked the scent.

I crossed my legs and slid my head to the side. 'That's what everyone says. You didn't believe a word my client said in there, did you?'

'Do you?'

I was caught off guard, and caught off guard that I was caught off guard. 'That's not the point . . .'

He took a sip of his coffee and his warm honey eyes sparkled. 'You don't. Doesn't surprise me. You're smarter than everyone else who was in that room. Including me. You should have been stood on that podium. I hear you tell the best stories. In fact, don't they call you The Storyteller?'

Ah. I nodded slowly, smiling. He wasn't just a sweet college professor, he was *me* . . . He was me on a different tier – not higher, but different. His organisation was in direct opposition to mine, equally as dangerous and covert, but his role demanded a little more discretion. It was why he also had the professor job. It was also why he knew who I was, and I had no idea who he was. A thrill ran through me. It had been a while since I'd faced a challenge.

'Are you going to be a problem for me, Shahryār?'

Shahryār grinned at me. 'Let me buy you that coffee.'

It started off casual. It had to be. Though we represented two people who were technically on the same side ideologically, they were opponents locked in a civil war, arguing over semantics and delivery. Escalation could have been ugly and often it threatened to be, but that's why they had us. We kept them in line. We were their generals, and so we had no time for anything as plebeian and ordinary as dating. What, were we going to do 'dinner and a movie' after a day of strategising how our clients would destroy each other? Impossible.

Shahryār couldn't hold a girlfriend down and I didn't want a boyfriend to hold me down, and so it was agreed that we'd only hook up if we bumped into each other at events. We bumped into each other at events a lot. Soon we started booking hotel rooms in which to bump into each other more, and then one day he bumped into me at my house, cooked for me, and we bumped into each other on the floor of my kitchen.

One day, after we'd bumped into each other in his house a few times and we were curled up on the sofa together – me watching TV, him reading a book – he stroked my hair and murmured into it, 'This is good. Isn't it?'

My body and mind relaxed around him so easily that it took considerable effort to heave my barriers back up. I did it, though, because this set me on edge. I said, 'Yeah, it is . . .' while I pushed myself off his chest and leant against the back of the sofa in what I presumed would seem like a carefree manner. 'I think what makes it so good is that we both know what it is, you know?'

Shahryār put his book down on the side and folded his glasses away, adjusting himself on the sofa so he could look at me through those sweet amber eyes that always made me want to furl myself into him. His face didn't betray a mite of emotion. 'Right. What is it again?'

I shrugged. 'We're casual. Two friends whose mutual interests align considerably, and one of those interests happens to be sex with each other.'

He was quiet for a few moments before nodding slowly. 'Of course. I'm actually talking to two other women right now.'

I smiled brightly, perhaps too brightly. 'Good. That's great. I'm happy for you.'

I snuggled back up against him and inhaled the soft cottony heat of his chest. He had stopped stroking my hair.

When I told Shahryār to keep talking to those women, I truly believed I meant it. It was painful, but it was that pain that assured me I was doing the right thing. I saw it as a necessary bloodletting to maintain my health. I had to cut the infection out, and in this case the infection was deep affection for Shah. I'd got this far by being on my own and not allowing myself to be softened. That was what I knew and what I grew up with. That was where I was safe. Aloneness. The fact that I was unnerved by how I felt at the thought of him kissing these women, or whispering softly in their ear like he did with me, was confirmation of my wise decision making.

It was incomprehensible that I should care. As I perused his (few

and limited) social media pages at night and went through his fol-
lower list with monomaniacal determination, trying to see who
looked like they might be his type, I was certain it was my professional habit having its way with me. I was just researching; I was
just thirsty for knowledge. Was having a curious mind a sin and . . .
Okay, am I crazy or does that girl Ziba look *exactly* like me, except
that I can actually pull off that haircut?

It was turning me into a bad person, and not the fun kind of bad
person either, but the kind of bad person I abhorred: jealous, petty
and critical of another woman's shade of lipstick. So, I did my job
and fixed it. I moulded the narrative to one that served me. We were
both equally available and it just so happened that I was pickier than
he was. It wasn't that I thought of him and smiled in public like a
loon, it wasn't that I skipped home after work on days that I knew
he was coming over. I believed the story I sculpted because I had to.
The alternative was that I had lost control of my own narrative, that
our story was spilling beyond my set limits, that it may not *have* a
limit. It would be out of my hands; I would not be able to protect
myself. That was something I refused to allow.

Now, however, looking at Shahryār across the kitchen island
and seeing how he saw me, eyes blistering through me, I realised
that there was no way I could be protected from this, and, worse
still, I didn't want to be. He shook his head and rubbed the bridge
of his nose, pushing his glasses up in the process. 'Let's talk about
it, Scher.'

I twitched a shoulder and blinked innocence at him. 'Talk about
what?'

Shahryār shrugged. 'Talk about how my toothbrush is in your bathroom. About how I keep the yoghurt that you like to eat for breakfast in my fridge.'

'That kind of seems like a boring topic of conversation . . .'

'Okay, here's the thing: I like this. I like us. I think you like this and you like us too. I think this could be a lot easier if you stopped sabotaging and manipulating yourself out of it. I know you told me that you hooked up with someone else thinking I'd get mad and end this, but I won't be the one to do that. It has to be you. I'm not a political pawn that you can mould and shape; I am a man who is in love with you. You can't do what you do out there in here,' he gestured to the space between us. 'In here it's *us*. In here it's sacred. You and me. Don't insult us by doing that. If you want to call it quits, then do it, but I won't let you make me do it. If you want to walk out right now, do it, but you're not going to make me push you out. I thought this was a love story, but if it isn't, tell me I'm wrong. If I'm right, though, I can promise you that it will never end with me leaving you. I will want you forever.'

I stared at him across the table with my eyes glistening. I hadn't known my tear ducts still worked until then. What a way to find out.

'The two other women don't exist, do they?'

'You tried to find them, didn't you?'

'Asshole. That was very clever.'

He smiled. I cleared my throat. 'This is my kitchen. I can't walk out.'

Shahryār nodded, and drew back his chair. 'So tell me to leave.'

I pushed my own chair back and moved around to his side of the table, placed myself on his lap and kissed him deeply, tasting the herbs and the spices and him. He wrapped his arms around me and pulled me in flush. I rested my forehead against his. 'I'm sorry. I'm not good at this.'

He pushed my hair from my face. 'I'm not either. Let's learn together.'

I nodded. 'Okay. Let's do that. I hated kissing him. And I didn't let him feel my boob. Not even once. I just thought doing it would make me un-fall in love with you.'

Shahryār brought my lips to his once more, softly, sweeping his thumb against my jaw. 'How did it go?'

'My first failed mission.'

'I am supportive of all your endeavours and I am proud of you for being incredibly successful in everything you do, but I'm glad to hear that. I hope every time you try to un-fall in love with me you fail. And I know you'll probably try it a lot.'

I started unbuttoning his shirt. 'Hmm. You're probably right.'

'Can we agree not to kiss anyone else apart from each other now?' He tugged at the belt of my wrap-style sweater dress.

I laughed into his mouth. 'Sure. Sex is okay, though, right?'

'Of course.'

I didn't like doing things I wasn't good at, but it turned out I loved learning how to love with him.

I'd told him everything about myself; not on purpose, it just happened. It was a natural reaction to the ease I felt around him and it was irresistible, being that free. It felt so good that I didn't trust it and I treated it like a vice, when actually, maybe it was good for me? Maybe it was a good thing I deserved to have? It just felt too good, too fairytale, too storybook, too *too*, because I wasn't used to it. My constitution had to adjust to it.

The transition from not knowing him to knowing him was a seamless transfiguration. Pieces of me fell into place; I was growing into what I should be. We were growing. It wasn't as if our love built me, it's that it galvanised me, making me stronger because he saw me fully, the best parts and the worst parts. I kept count of the nights we slept in the same bed. He was the first man that I'd ever allowed to sleep over and sleep over and sleep over, and it seemed to me, at first, such a remarkable, unexplainable phenomenon that I had to retain a tally. I thought that, at some point, I would get bored. Deep down I believed that, at some point, he would get bored. 1,001 nights. Each one felt unique, even in the growing comfort and familiarity; it was a widening tapestry and a deepening of our story. We were building our world. Some nights we would talk with words, others just with our bodies, developing our language, discovering new ways to say I love you; I see you, I hear you, me and you. A lot of nights, we would just collapse into bed silently and curl up into each other, and often those were the nights I understood most how staggering the thing between us was. I fell asleep so deeply next to him, safe and content. I never thought I could have a peaceful sleep with someone else by my side. 1,001 nights. About two years and seven months of what I reckoned would be a two-week fling. 1,001 nights in your arms and each one felt like a great eternity. I felt like there was an infinity within our affinity, that our connection was so deep and so fathomless that there was no way we could be bound by something as mundane as dawn. We were our own suns.

But our line of work was dangerous. We didn't talk about it much because it was a given, we didn't talk about it much because what was the point? We both knew that being together made us powerful and therefore it exponentially increased the risk. We were double the threat to a lot of people in the tall glass towers. We didn't talk about it much, but when we chose somewhere to live, it was a sweet neighbourhood just outside of the city, gated with security. We didn't talk about it much, but we agreed we didn't want children, even though we both cooed over your nieces in the same way. I saw the look in your eye. We didn't talk about it much, but one day you started kissing me longer before you left the house, started telling me to 'be careful, baby', brushing your thumb across my lips in a way that pulled a smile out of me and then made me pull you in and say 'hey, *you* be careful, baby, or we'll have a baby'. We didn't talk about it much, but one morning, you pulled me back into bed, whispered into my neck that we should both miss work. Our clients were going at it again, which was frustrating, as they had bigger, common enemies to focus on. It was stressful for both of us, to the point where we were starting to bring it home. We spent the whole day in our bed, white and cushiony, within the clouds themselves. I'd never felt more alive than when you made me breathless; and taking your breath away made me feel like God must have when he poured life into the earth.

When I got a call that said that you had been in a car-crash, a non-accidental car-crash, all the iron in my blood drew together in blocks and dragged me down to the floor, weighed me down and kept me there. I no longer felt like God. I was so pathetically mortal. We were so pathetically mortal.

And you knew, didn't you? I've found things out, done research and gone digging in your locked drawers. How could you keep it from me? They were after me, but you found them first, and dismantled their operation. 1,001 nights you kept me alive without me knowing. They found out it was you and figured that killing you would be worse than killing me anyway. They don't know me. Only *I* take your breath away. Only *I* have that right. The universe knows it. I've made them pay. It was easy; they're weak. They won't come near us again. My turn to protect you.

So here you are, my darling, in the in-between of life and death, with tubes and wires and beeping, soft amber eyes shut from me, your storybook closed, and I need your eyes to open, because we are not a once upon a time, we are a forever within an *ever*, and I drank the whole bottle of wine yesterday to see if I could taste me through you, but all I did was get heavy and slow and cry on your side of the bed . . .

I hate you.

Do not break your promise.

They said that I should talk to you every day, that it might get you out of this indefinite state, that you may hear and come back to me – please come back to me – so I've been talking to you. At first, I didn't know what I would say. I struggled. Every time I tried, I cried. I don't cry. You know that. So today I told you the story of us, talking about you like you were another person, because somehow it's easier to divorce *my* you from the you lying here in this bed, breathing through a contraption. But they are both my yous. 1,001 nights, but there has to be more. This is sacred.

This is a love story.

Psyche

THIS COULDN'T BE HAPPENING.

Psy watched as the non-fat soy latté seeped and spread into the white of her top, which in turn stuck to her skin. She stared down at it as if she could make the stain disappear through mere willpower. Somehow, she had already ruined her Promotion Outfit. After two years of coffee runs, late-night calls about fixing copy, and inserting anti-anxiety suppositories into the anus of a grouchy Pomeranian, Psy had decided that today was the day she was going to ask Venus Lucius – her boss, (tor)mentor and *Olympus* magazine's fashion editor – if she could be promoted from her assistant to an editor in her own right. While it was true that for two years she'd told everyone her job title was 'editor' anyway, she figured she was finally ready for this not to be a lie concocted to impress aunties, old high-school frenemies and men from dating apps with MFAs. She'd dressed for this occasion, hoping her outfit screamed 'ready to not pick up your dog shit, Venus – seriously, stop feeding her caviar'. Her sleeveless white mock-turtleneck top was meant to show she was a sophisticated, empowered woman unafraid to embrace her femininity, but, with the coffee stain, it now screamed: idiot who can't be trusted to not spill hot beverages, never mind be trusted to not spill crucial industry tea.

'*Shit!*' She grabbed a handful of napkins from her tan leather tote, a result of late nights at the office and fast food, and dabbed with frantic futility. She knew the stain wouldn't go away, but maybe she could reduce the stench of inner-city coffee shop on her skin.

Alongside missing her morning coffee, Venus hated misattributed scents – lipglosses that smelt like strawberry, candles that were meant to smell like 'Christmas', and as such she would inevitably abhor assistants who smelt like non-fat soy lattés. Once, Psy had made the mistake of switching up her daily perfume and Venus had called her into her office and asked why she was 'disrupting her olfactory peace' with a foreign scent when she had just got used to Psy's '70%-off suburban department store effluvium'. It had been a *long* couple of years. When Psy had passed her probationary period, which had involved trials such as sorting a heap of mysteriously label-less clothes by designer (and then by season, and then by year), she'd thought that things were bound to improve. However, just like when she thought Venus wouldn't mind a spinach salad when they ran out of kale at the deli, Psy had been *very* wrong. It seemed that the more capable Psy proved herself to be, the more Venus sought to test her. If Psy was forever three steps ahead, Venus ensured she elongated the path to success. So, this time, Psy had decided to take the leap and create her *own* path, pitch an actual idea rather than trying to hitch on to an existing one, and she had a feeling Venus might be more inclined to hear her out if she didn't rock up with a stained top.

She was scrubbing aggressively at the stain when Eros's low, smooth voice swooped into her earshot with 'What a statement. Is it a transformation of nude? A splash of brown against a white backdrop. Poetry. Subversive.'

Psy looked up to meet the gaze of the owner of the buoyant voice. Irritatingly, even at 8:45 in the morning and under the ugly fluorescent lights of the corporate lobby, the guy was still pleasing to look at it. His dark curls were immaculately dishevelled and moisturised, his bronze skin looked like he'd just come back from Mykonos, and he was dressed with urbane casualness, in a khaki shirt layered over a thin white tee that grazed the contours of his torso. There wasn't a coffee stain in sight.

'Great, thanks, Eros. Very cute,' she said.

'Thanks, and so are you. Actually, you remind me of coffee. Hot, dark, sweet, gets my heart racing—'

Psy groaned, rolled her eyes and laughed despite herself. This was their friendship: Eros flirting with Psy as some kind of exercise in rakish coquetry, because there was no danger of her thinking it was real, and Psy acting as if Eros was a creature to observe on some kind of playboy safari, taking notes, learning what to do when she encountered them in the wilderness.

'Stop. Do girls usually fall for this? Really?'

He twitched his shoulder. 'I mean . . . yeah. They find it charming and disarming and then it usually leads to me asking if I can replace their coffee, which they graciously accept . . .'

When she looked unimpressed, he changed tack. 'Isn't today promotion day?'

'That *was* the plan,' Psy huffed, before gesturing to Eros's outfit as an idea struck her. 'And this is what we're gonna do to make sure that's still the case. You're gonna give me your khaki shirt for an emergency fit. I'm gonna change in the downstairs lobby toilet. I can't take the risk of going upstairs and having Venus see me like this. She's ended careers for less. Remember when that intern came in in jeggings?'

Eros was already shrugging off his shirt and exposing arms that were almost too obscene to look at at this hour of the morning. 'She is . . . difficult, yes. It's just a case of managing her.'

Psy forced her eyes away from his arms, grabbed his shirt from him and quickly made her way to the toilet in the corner of the lobby, with Eros following suit. 'Maybe it's easier for you to manage her because she's your sister . . . But you know what? Maybe you're right. It's all about a positive attitude. Maybe if I dig deep enough, I'll find that there's something fulfilling about living my life in total servitude to a woman who once said I had a *"hard-working nose"*. What does that even mean, E?'

Psy was in and out the toilet in a matter of minutes. When she emerged, her coffee-stained top was squished into her tote and Eros's shirt had been transformed into a cute tie-waist number with a few buttons tastefully undone. Their conversation continued without pause, although Eros took a moment to silently decide that he would never ask for that shirt back, despite it being a favourite, that Psy should keep that shirt forever, and that it looked better on her than it would ever look on him or on anybody else. He cleared his throat. 'Well, I think you have a very cute nose.'

Psy levelled a cool look at Eros. 'So, what, she's saying that the rest of my face is so unattractive that my nose has to do a lot of the leg work in making me look half-way decent? Also, later on she told me that the magazine staff get discounts for non-surgical treatments at a certain clinic. Why would she say that?'

They made their way to the elevator together and Eros swallowed and shrugged uncomfortably. He knew exactly the kind of person his older sister was and knew that, if she hadn't been related to him, they probably wouldn't have been friends. Venus was strong, smart and capable, but also incredibly ruthless and self-involved, in a way that could manifest in being borderline cruel.

Psy was also strong, smart and capable, but unlike Venus, she was also well-liked and charming. She worked harder than anyone, managed her own popular fashion blog on Instagram (Psy's Style: 20,000 followers and counting), and after two years, she was definitely due a promotion. Venus saw her potential and knew that she had the same skillset she did but without the side of vaguely murderous energy. Eros knew his sister well enough to know that she felt threatened, and that's why she did everything in her power to suppress Psy. The only major schism in Psy and Eros's friendship was that it was his own flesh and blood who made Psy cry in toilets and made her feel like she wasn't good enough. He was conscious of Psy looking at him and seeing a reminder of the woman who created the chasm between her and her dreams. The thought of Psy resenting him even for a split second made him feel sick.

They entered the lift and Psy punched the button that would take them up to their floor. They were the only ones in it, a precious rarity that comprised the best part of Eros's day. Two shots of espresso in the form of a sweet, kind, sharp-tongued, diamond-eyed girl who knew how to look at him in a way that held his senses to ransom. Now she was looking at him with some distance, not quite meeting his gaze as she took his coffee from him and took an absent-minded sip.

'Sorry. Talking about your sister like this isn't fair on you. You being my work bestie and the brother of the worst boss in the whole world gets confusing sometimes—'

'I thought I was your work husband?'

'You would be, but we only ever end up hanging out when you're not too hungover from the night before, schmoozing and hosting at some new boujie bar that's opened. Which, by the way, you never invite me to—'

'You hate those places! And so do I! I only go for work! It's part of my job. I'm the PR Director, remember? It's about building relationships—'

'Ironically,' Psy muttered, with a sardonic snort.

Eros stilled. 'What's that supposed to mean?'

A shadow flitted across Psy's face before she laughed and shook her head, defusing the tension. 'Nothing, you're just clearly not a relationship person. I would hate to tie you down as my work husband. I have a constipated Pomeranian as my work husband, but you can be my side-piece, if you want.'

'What an honour. I'd really like that.' Eros smiled, but he knew it came across as strained. 'And don't worry about this job thing, Psy. It'll be calm, I promise. Just shoot your shot.'

Eros quickly saw that relaying his mantra to 'shoot your shot' had potentially been the wrong thing to say on this occasion, because Psy was looking at him like he'd just said she had three-and-a-half braincells. 'You think shooting my shot is all I need to do? Eros, I'm not *you*. You don't get it. Nothing is *ever* at stake for you. Whatever you want, you get. Jobs, girls; it doesn't matter—'

Eros knew from experience that it was best to let Psy continue speaking, to let her words run out till the edge flattened.

The elevator doors pinged open.

'—meanwhile, I don't even have *time* to date, even if I wanted to. I've been grinding my butt here for two years, and nobody's actually grinded my butt for almost as long—'

Despite the gravity of the conversation, Eros couldn't help but interject with: 'That was good.'

Psy released a sigh as they made their slow way down the corridor to the junction of the office where they would be forced to part ways. 'I know.'

'I also don't believe that you haven't hooked up with someone in two years,' Eros challenged.

Psy shrugged. 'I don't want to just hook up, though. If I'm gonna expend energy on a guy, it has to be worth my time. Because, at the end of the day, when their tongue isn't in my mouth, I'm gonna have to hear them speak at some point, and I'd quite like to actually enjoy a conversation with them, you know? Because I have a lot to give and I want someone who is able to match that.'

Eros nodded. 'You're right. But I find it hard to believe that nobody's risen to the occasion. You're worth it.'

Psy knew she should swallow the words that were clawing up her throat, but she couldn't. It was early, she hadn't had any sleep the night before, and now Eros was being a patronising prick about the Greek tragedy that was her romantic life.

She froze, blinked up at Eros and released another humourless laugh. 'You think I'm an occasion to be risen to, like falling in love with me is a massive feat? I don't know why I'm still single, Eros. Maybe you can help me out? One time I did think about dating a guy at work, because I thought we got along. I thought he was cute, and he made me laugh. I thought that maybe he felt the same way, but he *ghosts* me for a month . . .' Eros felt a little queasy. 'And when he came back, we just went back to being friends and he acted like nothing happened. Do you have any theories about that?'

Psy's stomach dropped with regret, just as the doors to the elevator behind them pinged open again and their colleagues started streaming out. Psy's mouth parted slightly. *Hades.* She hadn't meant to say all of that and now she had accidentally let the thing that they never spoke about slip.

It had happened about six months ago, after they had both been working late. Eros had knocked on the door to the office she shared with Venus with a pizza and a bottle of wine; the good stuff, stolen from a hamper gifted to Venus. He'd asked her up to the roof.

They'd talked, they'd laughed, they'd listened to music, and then they'd kissed and kissed and kissed, and it felt so right it almost felt obscene not to consider doing it again.

Until, the day after, when Eros disappeared. Apparently, he had to go on a last-minute month-long secondment. Psy would have been fine with this if Eros had actually bothered to *talk* to her while he was away, but the few times he had replied to texts, the replies had been monosyllabic, casual, veering on cold. Eventually she had just stopped trying. She respected and loved herself far more than she loved Eros. It was fine. They were fine. She was more than fine. She was grateful she wasn't on the receiving end of his rejection-by-rote monologue that he sent to his casual hook-ups. When Eros got back from his time away, he had stopped by her desk and looped her into an easy hug, and told her that he'd missed her, that he was sorry he was so errant, but his schedule had been hectic. He had said it breezily, in a way so devoid of awkwardness and tension that she knew he'd meant it as a friend. She'd rolled up her feelings and then rolled her eyes and said, well, she hadn't missed him at all, arrogant prick. He'd smiled and called her a liar. Which she was. She was a liar. She had missed him as much as she loved him. Which was a lot.

Eventually they had just slipped back into their usual banter. They both operated within the tacit agreement that the friendship they had was too valuable to lose. At some point it got easier for Psy to be around him, to breathe around him, for her heart not to sting around him.

Now, for some reason (maybe the repressed memory had become

tired of being suffocated), that night had unfurled in Psy's mind, crept out of her mouth and calcified into a crisp awkwardness between them.

Psy swallowed. 'I, uh . . . I was joking. I didn't mean to bring that up, E,' she stuttered, as the people from the lift streamed past them. 'Sorry. I just . . . I guess what I'm trying to say is that I have given up a lot for this job. It means a lot. I know you're trying to help, but . . . maybe don't trivialise it? Understand that it's a big deal.'

'Psy—'

Psy passed the coffee back to him. 'Nope! We— Let's not do this. Seriously. I'm good. We are good. I'm really nervous about today and I'm saying things I don't mean. Thank you for the shirt. I appreciate you. I have to go.'

And Eros let her go, just as he had six months before.

When Eros offered Psy a tour, the first day they met, she looked at him like he was a specimen for scientific study, with sparkling, shrewd eyes that ran across him in fascination. It was like she was saying, so *this* is what a Shallow Fuckboi is like . . .

'Is that what you do with all the new girls? Give them a tour and, in doing so, point out all the best spots to make out? Establish yourself as a friendly, welcoming face, so they imprint on you like a duckling?' Her voice was gently enquiring and non-accusatory. She was holding a coffee as she leant against the copy machine.

Eros wouldn't have put it in exactly those terms. He opened his mouth to smile, disarm, but the way she was looking at him made him acutely aware of the taste of his own bullshit. He rubbed the back of his neck, ran a hand through his curls and nodded. 'Yeah. I mean . . . that's usually what happens. But the beauty of it is that, by doing it, on the first day they get tired of me quite quickly. An office romance is a rite of passage, so I just help them get it out of their way so they can focus on the corporate ladder—'

'Ah. So you're doing them a favour—'

'Exactly.'

'You think you're easy to get tired of?'

Psy never let him get away with anything. She had a way of sharply swerving the journey of the conversation, making it more interesting, making him unsure of the destination. All his usual breezy, self-deprecating flirtation got heavier when she got a hold of it, turned it around in her incisive, curious mind and gave it back to him, showing him his own soul. It freaked him out, but he kind of liked it. He really liked it. He wasn't the god of his own destiny when she was around.

Before he figured out a reply, Psy was smiling. It was warm and soft, and to Eros it looked like the perfect place to lie in and just be. He wanted to sink into it. 'Show me all the alcohol stashes in the office. I think I'm gonna need them.'

Eros fell in love the moment he met Psy. He knew enough about what love wasn't to know exactly what it was. He had had his flirtationships, transient stints, late nights, tequila-tainted kisses, quick unzipping and clothes ripping, but it was all empty, with both parties knowing that their connection wouldn't last until the morning. It was clean, it was controlled and Eros had been certain it was enough. Until he met Psy. Then he became intensely cognisant of the gaping vacuum surrounding the Enough. He realised that it was possible to be connected to someone without being physically connected, that when it was real, when it was true, there was no clean, no control, it just happened and it was beautiful and messy and spilt out of him, making his game malfunction.

Psy saw through Eros without trying, and Eros never had a chance to use his flirtation techniques on her because she had an energy field surrounding her that reacted with him in a manner that destroyed any pretence. Any smoothness that Eros thought he had became clumsy around her. He bumbled, incapable of saying anything but the bald truth, and the truth always came out cheesy, but he leant into the cheesiness, because it made her laugh. He liked her laugh. It pierced his skin and lit him up from within. Eros knew that Psy enjoyed his company, but part of him felt as if it was anthropological. She was ambitious, driven, and strong enough to withstand Venus's petty tests of endurance. There was no way she would genuinely see Eros as a viable option. Eros was a connecter, the Mr Right Now you went through before you met Mr Right. He was the guy for fun anecdotes; soft memories with no hard feelings. Girls were never upset that whatever they had with him didn't last because they never believed he was capable of anything more than transient romance. His friendship with Psy, however, made him feel like he had been running on 30 per cent. That he had untapped reserves. That there was more.

That night, sat on a blanket, up on the roof of their building, before they kissed, with his tongue loosened by wine and the stars blurring through tears of laughter, Eros had told Psy that she was the best person he'd ever met. He'd told her that he was glad they never hooked up because the thought of her never speaking to him again scared the shit out of him.

Psy had held very, very still and looked at him curiously for a few seconds, eyes narrowed and so sharp and scintillating they provided fierce rivalry to the stars that were surely watching them agape. As if in a kind of bodily self-protection response to the intense awkwardness he was unused to, Eros had suddenly felt like he had stepped outside of his body and was watching the scene like a spectral spectator. His body somehow knew that, if his soul remained fully inside of his body, he would have combusted from the sheer mortification; and so, it expelled it. An incorporeal version of Eros watched the scene from above as some idiot whose shirt was unbuttoned too low waited for the only girl he had ever truly cared about to try to figure out the best way to let him down easy.

The gentle night breeze had provided the only movement that night for a few moments as Psy stared at him, before the sharpness in her eyes melted into something softer.

'Is that the only reason you're glad we never hooked up?' she had asked, lowering a plastic cup full of warm rosé from her lips, black and pink, molasses and berry. The atmosphere between them tightened and drew Eros's soul back into his body, just so it could be close to her.

Eros had responded, 'That's the only reason.'

Psy had simply nodded, put her plastic cup down and said, 'I'm never gonna get tired of you, E. So there. Now you have no reason not to kiss me.'

Eros had skipped to work the next morning and found that the dirty pigeons were cooing a Stevie Wonder song. The inner-city air smelt like an orchard instead of a construction site Portaloo with base notes of deli meat. Life was, by all accounts, good. The night before, he and Psy had kissed. It had been languid but fervent, tipsy but not drunken; it made him feel tethered, but it also gave him wings. He soared with the knowledge that Psy wanted him back. Usually, when his attention was drawn to someone, he found that he already had theirs, that the 'yes' had already been released before the question was posed.

With Psy, however, it was different. She was different.

The kiss was still looping through his mind as he entered Venus's office, having been summoned for a meeting. Psy wasn't in yet, he knew that; she'd sent a text earlier informing him that Venus had sent her on an intricate errand across the city that would take half a day. He couldn't wait to see her, to cement the new iteration of their relationship and, maybe, if she wanted to, sneak into an accessories closet and talk about it, and – if she wanted – make out about it.

'What's up, sis?' Eros plopped into the seat opposite her desk happily, and Venus rolled her sharply lined eyes.

'Sis? What are we, in a cable kid's network sitcom? I really think that you formed some kind of brain problem the day that I accidently dropped you down the stairs as a kid, which has made you, like, idiotically chirpy all the time.' Venus's voice was flat, cool and unemotive.

Eros smiled. 'Why, thank you for telling me that my being a

non-monstrous human being is a result of possible sibling abuse. What did you want to see me about?'

'I need you to take down that throwback picture you posted of us on Instagram from when we were teenagers – the one with my original nose.' Venus's naturally thick curls were flattened into a seamless curtain that slinked around her angular, flawless face like a waterfall, and she flicked it off her shoulder.

Eros reclined, grinning wider. 'I think it's adorable. It humanises you.'

Venus stared at her brother incredulously. 'Exactly.'

Eros laughed and shook his head. 'Fine. Anything else or can I go now?'

Venus looked down at her computer. 'Yes. You need to stop doing whatever you're doing with my assistant or I'll fire her.'

Eros straightened up, his smile melting from his face. 'Excuse me?'

Venus's eyes calmly lifted from her screen. 'I have eyes everywhere. I need her focused. Plus, if she has a relationship with you, she's going to feel like she has some kind of affinity with me. People are already mentioning her name to me in my circles—'

'Isn't that a good thing? You should be proud—'

'Of what? An upstart who hasn't paid her dues being seen as of the same stature as me because of a little blog? Our name is power, Eros. I can't have her further connected to my legacy and, unfortunately, you're tied to that. So let her go or I'll fire her.'

Eros's jaw tightened. 'Come on, Venus. This is messed up. Even for you. You can't do this—'

Venus's gaze flashed sharply in amusement. 'Or what? You'll quit?

We both know you're not going to do that. This job is too convenient for you, and you get paid way more than you're worth, thanks to me. And if you quit, I'll fire her.'

'No you won't.'

Venus didn't blink. 'Try me.'

Eros had never truly despised his sister until that moment. He had honestly loved her, but now he definitely hated her. She was obsessed with power for power's sake. This job meant everything to Psy and Venus used it to punish her, to keep her captive. She knew she would never have another assistant more dedicated. The fact that Psy and Eros cared about each other was just another chain to Venus.

Eros nodded. 'I'll end it. But just know that I'll never forgive you for this, Venus.'

Venus smiled for the first time during their entire interaction. It was dazzling, alarmingly beautiful, and if you didn't know any better, charming. 'I don't need your forgiveness, Eros. Oh, don't look so sad: it's messing with my office aura. Look, I've sorted out a month-long assignment for you. It starts today. I've had a flight booked for you. You'll enjoy it and you'll be away long enough for whatever you think you feel for her to die. This way you won't actually have to reject her. See? I have a heart. Love you, *bro*.'

And so, Eros let Psy go.

Psy couldn't breathe. She shouldn't have said what she'd just said. It was just *him* talking about how it was nuts that she hadn't found anybody, as if she hadn't found him six months before. It had roiled up emotions she thought she'd buried. The hurt and anger spilt out of her and over their friendship, much like, say, a non-fat soy latté on a high-end high-street top she'd got on sale. Psy knew she shouldn't have resented Eros for not wanting her the way she wanted him: she wasn't his type and she knew that. He liked women who had fewer sharp edges, who were bubbly and preferred matcha-and-flax-seed smoothies to doughnuts, and that was entirely his prerogative. Eros was fun and sweet and Psy was focused and acerbic. Knowing this didn't stop her from going over that night in her head, wondering what she'd misread. She could have sworn she noticed something in the way he looked at her, tasted something in the way he'd kissed her, his arms immediately drawing her close to his body. It was as if he was as hungry as she was, as if he'd been waiting as long as she had.

Psy took a deep breath outside the glass walls of the conference room. She'd arrived just in time for the general meeting. Her plan was to propose an idea that would wow Venus and the team so much that, when she asked for a promotion, Venus would find that she couldn't say no. Psy decided she was going to pull herself together and think about the mess she'd made with Eros later.

She opened the door and beamed brightly at the team. 'Morning everyone!'

'Love the fit, Psy!'

Psy smiled at Pheme, a celebrity gossip reporter who she didn't trust with a lick of information. Nevertheless, at this moment, Psy was grateful for Pheme's warm, welcoming face, because Venus was currently staring icicles into her chest.

Venus's chin was resting on a single elegant finger, the shiny black talon on it seemed like a weapon ready to go. She tilted her head to the side, voice cool. 'Nice of you to join us.'

Psy was quite literally perfectly on time. She'd also sorted Venus's documents and briefs the night before and placed them in the conference room ready for her.

Psy smiled sweetly anyway. 'Sorry I'm late.'

Psy attempted to focus throughout the meeting while trying to balance conjuring the energy she needed to pitch with the energy she needed to get over the fact that she'd just basically confessed to Eros that she was in love with him. She failed at all three things, which meant that when Hera, Founder and Editor-in-Chief of *Olympus* magazine, asked if anyone had anything to add, it was only Pheme's pointed cough that alerted her to the moment. Psy swallowed.

'Um, I do.'

Venus's eyes swivelled to Psy's and she slid her head to the side, ever so slightly. 'You do? Aren't you meant to run things past me first?'

Hades. Psy had hoped that she was demonstrating initiative, but apparently this translated as insubordination in Venus's perfectly lined eyes.

Hera released a genial smile. She was an exquisite woman with thick, grey locs swept up elegantly on top of her head, and wide, sage eyes that seemed to see everything, even if she didn't always say anything, wanting to see how you fared on your own before deigning to intercede. Hera allowed room for growth, as more of a benevolent overseer. 'Go ahead, Psyche.'

Psy cleared her throat and tried to ignore Venus's cool glare as she scrolled through her notes on her tablet. 'Uh, so, *Olympus* takes up such an important space in this industry. Hera, when you started it, you wanted to make a statement about how powerful women could be through their choices, their freedom to make those choices, and how those choices can be reflected through style. Recently, um, I've noticed that our covers boast a very . . . homogenous sort of beauty. I get it. But given our power, I think we have an opportunity to change that, to push and evolve our industry landscape, like we used to. Which is why I'd like to propose a new campaign called *"Muse"*, with the aim of centering the everyday woman. She can be her own muse. She doesn't need to look outside, she can look within, and we want to inspire all women to do the same. Activists, humanitarians, thought-leaders, in the clothes and make-up that make them feel the most powerful.'

Psy noticed Hera's right-hand woman – the Chief-Strategy-Officer of *Olympus* – Athena, nodding, intermittently, infinitesimally, sharp green eyes narrowed. Psy felt bolstered to continue. 'I think that, if executed carefully and thoroughly, we could potentially revolutionise and challenge the concept of a universalised beauty standard. I mean, what really *is* beauty? We have a chance to assert that sartorial and aesthetic inspiration should ultimately come from who we are—'

Hera held up a single hand, just as Psy was convinced she was hitting her stride. Psy felt as if she'd run up and smacked up against Hera's palm and fallen on her butt. She knew she had crossed a line.

Hera's eyes were placid as she looked squarely at Psy. 'So, you're saying that my magazine is archaic and needs rejuvenation? And you . . . think you're the person to do it?'

Psy swallowed. 'Uh, no, I just . . .' Psy was so used to backtracking under Venus's glare that it took her a few seconds to realise that Hera was looking at her calmly, with no judgement or vilification. Psy saw a wide-open space in Hera's eyes that was calling her to press forward. 'I don't think your magazine is archaic, but I do feel that we can help mould a conception of beauty that takes our souls into account. Who we are and what we bring to the world.'

Hera nodded. 'You want to start your own platform within the *Olympus* outfit?'

'No, I . . . well, no, but, actually, I think a platform affiliated with *Muse* would be beneficial. I don't need to run it, but I would love to be able to facilitate—'

'Why not?'

Psy almost choked on her own saliva. 'Excuse me? Ma'am. Ms. Um, I—'

'Why don't you need to run it? You've worked hard for two years. You've consistently proved yourself in what is a difficult role. I've been watching you. You should definitely run it. We'll set a meeting up later to discuss it further. If you're happy with the terms, I'll have Moirai from the HR department draw up the paperwork. It will involve building your own team and working within the social media department.'

'*What?*' Venus's and Psy's voices merged, one icy, the other in soft disbelief.

'Th-thank you, Hera.' Psy could hear her heartbeat pounding in her ears, as the adrenaline coursed through her.

Hera inclined her head and let the corner of her mouth flick up ever so slightly. 'You've earned it.'

As Psyche left the meeting room, she saw Venus working hard to hide her ire and asking an impassive Hera for 'an emergency meeting of high minds'. Attempting to look like Psyche's success wasn't consuming her from the inside made Venus's beauty suddenly look askew – she looked slightly demonic. Psy smiled to herself. She was *free*. She'd done it. She'd wrenched herself from the claws of an unhinged tyrant, and with this knowledge she felt lighter, emboldened, her knowledge of her capacity made more acute.

By the time she reached her desk, she felt like the most powerful woman in *Olympus*. She was going to tell Eros how she felt, tell him that he hurt her and that she *wasn't* okay with how they left things all those months ago, and though telling him might destroy their friendship, it would be better than enduring the steady erosion of her heart. If she'd impressed Hera, then her situation with Eros wasn't anything to be freaked out by. What was a small workplace will-they-won't-they romantic entanglement compared to pitching to the most influential woman in the media world? Nothing. She was ready. Before she grabbed her phone from the desk, she noticed a small white jewellery box resting on top of her laptop. In gold cursive, *'Ambrosia'* was emblazoned on the cushioned leather of the small case. Psy knew a gift from one of the most prestigious luxury brands in the world had to be for

Venus, but she couldn't help but flick it open, in one last act of assistant privilege.

Within the royal blue velvet encasement glinted a dainty gold chain with a beautiful, delicate bow-and-arrow pendant hung from it. It took Psy's breath away. And when she read the blue post-it note folded up inside of it, her pulse jumped:

I knew you would do it. Can we talk? Roof?

'Did Pheme tell you?'

Psy's voice pulled Eros out of his own churning thoughts as he paced the roof, trying to excavate his emotions and iron them out into actual words he could say. Eros stopped pacing and turned towards the heavy industrial doors that Psy had just walked through. The morning sunlight shone directly on her, causing her brown curls to glint golden as they bounced with each of her steps towards him. The closer she got, the more of Psy the sun released to Eros – proximity revealed the bright of her eyes, the slanted twist of her lips into a smile that was half teasing, half delighted and the sparkling bow-and-arrow necklace that hung from her neck, its gold bringing out the deep copper tones of her skin. All the words that Eros had figured out to say so far dissipated through his deep exhale. She was so lovely.

Eros straightened up and tried to coax his body into a casual stance. 'Uh, yeah. She literally tweeted it as the meeting was happening. Hashtag "PsycheSlayed".'

Psy laughed and it soared over the city sirens and the bustle of the street below. 'Of course she did . . . Thank you for this necklace, by the way. It's stunning. I love it. How did you sort it out so fast? Do you just have a bunch ready to give out to girls as some sort of Eros Experience souvenir?' Her voice was jaunty, but tentative, and the vulnerable way she looked up at him made the air feel heavier and harder to haul down his throat.

Eros swallowed. 'No, uh, I got it a while back. For when you got your promotion.'

The playful smile melted off Psy's face as her lips parted slightly, her eyes glistening. 'What? Seriously?'

Eros shrugged. 'I knew you would get it, Psy. I knew something would happen for you. I knew that you would shoot your shot and *Muse* would be a hit because you're smart and brave and incredible. Speaking of . . . I feel like we need to talk about earlier—'

Psy shook her head, still looking slightly dazed as she scooped a tear up from the corner of her eye. 'Yeah, yeah, I think we do. You're really sweet. Like, the sweetest guy I've ever met and that's part of the problem. You can't keep doing things like this and expect me to forget that the kiss ever happened just because you have. It's not fair—'

Psy's chin lowered and her voice cracked, and Eros's heart cracked with it. Though he still hadn't discovered the formulation of words that would accurately convey how he felt, he realised that it didn't matter. All he needed to do was to prevent there being any more moments where Psy didn't know that she was the most important thing to him. He stepped closer to her.

'That's what I wanted to talk to you about, Psy. I didn't forget about it. I haven't forgotten about it. It's all I've been able to think about for six months. It's killing me that you think it was nothing to me, because it was everything to me. Venus found out about us and said that, if I pursued anything with you, she'd fire you. She sent me away. I didn't talk to you for a month because I didn't think there was any way I could talk to you without letting you know how I feel about you. I just felt like it was easier if I just pretended that it didn't happen. But even saying that out loud sounds stupid. And selfish. And I'm sorry for making you feel like it didn't matter. I think deep down I was . . . Kind of relieved, because it meant that I didn't have a chance to mess this up or let you down or give you a chance to see something in me that you didn't like. I was insecure and an idiot. Anyway, I quit. It was actually before your meeting. I went straight to HR. I realised that Venus had power over me because I let her believe that she did. But, mainly, I realised that there was no real way she was actually going to fire you. You're powerful and she fears that. Keeping you under her control benefitted her. Besides, I talked to my mate Ares in the legal department – the big guy I play basketball with on Thursdays – and *he* said that—'

Psy stared at Eros incredulously, and inched closer to him. 'Wait, I'm . . . I'm still digesting. She *blackmailed* you? Also, you *quit*? For me? That's insane. You know she's gonna blackball you, right? Why would you do that?'

Eros shrugged. 'I'm in love with you, Psy. Also, my sister is a witch. But, yeah, it's mostly the first part. I'm pretty sure you're the love of my life. I, uh, like your face and I like when words come out of your face. Sorry, that didn't sound romantic at all. I just . . . is it hot out here?'

Psy's eyes were prickling and she bit into her smile. 'No. But I guess this is a very intense conversation and it isn't even 12 yet, so—'

Eros forced nonchalance into his voice. 'You know what? Enough about me and my undying love for you and the fact that I am now unemployed. Let's change the subject. Tell me more about Venus's reaction in your meeting.'

Psy grinned. 'She was spitting blood when Hera announced she wants me to run *Muse* as a new social media-based platform. It was incredible. Um, what else is new with me? Oh right, the guy that I've been in love with for two years just told me he loves me back. But he also just told me he's unemployed, so . . . I may need to rethink some things. I'm a boss bitch now.'

Eros felt his heart push out a smile that spread across his face and pushed a light so bright through his eyes that it made Psy giggle, grab the front of his T-shirt and tug him closer to her. His arms slid around her waist and pulled her till their chests touched. 'Damn. Is he at least good-looking?'

Psy shook her head. 'Not at all, no. Very bad dresser too. He's sweet, though. Great taste in jewellery.'

Psy's hands were sliding up his chest to hook themselves around his neck and she smiled against his lips. 'You know what, though? You can be my assistant. It will be a significant pay cut, but at least the benefits are basic. How does that sound?'

'It would be my honour. What do you need me to do first?'

'I mean, the list is long. Coffee. Dry cleaning. Feeding my guinea pig – and you know Nymph's a biter. Making out with me—'

Eros nodded thoughtfully. 'Uh huh. So how do you like your coffee, because I can go do that right now—'

Psy laughed into his mouth. 'I've had enough coffee for one day.'

Eros pulled Psy so close to him there was no real demarcation between her heartbeat and his, and when they kissed, with *Olympus* beneath their feet and the sky surrounding them, Eros felt as if what they had was not just above the world as they knew it, but beyond it, out of its touch, its scope, itself a propelling energy that catapulted and vacuumed them into their own universe.

Attem

ITUEN KNEW THE SCENT OF WEALTH. The corner of his mouth curled up in tandem with its aroma. It was delicious, earthy and tart as it swirled up, into and around the curve of his nostrils, before settling sweet inside him. It was undetectable to the untrained nose, mingling with the cacophony of heady scents that saturated the bustling marketplace. He was able to expertly distil it from the other scents: corn, roasted by one of the wiry village boys, sweat seasoning the snack with salt as he turned and twisted the cob till its yellow burnished into gold. He could separate this particular aroma from the spiced meat, speared through a stick and barbequed till its juices ran clear.

With an expert eye and leaning his muscular back against the smooth wooden post of a stall, he cast a deceitfully casual gaze across the scene. It was all familiar to him, mentally imprinted on his mind. Every marketplace in every town looked the same. There was fresh fish and meat furthest up the strip, and if he were to progress down the thoroughfare, there would be stalls filled with clothing, jewellery, brass, exotic wares and art. He noted where the gaps were between the wooden stalls: he knew the easiest route back to the forest and had rightly judged which Uncle stored a cutlass at the back of his shop and which Mama carried a dagger tucked into the folds of her wrapper.

It was high noon on the Fourth Day. The marketplace was at its busiest, with the townspeople out to purchase goods with their week's wages. He could hear the clatter of cowrie shells and that clatter was the rhythm his heart beat to. Ituen was a hunter by trade. When his arrow was pointed towards an antelope, he was taking from the forest. This was part of the forest's cycle and he was integral to its nature. People needed to eat, and the forest had to purge, lest it sank into itself. And when Ituen stole from humans, he was helping them re-value what they held dear. Can you properly cherish and relish and revere something without the fear of losing it? It is the fear of losing ownership that gauges integrity. It defines whether a man is greedy or if he is generous. It defines what defines him. The world needed him.

In his mind, the hunter and the thief were blended, melded. His manner of operation meant they were just as noble as each other. Ituen targeted the strongest animals just as he targeted the richest of men. In the moment between the draw of his bow and the piercing of skin and sinew, a temporal vacuum was created, one within which all he could hear was the panting of his own breath, the beating of his heart. If it wasn't so fanciful, he would have sworn he could also hear the heartbeat of the animal synced with his. It almost felt as if the spirit of a god moved him, if not that *he* was a god.

When he stole from the rich, he felt the same sensation. Except, in that instance, it wasn't a sense of control over life and death that made him feel all powerful, it was the fact that he, Ituen, the only son of poor farmers from a small, exploited village, was taking something away from those who thought they were superior. He was usurping – in his own small way – the chiefs and kings that unfairly taxed his people back home and fattened themselves on their people's suffering. Ituen took their riches and used them to free those who were indentured to pay off debts. Ituen was in the business of balance.

'Sir, are you buying?' a sweet cajoling voice called out to him from the stall opposite. Ituen squinted against the sun to look at the bead-seller. He could tell from the way her yellow-and-blue head wrap was tied elaborately and from the layers of red beads that dripped on to her ample chest – tightly wrapped to lift and accentuate – that she was unmarried. She gestured to her wares splayed across a woven mat.

' . . . for your wife,' added the coquette, with a tilt of her head.

Ituen threw the picking stick from his mouth on to the dust and flashed an easy grin. He knew this call and response song. He had been practising, learning and honing his lines since he turned fourteen and his face became angular and his muscles became tauter, maidens' eyes lingering upon his for longer, with soft eyes and sharp smiles. Ituen cast a quick eye across the market and ambled over to the stall.

'I am still searching for a wife, queen.'

The bead-seller smiled wider still and ran her eyes across his trim, muscular form. 'Then you must be a blind man.'

Ituen laughed, leant a hand on the post of the stall and looked deep into her eyes. 'I'm just looking for someone who sees me as I see them.'

The woman nodded and giggled, hearing but not listening, her eyes running across Ituen's bare chest. 'I see you, sir.'

Ituen smiled. He knew his best camouflage was his looks, because no one cared about who he was underneath them. He introduced himself to villagers, winked at the girls, drank palm wine with the men and let the mamas squeeze his cheeks, feed him and lament that they weren't twenty years younger. It allowed him to slip in and out unnoticed. But there was also a part of him that enjoyed being part of a community, if only for a day or two. His parents had died when he was young and his hamlet had been robbed dry, a home turned into a wasteland because of greed and self-interest. There was nothing for him to go back to after his own family told him he was better off venturing out on his own. He wondered what it would be like to be welcomed into a home because he belonged there, not just as a guest.

However, he had a role to play in order to survive. There was only so much he could give. He had to be a shadow of himself to pass easily in and out of these villages, and so the friends he made were also shadows. He accepted this and made the most of his transience. He worked hard to convince himself that it was an adventure.

Ituen leant into the stall, about to ask the bead-seller what exactly she saw in him when he felt a shift in the atmosphere. The scent of wealth had intensified. He could also tell there was a change by the ripples in the air, the slight murmurs in the marketplace when someone from the king's company was around, the reverent jealousy and the gossiping. The bead-seller rolled her eyes and kissed her teeth in a way that immediately informed Ituen that she was looking at a woman she either hated or wanted to be.

When the bead-seller spoke again, her voice was no longer sweet. 'That one, I don't know who she thinks she is.'

Ituen straightened and turned to the brassware stall the bead-seller was looking at. He saw where the scent of wealth was coming from. She had skin as deep and as rich as the earth in the forest, as smooth and full as fruit about to drop from branch, and it gleamed and glistened in the midday sun. He only caught her profile, but it was enough. He noted the rich, textured red cloth she was wearing, designed with white nsibidi characters that boasted a royal history of wars and celestial beings. Usually that cloth was only worn by men who belonged to the upper echelons of society. The material swathed around a waist that dipped and hips that bloomed. Her arm was smooth and elegant as she picked up a sculpture of a brass leopard and turned it around in her hand. She was stood under a parasol constructed out of dried palm branches, paled by the sun. The parasol was held up by one of her ladies, who wore an outfit sporting a yellow sparrow print, the royal cypher of King Offiong. Ituen felt his heart stop and, in that moment, all the truths of the universe came rushing to him. Then he came alive again and all truth fell away until the only one that remained was the woman he was looking at.

The bead-seller continued, voice low and compressed with resentment, revealing intricate personal information in a manner only one's enemy could. 'It is King Offiong's youngest wife, Attem. An insolent girl. During the Harvest Festival, the old king saw her dancing and immediately fell in love, so he took her as his seventh wife. You should have seen her dancing. Ah! Shameless. Right in front of the king, in front of his wives. I don't trust her. Now she moves around the town as if she owns it. She has become the most prominent wife. No wife but the first is permitted to travel to the market, and yet every Fourth Day she comes.'

Ituen couldn't take his eyes off Attem, now in full view. She smiled at the brass-seller and said something to her handmaiden that made everyone laugh. 'And does the king mind?'

Ituen could hear the bead-seller roll her eyes. 'No. The king is not thinking with his mind, so how can he mind?'

Ituen smiled and walked towards the brass stall.

Attem smiled.

'He really is beautiful, isn't he?'

Her handmaiden, Affiah, put the small wooden elephant carving back onto the table and turned in the direction Attem was looking in, until she spotted Attem's target. A sharp intake of air confirmed to Attem that Affiah had seen what she had seen. 'Oh yes, madam. A fine choice. Tall. Strong looking. Handsome.'

Attem moved a little further on to a garment trader and picked up a thickly woven purple cloth, the most expensive within the spread, rare, really only displayed for proof that the trader could obtain it.

It wasn't for sale, but served as a bar against which the trader would set his prices. Attem picked it up.

'Well, all my choices are tall, strong looking and handsome, but this one also has a different air about him. Quiet. Nothing to prove. Most would never be able to tell he was a thief.' She knew he was; she had been one herself not so many moons ago.

They were whispering despite the fact that Attem's royal guards were quite a way behind them, by Attem's request, and so far, nobody had discovered the real reason for their Fourth Day market expeditions. They could take no risk of being overheard.

Attem was twenty-one and married to a withered old man who repulsed her. A king, yes, but a man nonetheless. Men, Attem found, were fools in general, and Offiong was perhaps the biggest fool of them all. This worked well for Attem. He was so bewitched by her mimicry of affection and so arrogant in his belief in his desirability that Attem found she could virtually live her life the way she pleased. She could keep him distracted by his base desires while she attended to hers. Attem felt that she should not waste her gifts as a beautiful young woman, or live a life absent of pleasure, and so she set out every Fourth Day to shop for more than just trinkets.

She would pick out a man on sight and send Affiah to interview them later. When Affiah was satisfied that they met Attem's requirements, she would bring them, under cover of darkness, into Attem's secret quarters: a cave in the hills above the village. In the morning, they were smuggled out. It was a smooth operation that depended on the cunning of the women courtiers that Attem kept close. Shunning the offer of being tended to by the daughters of the most prominent businessmen and chiefs, Attem's indoor equerries and guards were mostly servant women that Attem freed, educated and trained to be part of her retinue. She dressed them in fine uniforms and ensured they were well fed and happy. Attem made it known that, if the male guards so much as touched her women against their wishes, she would call for their manhood to be cut while they were alive. King Offiong initially resisted when he was met by the consternation of his court. They argued that Attem was disrupting the order of their land, that it would anger the gods. Attem was undeterred and unruffled, holding her head high against the weighty glare of the king's raging men. Attem had swept a soft hand across Offiong's cratered, sagging cheek, cupped his chin and whispered into his ear that she felt safer with women around her because the only man she ever wanted close to her was him. The oaf had lapped up her ego-fattening words from her palm and ordered the men to obey.

Affiah did the due diligence needed to ensure that the men Attem chose were discreet – and they were. Discretion was easy to come by, even without consideration of the mild fact that these men would certainly be flayed alive if the king discovered they had consorted with his wife. The secret was kept due to its sheer essence: they had been chosen by Queen Attem.

Attem was under no illusion as to what their attraction to her was. It was uncomplicated and she enjoyed the clarity. What was important to her was that it was her choice, a tangible flex of the only power she possessed. Her marriage to Offiong had happened because of her complete lack of choice. Her parents had been humble craftspeople who had found themselves in crippling debt to the throne after they entrusted someone they shouldn't have with their life savings. King Offiong's regime gave them two options: to give up the compound that had been theirs for generations and live the rest of their days enslaved, or run away. Meanwhile, Offiong's estate fattened with the luxuries he plundered from everyone else. A benevolent king might have waived the debt, but Offiong wasn't a benevolent king. He was the son of a man who had killed and manipulated his way to the throne; he was a violent liar, his kingship sired by blood.

Attem knew her proud parents would rather have been taken than run. They encouraged her to flee with her younger siblings, but leaving her mother and father to be enslaved was unthinkable, and she could never leave her two younger siblings to fend for themselves. Soon, Attem realised she had only one option. She would seduce the king. At the Harvest Festival she had pushed herself to the forefront of the assembled group of sickeningly young and coy girls and used everything in her possession to stand out. She had no other choice: be bold or leave her family in destitution. Either the lascivious old man fell for her or her entire world be destroyed. She had repressed her disgust and met his eyes flirtatiously. Adrenaline made her hips sway with more verve; her feet slapped the dust with increased vim. She was dancing for the life of her family.

King Offiong paid a handsome dowry. Her family were not happy about the arrangement, but could not argue with the facts: all their worries were to be quelled with this marriage. They retained their land and were able to help others in a similar predicament. All Attem had to do was drink contraceptive herb-spiked palm liquor daily, close her eyes and allow Offiong to pump into her once a week as she willed away the two-minute nightmare.

Attem's expeditions to the marketplace gave her choice, power and freedom. She was fortunate enough to win Offiong's leniency and favour. He said he liked her sass (the other wives tutted and rolled their eyes and said it wasn't her *sass* he liked) and so he allowed her to roam town once a week. She decided that being bound needn't mean that she had to be trapped.

This man, at the marketplace, with skin like silken copper pulled taut over muscles, looked like a perfect choice. She saw the fire in his eyes as they darted across the market, the slope in his mouth as he took it all in. He was a man with ambition.

Attem nudged Affiah. 'Let's move closer to him.'

Affiah looked at Attem curiously. This was not how they operated. Proximity could tempt suspicion, and this was not something that they could afford. Despite knowing this, Affiah trusted Attem implicitly. Affiah came from a herding family, but Attem never made her feel as if she was anything less than high-blooded. During the first few weeks of her marriage, Attem had seen Affiah give a man a dressing down after he tried to swindle her on some cows at the market: she had taken a stick and thwacked him in his privates. The man had tried to get Affiah arrested, but Attem intervened and called her to her court. Affiah was sure Attem was going to personally punish her for disgracing their gender in her proximity, but Attem stated that she needed women unafraid of men to be close to her. Soon after, the man that tried to rob Affiah of her livelihood disappeared. Affiah knew Attem would never put them in danger, so she nodded in assent.

'Let us move to the brass stall opposite. He will meet us there,' Attem announced.

Affiah was about to ask Attem how she knew that he would meet them there, but then she remembered: Attem always just knew what she knew.

Ituen knew this was a risk, but what was life without stakes?

Ituen strode towards the stall as the plan formulated in his mind. A casual, cursory glance informed Ituen that the queen was moving with three male guards who stood some ways behind her. This was unusual and he liked it; she was clearly a woman with confidence and power.

She was running a hand across the sculptures and chatting with her handmaiden when Ituen moved next to her. There was a respectable distance between them – not close enough to arouse suspicion, and not so far away that striking up a conversation would be awkward. She held still for a few moments before continuing to browse, chatting to the trader about the craftmanship, the detail. She was a woman who knew art. Ituen cleared his throat and picked up a bronze leopard. It was an elegant piece; the creature had a long-arched back that was ready to spring into a pounce, eyes sharp and focused, minute claws extended.

He turned it around in his palm and looked up at the trader. 'Oga, how much?'

The trader flicked an incredulous look at him. Queen Attem still had not glanced his way. He felt exposed by her lack of attention, and it was then that he realised how badly he wanted it.

The trader clucked his tongue against the roof of his mouth irritably. 'Can't you see I'm busy? Mannerless boy. You want to interrupt my trade with a queen—'

It was then that Queen Attem raised her chin. Ituen could tell from her profile that the corner of her mouth had flicked up in what seemed to be amusement. Her handmaiden was smiling too. This was objectively a good thing, but it surprised and unnerved Ituen. He had predicted an annoyance from her, which he had plans to soothe, but she had bucked his control of the situation with the curve of her lips. Ituen desperately wanted to see the rest of Attem's smile. The half that he had seen had hooked into his chest and drawn him to her. He was being baited. For once, he felt like the prey.

'No,' her voice was as sweet and husky as a night breeze that pushed through the forest. It wrapped around his pulse and squeezed tight. 'Let him go before me. I am still trying to decide.'

Ituen tried to reformulate his plan – her voice had scattered it, blown it to pieces. 'Thank you, Your Highness.' She nodded, still not looking at him. Ituen asked the trader again: 'How much?'

The trader stared irritably at Ituen, frown set in between the old folds of his leathery face, arms crossed. When he spoke, it was a snarl. 'Twenty.'

'Ah, Baba, now. Please. I am going to visit my mother's family and still have some ways to go. I need to save some money for food. Ten, abeg—'

The trader's face creased further with irritation. He wanted to get back to the queen for the ensured sale, but he knew that to be rude to this man would be an affront to her.

'Then save your money for food by not buying it. Ah! Do you not see the craftmanship? Have you ever seen features like this?'

'No, sir, and that's why I need it. It reminds me of a dream I had of the woman I would one day fall in love with. Her curves,' he tapped the dip in the back of the metallic creature, 'are as smooth this. She has the leopard's savagery and elegance. Eyes that . . .'

It was now that Queen Attem turned to look at Ituen. Her gaze pinned him, pressed against his chest and pushed the air out of him in a heavy exhale. She was even more beautiful up close, lips full and smirking, a round and majestic nose that spread a little with her smile.

'Eyes that what?' she asked, her smile now rolling around in her mouth and flavouring her voice.

'Eyes that,' Ituen swallowed, 'eyes that look like the night wrapped around the sun.'

Attem glanced at the leopard in his hand. 'Interesting. I didn't notice that. You must have a taste for the exquisite. What is your name?'

'Ituen, Your Majesty.'

Attem nodded. 'Hawk. So, you are brave, eh?'

The ground beneath them seemed to contract and draw them closer together. Ituen could hear his heart beating in his ears. Attem felt time still. Neither of them could tell who was ensnaring who.

Ituen stood strong. 'I do what I have to do, Your Majesty.'

'That is something that brave people say, Ituen. Are you hungry?'

Ituen inclined his head. 'I could eat. Thank you, Your Majesty.'

Attem grinned. 'Listen, I have a proposition. My girl Affiah,' she gestured to the woman beside her with the pretty braided knots on her head and wry eyes, 'is looking for a husband. I am the closest thing she has to family. All her elders are dead. I think you pose a possibility as a suitor.'

Affiah's eyes widened in well-practised flustered shock, before seeming to remember herself, and looked at the ground shyly, releasing a small smile, playing her role perfectly. Ituen opened his mouth to speak, but for once he was lost for words.

Attem gestured to the trader. 'Baba, please bring me the leopard, and Affiah, please pay this gentleman.'

The trader's testiness immediately fell away.

Attem finally turned to an intrigued Ituen. 'My women will collect you from this spot at sundown and bring you to eat with the men at court.'

Ituen opened his mouth to speak, but Attem's voice leapt in front of whatever clumsy words he was about to release.

'Come and feast tonight, and we can discuss the possibility of a courtship.' She took the bronze leopard from Affiah and handed it to Ituen.

'A gift.' She turned to her handmaiden. 'Come, Affiah, we must inform the guards that we have invited a guest to court this evening.'

With that, Attem and her entourage withdrew and Ituen was left with the complete certainty that any illusion of control of the situation he thought he had was gone.

*   *   *

Though he tried to stay away, Ituen found himself always returning to Attem, as if by gravitational force. It was like a compulsion. On that first Fourth Day, it didn't take him long to discover her ruse, the same way it didn't take her long to know that he was a thief. When Ituen first entered her secret cave quarters, Attem was lying on a rug with an abundance of trinkets to give him for his service. 'Since,' she said with a smile, 'I've interrupted your trade.'

She was sharp and direct. He had wondered if it was some sort of convoluted trap. He had assumed she was like the rest of the high-borns, vapid and imperious, but she had rolled her eyes at his shock and laughed. 'Come, sit, relax. Don't look so worried. This isn't a trap. I was a thief myself for a time. Before being a king's wife put food into my family's mouth, stealing from the market did. It just didn't turn out to be sustainable. I don't judge you. We do what we have to do, like you said. It's survival. But I feel like we need to do more than survive, don't you? We deserve some pleasure. Of course, you have the choice to decline. You may take the treasures either way.'

This was a new experience for Ituen; the hunter turned into the hunted. He surprised himself by enjoying the sensation of being chosen, of being seen clearly as himself. She had seen through his mask with ease and embraced what was beneath. After they lay together, they found themselves speaking, their thoughts finding places to be held within each other, their philosophies finding companionship. He learnt of her abundance of wisdom, the steely softness and immensity of her heart and, above all, her strength. He discovered a new form of wealth; one he had never contemplated the existence of, one he never knew he was searching for.

She requested he stay for one more night. A part of himself he hadn't known existed had leapt alive. When he left, the treasures she'd brought him were untouched.

'I missed you,' Ituen said, as he entered Attem's cave-quarters, six months after they first met.

Attem awaited him in the hillside cavern that she had discovered during her first days of being married to the king. It was lit with torches that made the rocky walls glow gold, was decorated with plush mats, rugs and cushions that transformed the lair into a queen's quarters. Palm wine and fruit were plentiful, and incense burnt. It was her haven. After dinners and festivities, she often retreated there, into the mountains with her handmaidens, telling the king she sought to meditate and commune with her spirits. 'How could I not be devoted to the gods when they brought me to you?' she would purr.

Attem lounged on her mat and sipped from her goblet. She smiled and gently shook her head. 'You and I both know that's against the rules, Ituen.'

Ituen grinned, and shrugged off his tan, hide-skin waistcoat. He laid it down in its usual spot, slipping off his sandals by the entrance.

'And since when do we play by the rules, Leopardess?'

Attem rolled her eyes at Ituen's nickname for her. 'I need to talk to you about that. As fun as this is, we have to be careful. You can't just appear like you do. We said the last time was the last time.'

Ituen sat himself by her on the mat. Attem's wrapper was tied low on her chest, her smooth skin glowing under the warm amber of the torches. Ituen dipped his head to kiss her shoulder, then her neck, inhaled her scent of crushed ylang ylang and sandalwood, and smiled against her skin as she relaxed and released an exhale as soft and full as her body.

'We said it was the last time the past five times,' he murmured against her throat.

Attem swallowed, trying to resolidify herself from her increasingly molten state. She gently pulled back from Ituen and held his chin. 'You shaved your beard.'

'You said it scratched.'

Attem smiled against his lips. 'Ituen, we're being reckless. We have to talk about this. Repeats are dangerous for the both of us.'

Ituen nodded. 'Are we risking getting caught? Or risking something else?' He swept a thumb across her jaw. 'I fear the something else may have already happened, Leopardess. Let's save ourselves the pretence.'

Attem ignored his implication, ignored the way her heart skipped at the endearment, and shook her head. 'With a tongue so golden you should keep your mouth shut. Protect it.'

'Ah, but then how could I kiss you?'

He leant closer to her and Attem smiled and teasingly pulled away, drawing on the power of anticipation. 'You are a ridiculous man. How were your travels?'

Ituen sighed and reclined on the mat, popping a de-seeded star apple into his mouth. 'Tedious. I infiltrated a royal court seven villages east. It was very easy. Rich people are terribly stupid. All you need to do is act the part and they don't ask questions. They are also boring. And greedy. *They* are the thieves. All they talk about is the ways they exploit the poor, the women they pay to sleep with and the wives who would rather they stop. Got a gift for you, though.' Ituen procured an onyx bracelet, tucked into the cloth wrapped around his waist, and held it high in front of Attem. She smirked as he tied it around her delicate wrist.

'Thank you, sir. But we both know you have to keep that. For the last time, I don't need anything from you.'

Hurt flashed through Ituen, but he attempted not to show it. 'No. It's for you. I want to give you something. To pay you back for the leopard you bought me, months ago.'

'It was to remember me by.'

'I want you to remember you by.' Ituen was frustrated: he had finally found a way to live life as more than just a shadow. The carefree, reckless life he had told himself he enjoyed faded into a colourless, flavourless existence in comparison to his snatched moments with her. 'Attem . . . you deserve the world. I hate that I cannot be the one to give you that.'

Attem ran the back of her hand across his jaw. Ituen was far more tender than when she had first met him. 'You give me what I want. That's more than enough.'

Attem always felt free with Ituen; nothing compressed, all her emotions flowing, unbound. There was no duty here, no mould, no rules. Here, they were their own jurisdiction. When she'd met Ituen all those months ago and chose him as her next conquest, she'd surprised herself by asking him to stay the following night. He'd surprised himself by saying yes. They'd both been surprised by the fact that their minds got along as well as their bodies did, that they'd ended up speaking till dawn, laughing into each other's skin and talking about their theories on the universe. Each time they were careful to avoid talking about the future, not wanting to corrupt the startling sublimity of the present. Every morning when Ituen had to leave, they said their goodbyes and held their own quiet sadness close to their chests. They knew how dangerous it was, and so each time felt like the last. Attem was never sure if she was going to see Ituen again. And so they told themselves that there was no heart involved in their arrangement. A sweet lie that protected them from love as well as a mouse could fight a hawk.

Ituen released a small smile, designed to dissolve the direness of their reality, the gaping schism between their worlds. 'It's funny. Though I ate well at the feast Affiah brought me today, I still remain ravenous.'

Attem laughed and allowed Ituen to tug at the wrapper loosely tied at her breast.

'You're a fool. I'm afraid I have nothing for you to dine on here, sir.'

Ituen gently pushed her towards the mat. 'I'm a hunter. I'll find something.'

His lips bumped against hers, and it didn't take long for her mouth to welcome him, for her body to beckon him. Only around Attem did Ituen feel calm, no longer desperate to move on to the next village. She was so strong, so he sought to be strong for her. She was so smart, so he found himself wanting to be smart for her. Kind, so he sought to be kind, like her. Getting to know her was his riskiest, yet most fulfilling adventure thus far.

With dawn's chorus came a now familiar heavy, stodgy dread that weighed Attem's stomach down. Ituen stirred and pulled her closer to his chest. She could feel his heart beating close to her spine, his breath warming her neck. It was agony ensconced in bliss. She stared directly into the morning light at the opening of the cave. It was strange, that the open air represented freedom, when she really only felt free in the dark, within Ituen's arms. She thought she had this situation controlled, that she could live two lives simultaneously, survive one if she had another, but since knowing Ituen, the life she lived with the king had become increasingly empty. It wasn't just the fact that she had fallen in love; it was the growing dissatisfaction of having to please Offiong, a hateful and disgusting man with no dignity and no respect for his people. Ituen, meanwhile, gave more than half his spoils away, only keeping what he needed to live. If he wanted, he could have lived like a prince. Settled. Obtained a wife – *wives*. He had chosen not to. These moments with her chosen men were meant to be an escape; a dream world she could enjoy for a time, but with Ituen this dream was starting to solidify into a reality. A reality that she fought the urge to reach out and grasp, lest it was a mirage.

'What's on your mind, Leopardess?'

Ituen's voice growled against her back, chased by his soft lips, Attem turned around and faced Ituen.

'Ituen . . . I haven't chosen anyone else aside from you since I first met you.'

Ituen picked up Attem's hand and kissed it, eyes bright. 'Me neither—'

'You don't have to lie to me. I would understand if—'

Ituen's eyes glowed like iron on a furnace. 'I swear it, Attem. May the gods strike me down if I'm lying.'

Attem felt something fierce and galvanic warm her from her stomach. She felt the bond pull tauter and wrest them closer. 'Ituen, I want you to know that you could have your freedom if you want it. Every time you come here you risk your life.'

Ituen's gaze seemed to switch dimensions, became all of a sudden deeper, fuller, overflowing with something that poured into Attem's heart till it felt it was going to explode. His grip on her became firmer, and he leant his forehead against hers. She found that air was sweeter when it came directly from him.

'Attem, listen to me. I wasn't living before I met you. I was hunting, going from village to village, hungry and wild, trying to fill myself up with trinkets. And then you arrived, and I realised that I was looking for you. I want to find a way to be with you.'

The sweetness filled Attem up till tears pricked her eyes. For a moment she truly believed that perhaps reality and fantasy could merge, that together they could breathe life into the impossible. 'This is what I want to talk to you about—'

'They're coming!' A frantic voice split the air between them, which made Attem and Ituen spring apart and Ituen run towards the cave opening, where Affiah stood panting, eyes wild, her clothes slipping off her body and her hair in disarray.

Attem's stomach solidified into rock. She barely felt the words leaving her mouth as she hastily tied her wrapper around herself. 'Who?'

Affiah's eyes glistened as she ran into the cave and pulled her mistress up. 'Attem . . .'

It was serious. As close as they were, Affiah never ever referred to Attem by her given name.

Affiah continued, 'We have to *move*. Someone has betrayed us and informed the king. They are coming. They are coming . . . oh!' She was wailing now. 'Offiong's men are coming. They are expecting to find something. Let us be going, please!' She grabbed Attem's arm and tried to drag her towards the opening of the cave, but Attem held still. Affiah looked at Attem as if she had grown five heads. Attem attempted to calm her friend down, but this only made Affiah more panicked. Attem gripped hold of Affiah's shoulders, hoping the pressure would assuage her own trembles.

'Affiah. *Affiah*, look at me! I have never ordered you to obey me. Now I will. I have to stay here. If I move, I look suspicious. I told Offiong I was worshipping and that is what he will find me doing. The fruit and the wine are offerings. You hear me? I must stay. You go.'

Attem could hear distant marching, faint chants. Her blood pounded in her ears. Affiah nodded, her breathing only slightly slower. 'I will stay with you, ma. They will be more likely to believe then.'

Attem could not argue with this. She turned to Ituen, who had somehow found the time to go to his knapsack and procure a dagger. His eyes were flinty and dark; he was ready to make his final kill. She shook her head. 'No. Put that away. You have to leave.'

He stepped closer to her. 'I'm not leaving you.'

'If you stay, we both die. My family dies. My girls die. If you leave, we still have a chance, but you have to promise me you won't come back here.'

Ituen shook his head, his eyes now glistening as the sound of marching became louder. They were close. 'I can't.'

His voice broke and Attem slapped his chest, her own tears falling freely. Ituen barely flinched. 'Wake up! Use sense. You have to, Ituen. Please. If you love me, you will leave and never return. If I survive this, I will find you, just please promise you won't come looking for me.'

Ituen drew her close to him, so she could feel his whirring heartbeat against her collarbone, pulled her head back and kissed her, wanting to be as near to her as possible, to feel wholeness before he became a lost man once again. His soul felt as if it was being split in half. 'I love you.'

Attem pulled away and kissed his wrist. 'Swear to me.'

Ituen nodded and swallowed. 'I swear.'

Attem sniffed and hastily shoved him towards the entrance of the cave, as she backed away into the darkness. 'Go. Don't turn back. Don't stop.'

In the moments before they came, Attem gave silent thanks to the gods for giving her the chance to truly live before she died.

*   *   *

Ituen heard the sound of laughing children squawking and giggling outside of his cottage. Slightly irritated, he put the chisel he was using to carve out yet another delicately eked leopard from the finest wood. He was a hunter turned carpenter; a destroyer turned creator. He had honed his craft till he was able to make an honest living out of it. When he first stopped at this village, he'd believed it was temporary. Attem would survive – she had to – and somehow she would send word for him. A month passed, and then three, and then six, and then thirty-six, still not even a whisper from her. At some point along the way he forced himself to stop feeling so his heart would stop breaking. He settled, took an apprenticeship with a taciturn old man with no sons who took to Ituen's newly acquired stoic sullenness. Ituen's wooden leopards were renowned for the elegance of their craftmanship; his patrons marvelled at his dedication to his skill, noting the heart that it took to create such a thing. He poured all his love for Attem into his creations, not knowing where else to put it.

Ituen left his workstation and walked to his doorway.

'If you don't keep it down, I won't make anything for you to play with. Is that what you want?'

The children were running directly to him excitedly, panting, talking over each other frantically, pointing at him and then gesturing towards the market. Usually they kept a reverential distance from Ituen, respecting him for the toys he made them for free, but wary of his muscular bulk and the thick beard that sprouted from his face, the way he growled his words. Now, though, they were tugging at his wrist, as if he was their playmate, pulling him towards the market square.

'Sir, sir! Someone is asking for you!'

'A *queen*! She is from a faraway village! She is so beautiful! How do you know her?'

'She doesn't even have a husband! She is queen on her own! I think she is a goddess!'

'She gave us sweet cakes!'

'She is asking for the man who makes the leopard. She said he is renowned. She said she has a comish-comissary.'

'Commission, you idiot!'

'She is asking for you, uncle! Come! Maybe you should put small oil on your face. You look dusty.'

Ituen stumbled into the marketplace, led by the tiny, chattering generals. Out of sheer terror, he tried to stop the softening of his heart – he could not physically survive mourning her again – but then he recognised the scent of wealth. It was an unmistakable bouquet of wisdom, kindness and strength. He knew it was her, even before he saw her silhouette, even before she'd turned around and hit him with that smile that jolted his heart into beating again, even before she said, 'Please forgive my lateness, my love. I got a little waylaid. You see, there was a revolution to handle and a coup to organise. I see you've grown a beard. We need to get rid of that as soon as possible.'

Ituen opened and shut his mouth, unable to move, fixed to the spot with all-consuming shock and happiness.

Attem smiled, eyes glistening. 'I also thought I should finally thank you in person for the gift you gave me.'

Ituen frowned in confusion, still stunned into silence, when he saw the small boy hiding shyly by her leg, with his copper colouring and with Attem's sunrise eyes. In just a few moments, Ituen's world came alive again, his withered heart bursting into life, growing bigger than his body. He could scarcely breathe with the force of his new joy.

Attem beamed, ruffling the boy's hair. 'The greatest gift anyone has ever given me.'

She bent down and whispered into her son's ear. 'Little Hawk, why don't you go and say hello to your Baba?'

Ituen knew the scent of home.

Yaa

YAA STRETCHED HER ARM OUT OF THE CAR WINDOW. She was on a road trip to Ankobra Beach in the middle of spring semester, second year. She was stressed with mid-terms, stressed about familial pressures; stressed about who she was supposed to be and who she was.

He had detected the dip in her mood – he always did. He always detected her shifts, the motion of her thoughts, without trying. He'd shown up at the door of her dorm room at 6 a.m. and told her to get dressed. It was almost a seven-hour drive to the beach. Yaa had insisted on splitting the drive, but he refused. And so she relaxed and slept peacefully on the way, as he played her favourite songs and intermittently reached over to gently sweep his knuckles across her cheek. She would smile in her sleep. To this day, Yaa couldn't recall a time where she'd sunk into such contentment.

When they arrived at the beach, they spoke about life, their futures, their wants, all while curled up with each other, hands tracing maps on each other's bare, sun-drunk skin, all roads leading to happiness. It was just them on their section of the beach that day – off-peak, during the week – and they were so tipsy with the heady cocktail of youth and love that they wanted to believe that God had created it just for them. They were the world's axis. They drank milk straight from the coconut, ate fried fresh tilapia and then indulged in the richness of each other, feeling nourished, galvanised.

She didn't hear the roar of the waves, only how sweet her name sounded on his tongue.

'Yaayaa,' he whispered.

They were each other's natural wonders.

'But how do you *know*?'

Yaa paused in perfecting the deep-wine hue of her lips and swiv-elled her neatly lined eyes away from her reflection to the phone lying on the marble of her bathroom counter. She knew her best friend couldn't see the incredulous look she was levelling at her through speakerphone, but she also knew Abina would feel it by instinct. After a few seconds, Yaa sensed her best friend roll her eyes as her voice rose from the phone.

'Abeg. Don't look at me like that. I hate it when you look at me like that.'

Yaa smirked. 'Then don't ask silly questions. How do I know Kofi is gonna propose tonight? Maybe because it's my birthday and we're going to the best restaurant in the city and he paid for me to get a manicure, oh, and I stumbled upon a ring hidden in his blazer pocket?'

Yaa

Yaa turned back to the mirror to finish up her lipstick and scrutinise her look. Her high cheekbones were subtly glowing in a manner that mimicked the glow of love. Her dark eyes were accentuated to look wider, brighter, which would assist in the expression of pleasant surprise that she intended on pulling later. Her deep skin gleamed smooth and poreless – ready for any close-up photos that might ensue. Yaa ran a hand through her straight, thin, waist-length twists to ensure that they weren't tangled at the bottom and inhaled deeply. She looked exactly how she knew this evening was going to be. Perfect.

'Oh yeah. The ring that you *accidentally* found because you just so happened to be going through every single blazer he owned.'

Yaa laughed as she carefully combed through her eyelashes with an inky-black bristled wand. 'It was an accident. I was looking for change to tip a delivery guy with, that's all. He should have been more discreet.'

Yaa's best friend scoffed. 'Sticking to your story, huh? Like searching his blazer pockets isn't part of your morning routine. Anyway, that isn't what I was asking. What I actually meant was how do you know you wanna marry him?'

The question stilled Yaa as she lifted up a bottle of perfume to spritz on her wrist. The question was so foreign it made her mind buck and recoil. It raked against life as she knew it. The knowledge that Yaa was going to marry Kofi was always an always.

Yaa and Kofi's families were the most influential in the Ashanti region and were considered something close to royalty in the province's capital, Kumasi. Kofi's family was a political dynasty of chiefs and councilmen and governors littered through generations, while Yaa's family was one that had grown from a plucky market-trader, who went from one stall in old Kejetia market to the biggest department-store chain in the region. Yaa's family had started unions and safeguards for traders, rattling the local government. Kofi's family was old money, old power, they represented a time in the past where there was a clear distinction between market woman and ohemaa, whereas Yaa's family blurred the lines and established a new world where tradeswomen could become queens, with her great-great grandmother – after whom she was named – leading the way.

For almost a century the two families were natural enemies, representing a war between classes, the people versus privilege, both units occupying the same space while resenting each other for it. Yaa's family served the people where they could, creating jobs and benefits where the government lacked, while Kofi's family begrudged Yaa's for stirring up the common people and for awakening disillusionment towards the ruling classes. However, by the generation of Yaa and Kofi's parents, the animosity weakened as Yaa's family's position in society strengthened and became sedentary. The families soon found a tentative closeness, bound by power and proximity. By the time Yaa and Kofi were born – within the same year, both to be only children – the two families had become allies and, ostensibly, friends, sharing beach houses and ambitions.

Ever since Yaa could remember, she had been affectionately known as 'Little Wife' to Kofi's family. Since Kofi's father's death, he called Yaa's father 'Pa'. The two families recognised that their best chance at continuing (and controlling) their respective legacies was to merge into one. So, Kofi and Yaa attended the same schools and, when they came of age – through nurture rather than nature – the two saw their relationship mature into romance. Save for the three years they'd split for university, when they pragmatically agreed to break up in order to eventually be better partners to each other – Yaa's idea, which Kofi eagerly agreed to – they'd always been together. It was never truly a friendship, but an understanding. A partnership. They complemented each other. Kofi had studied law and Yaa studied politics and business. Now, already a successful lawyer, Kofi had started formulating his campaign strategy to be the youngest councillor in the district, which in turn would set him steady on the path to be the youngest regional minister, while Yaa ran the CSR division of her family's company. Her plan was to work closely with Kofi – within the political role of his wife – to encourage the development of social relief measures. Yaa made Kofi more accessible to the common people. Kofi had the legacy and Yaa had the ideas. They were a team and they balanced each other. Kofi and Yaa, Yaa and – well, it was never Yaa and Kofi. It was Kofi and Yaa. Kofi's identity flowing into Yaa's, a fact that was entrenched and manifested physically in the couple's portmanteau sobriquet, which was typed below glossy hi-res pictures of them together at galas: *Kofiyaa*. They were the literal poster couple; young, thriving, in love and successful. Beautiful, aspirational, picture perfect.

Kofi's mother spoke about her grandchildren, as if they'd already been born; of how they would be a blend of Kofi's mind and Yaa's looks, with, perhaps, Kofi's family's colouring, which she would add in with an impassive smile. Yaa, after all, had the deep sun-steeped skin of an ambitious market woman. Yaa didn't mind, because she knew that Kofi's mother needed to believe that Kofi brought more to their partnership. Though their families were now, technically, societally equalised and despite all amicability, Kofi's family was still Kofi's family. Their alliance with Yaa's family had been a tactical necessity and was a bid to retain their throne. Years of authoritative positioning laced their blood with an elitism that meant his mother needed to assert that Yaa needed Kofi more than Kofi needed her. Yaa allowed her the small grace of letting her believe it. In many ways it was a compliment, for Yaa was proof that you could be more than a charm on a man's arm used to sweeten deals, or a tincture that made men seem softer, evidence of heart. Yaa could ignore Kofi's mother telling her that there were creams she could use to 'heighten' her skin, as she would supposedly be even more beautiful with 'some of the sun lifted out', because of the objective fact that Yaa had always gotten all the top prizes in school over Kofi. At political events, *she* was the one whose brain wanted to be picked, who engaged in debates that disturbed men enough for them to be both fearful and impressed. She knew this made the old lady uncomfortable – it agitated what she knew to be the norm, destabilised her contentment. And so Yaa allowed Kofi's mother her futile barbs. It didn't matter either way. Their futures were fused. The knowledge that she and Kofi were meant to be together wasn't so much imparted to Yaa, but built into her, and then enshrined as the only world she knew. It became intrinsic to her thought processes, vital to how she strategised her life and career. Yaa acknowledged her power but also saw that partnership with Kofi amplified it. She recognised that he helped the world open up to her.

All this was hard to summarise to her friend, even if she wanted to, so Yaa shrugged; a gesture she knew Abina would hear in her voice, but also one she hoped would disrupt the curious tiny spindles of unease that had started forming in her stomach. 'I just know. It just *is*. There is no world where we aren't a thing.'

'Well, as sweet as that sounds . . . that's a lie. There is. There was. The world I met you in. University. Remember that? Remember that girl? Don't you miss her?'

Yaa swallowed in an attempt to push back down the tension that had started to crawl up her throat. 'Hey, um, I just got an alert telling me that my Hitch ride is outside my building.' Mercifully, the truth gave her a way to evade the questions she couldn't answer.

'Yaa—'

'I have to go.' Yaa took her phone off speakerphone and propped it between her neck and ear as she ducked out of her bathroom into her hallway, where she slipped her black open-toed heels onto her freshly pedicured feet, her nails shining, pearly-white.

Abina sighed. 'I'm sorry. You know I just want you to be happy, sis. Does he make you happy?'

Yaa met her own gaze in the hallway mirror. Despite her eyes being carefully decorated to accentuate soft joy, all her elongated lashes did was tug at something dark in her eyes. It was sharp and stark, and it was a part of herself she'd grown accustomed to hiding. It seemed to be leaping out to try to tell her something. Yaa blinked and forced out a smile, something bright and wide enough to push the bad feeling aside. It was the smile she gave at dinner parties when Kofi squeezed her knee to get her to dial back what he called her 'social justice rant', the firm grasp that told her she was spilling out of the 'girlfriend who is smart but not enough to embarrass me' mould. Yaa smoothed out the scooped neck yellow kente dress that skimmed over her curves. The neckline was low but not too low, dress length hovering just above her knees. It was sexy yet still demure, fitting for a future minister's wife, ready for the photos that would be plastered on society blogs and Instagram roughly thirty minutes after the proposal. Kofi would definitely have hired a photographer. Yaa nodded at her reflection.

'We're perfect for each other.'

Running late at the office. Meeting overran. Have pushed the reservation. Another 20 minutes or so. See you soon. K

The car pulled away as Yaa blinked at the text from Kofi in the backseat. She rolled her eyes. Not *tonight*. Of all nights. Even if it wasn't *the* night, it was still her birthday. The knowledge that the two of them would be together forever meant that Kofi took Yaa for granted. He showered her with gifts, took her on luxury trips and they dined finely, but when it came to his time, to the listening, to the seeing, their long-destined relationship overrode any need for him to try. They were to be together and nothing would change that. He knew that. The parties she threw him, the way she talked him up to crowds of ordinary people at campaign rallies, the loud laughs and arm rubs she gave him at dinner parties and the uncomfortable lingerie she wore for him was the result of what was apparently her sole duty to put in effort. All Kofi felt he had to do was show up, and he couldn't even do that, apparently. All he had to do was pretend for one night that he wasn't fucking his assistant, but he couldn't even do *that*. She let him have the assistant fucking. The assistant was ambitious and smart; she knew this because she knew Kofi was paying for her after-work business management classes. Yaa found her useful. When Yaa made it clear that she knew about them, Yaa quieted the assistant's panic by letting her know that it didn't have to be a big deal; all Yaa wanted to know was the major meetings that Kofi sat in on but didn't tell her about. She wanted to know about the draconian policies he was angling to put into place that protected the elite and suppressed the poor, whom he had made promises to protect when he came into office. The assistant smiled knowingly and said: 'No problem, madam.' It benefitted them both.

Still, there was a base level of respect that Kofi sometimes couldn't be bothered to rise to, and that irritated Yaa. They'd known each other their whole lives and, for better or worse, they were in this together. That should count for something. The only time Kofi ever cried about his father was to Yaa, in the privacy of their unique intimacy. She was the only one who knew that his rage at his father's absence when he was alive had only been exacerbated by his death. And whenever his mother's jabs hit too close to the bone, Kofi would always fight for her. Regardless of anything else, they were a team.

But there was no apology at the end of the text. Why apologise if you felt like you'd done nothing wrong? Yaa swore under her breath. The swearing was impressive, her own a particular cocktail with particular stresses on certain words. Kofi always hated it when she swore, he said it was her market-woman blood coming out. Yaa was contemplating telling the Hitch driver to take her back home when, while stopped at a traffic light, he spoke.

'*Yaayaa.*'

The low, familiar voice pierced into her, curled around her heart and squeezed so hard that Yaa gasped. Only one person called her 'Yaayaa'. It was her, doubled over. Her at her fullest. It was a nickname that tasted like a sugarcane-whisky-laced kiss, both indulgent and intoxicating.

Yaayaa. The name had been buried for so long – suffocated, really – that when it was freed, it took up all the air in the car, made it difficult for Yaa to breathe. The screen of her phone began to blur as she looked up to meet the eyes of the Hitch driver. She needn't have looked to verify. She knew. The odds of this happening were far too unlikely for it not to be happening. It was a terrible joke, a torturous irony that would have made her laugh if she hadn't been its victim. Maybe she'd laugh tomorrow. Maybe this could be a bachelorette anecdote. There was a version of her that wanted to slip out of the car at this stop light and run back to her apartment, but that part of her was becoming less realistic with every second that passed. That version of her was beginning to feel like an imposter. Every inch of her was in a state of remembrance, reshaping itself to a former form. Just at the sound of his voice.

She looked up. '*Adric.*'

There were two people in the world who knew her, the potent her, the essence of her and the honest her. One was Abina, her best friend and spirit-sister, and the other was the man whose eyes were currently sliding from soft, warm surprise to something colder, a forced distance.

He nodded. She could see the tension in his face, the tightening in the sharp jaw she used to enjoy sliding a finger across, raining kisses down the trail.

'I saw the name on the app, but I didn't figure it would actually be . . .' He paused and looked at her in the rearview mirror. 'I knew it was you when you got into the car, but I didn't know if it was best to pretend I didn't recognise you or to say something. Then you swore and, well, I always liked it when you swore. Really disgusting stuff. Extremely graphic. Poetic, really.'

Yaa laughed and felt the knots in her belly begin to loosen. She saw his shoulder hitch up in a shrug. 'Yaayaa just came out. Sorry.'

She swallowed. 'Don't be. You're the only one who ever called me that. You will always be the only one who will ever call me that.'

Yaa and Adric first met at a student rally in their first year of university. He didn't know who she was; he knew her only as the girl at the front of the protest, creating pithy chants against elitist politicians who wanted to make the requirements for grants more stringent. The fewer people able to attend university, the more power remained in the same hands. He had no idea that she was protesting against the people who she was to be married into. He caught her eye, and she'd almost stumbled by the force of how he looked at her. It was more than preliminary attraction; it was a want to know. They went to the post-protest social at a student house and there Yaa found out that Adric was the son of a skilled carpenter and seamstress. Yaa told him her people worked in craft and trade too and quickly changed the subject. She knew she should have told him the truth straight away, but she was seduced by the bubble she was in and giddy with their flow of conversation. They had an immediate easy playfulness. She liked his mind, liked that he wanted to know hers. Love immediately pulled at her. It was a kind of love she'd never known; unburdened, pure and without expectation. Transparent love, unqualified love. They kissed for the first time that night at that student party, while dancing, in the corner in a room with dimmed lights and plastic cups full of warm liquor and flat mixer. The air was electric with R&B, possibility and promise. They were young people coming together to effect change, young people with their future in their hands, young people with their arms around each other, his wrapped around her waist, hers around his neck, drinking each other, rising up within each other.

They fell fast, heavily, startlingly into heady love, a love that thrummed through her veins and pulled her essence up to her skin till she was glowing with it, till her mother wondered why she looked different and her friends made fun of her. They discussed ideas, perspectives, learnt from each other, their minds calling and responding to each other, their bodies following suit. Yaa divorced her pre-written future from her world with Adric. When she was with him, she could pretend she was just Yaayaa, unencumbered. She knew it couldn't last. They had been dating a year when Adric saw a text from Kofi flash on Yaa's phone screen.

Yaa

Argument with my mum. Call? I need you. And miss you. No one gets it like you do. K

Though they weren't together, Yaa and Kofi still had an attachment they couldn't untwine themselves from.

Through ragged sobs, Yaa explained that she'd never cheated on Adric – that she would *never*. But she did have to explain that she had lied to him about who she was. He was confused, angry, heartbroken. He wasn't bothered about her background – Yaa was still who she was, still believed in what she believed in – but the fact that their relationship had to be finite killed him. She told him that she had a plan, that Kofi was just a means to an end, that she felt she could change the system from within. Adric had laughed bitterly and stared at her before realisation softened his eyes. He almost looked sorry for her.

'You really believe that, don't you? I've seen you mobilise students and have the faculty shaking and now you're talking to me about some archaic child betrothal shit. You have to be with this guy because of family alliances? You think you're going to marry him and change the world? You think it won't corrupt you? You think sacrificing us is worth it for a fantasy? Yaa, what are you even talking about? Who are you?'

She couldn't answer any of his questions. She just didn't see a way out of it. It was a world that she didn't know if she could extricate herself from without parts of her falling away with it too. Kofi was part of her scaffolding. Kofi made sure to check in on her, reminding her of her duty, of the ticking clock on her happiness.

Both Adric and Yaa cried the night she confessed. They sat on the floor and whispered, holding hands, they stood up and screamed in each other's faces, they paced, they embraced. They talked, and they talked, and they talked. Then, finally, in a low voice that reverberated through Yaa and made her heart shatter, Adric asked if their entire relationship had been an experiment. He asked if it was just an adventure for a rich girl who thought she would slum it to make herself feel better about her privilege. He asked her if she laughed at him behind his back, at his crappy car, at his bartender job. The tears were falling faster down Yaa's cheeks when she grabbed his face and kissed him in response. He kissed her back. It was deep, the kind of kiss that reached all the way to the heart and twisted it, the kind that you both find and lose yourself in. When they finally pulled apart, she shook her head.

'You're the best person I know. This was real, Adric. This is real. I am the realest I ever am with you. I'm messy with you. All over the place, with you. I don't have to be perfect with you, I just have to be. This wasn't an experiment. This was me, the purest me I've ever felt. For the first time, leading my life . . .'

'So, lead, Yaayaa. Choose yourself. Rid yourself of these people and their expectations.'

Yaa opened and shut her mouth. It wasn't that simple. Their families had deals together, their futures were tied up in each other. Kofi and Yaa didn't know a world without each other. Kofi had always been there: he was her first everything. Kofi didn't know how to love because his parents didn't, but he tried in his own way, made up for it where he could. There were worse ways to make a difference in the world. After a few lethally silent moments, Adric nodded, eyes steely, glinting.

'I'll miss who I thought you were.'

He walked out of her room.

Yaa didn't know what she'd expected to happen. The bubble was bound to burst. The rupture felt bigger than a break-up with a boy – it felt like a break-up with herself, not because the boy had been sutured to her like Kofi was, but because she'd been most herself with Adric. She knew she would never feel that again. The heartbreak was so brutal that Yaa had to split herself in two to survive it. She managed to pack away one half of herself, the Yaayaa she wanted to be, and subdue it with the half that had to believe that Kofi was her destiny, and Adric was not. Adric was the break she needed in order to focus on her duty. Frivolity was now out of her system.

She let the shrewd Yaa take over from then on; the version of Yaa who would later have it in her to ignore the fact that her boyfriend was fucking another woman on her birthday. Kofi had inherited his father's money and weak will, but Yaa knew that, if Kofi was going to listen to anyone, it was going to be her. He trusted her more than anyone else in the world. He was insecure, and as strange as it was, she knew that he admired her, relied on her strength. During their time apart at university, despite screwing half of the student body, Kofi had messaged her constantly, needing reassurance, needing someone who saw past his money and name. That Kofi-less time meant she had been able to grow without the spine of responsibility, learn who she really was. Now, she understood her purpose even more. Her power had to be channelled through him. Though Yaa now found herself having to cut and contort herself to fit back into her and Kofi's world, she found that this was the most effective way she knew to make a difference.

Now, though, she felt parts of herself growing back, unfurling in the back of the taxi, her body hot, her heart pounding.

'So, what are you doing – I don't mean – there's nothing wrong but . . .' She was tripping over her words, her tongue clumsy, as she tried to reacclimatise to being around Adric.

'I know there's nothing wrong with me driving a taxi, Yaa.' His voice was hard, and pushed at Yaa's heart till it fell into her stomach.

'Yes. Of course.'

There was a pause as Adric moved off from the traffic light. He sighed and rubbed his forehead.

'I teach politics at the City Polytechnic. Mama got sick a few months back. She's fine, don't worry, but I do this after work some-times to help pay some of the bills.'

Yaa had been lobbying for a bill for months that would support the elderly if they became sick and had to stop working and had been encouraging Kofi to include it in his campaign. He'd said, as he did about most of her suggestions, 'Everything in due time, Yaa.'

Yaa cleared her throat. 'I'm sorry about Auntie. I'm glad she's fine. I miss her.'

She saw Adric nod. 'She misses you too. Mentions you all the time. She likes seeing you on the news, talking about things that matter. Doesn't like seeing you on the news next to Kofi, though. She said she doesn't trust him. His ears are too small.'

Yaa smiled. Trust Adric to infuse some semblance of normality into the awkwardness, to calm her nerves. 'Hmm. They *are* kind of tiny, aren't they? Must be why he struggles to hear anything besides his own voice.'

Within the silence that fell, a rapper on the radio rhymed 'waist' with 'rotate' and offered to 'pound it till you're soft like fufu'. After a few moments, Yaa and Adric both laughed, hard, cathartically, at the absurdity, at the inappropriateness, and at the tragedy of it all. They stopped at another traffic light.

'Can you unlock the car please?' Yaa asked.

Adric turned around, eyes aghast. 'You serious? Yaa . . . at least let me drop you somewhere safe!'

'Unlock the car. Please. I'm uncomfortable.'

Adric blinked, startled, before he nodded and turned around. The doors clicked. Wordlessly, Yaa slipped out of the backseat of the car, and slammed the door behind her. She walked around to the front and slid into the front passenger seat next to Adric.

She exhaled deeply. 'Better.'

Adric shook his head at her, a smile spreading across his handsome face, so bright it was like her own personal dawn.

He laughed. 'You had me there.'

Yaa giggled, a sound she hadn't made in years. 'I couldn't help it. Sorry,' she paused as her smile faded, 'I am *so* sorry.'

The traffic light switched to green and Adric nodded as he looked out into the road, his jaw tightening again. 'It was a lifetime ago, Yaayaa. We were children.'

Yaa's throat tightened and she looked down. 'What we had wasn't childish.'

Adric released a long breath. 'No. It wasn't.'

Yaa lifted up her head and swallowed. 'What I did was selfish. I know. I just . . . for the first time I could live my life without all those expectations. For the first time someone was seeing *me*. I wanted to hold on to that for as long as I could. Hold on to you. I think I was scared of letting go of Kofi because I was scared of what I would be with my future unwritten. Once you have freedom, if you fuck up, that's on you, you know?'

Adric glanced at her, and as quick as it was, Yaa saw something warm and tender that balmed the long-cracked parts of her heart before he spoke. 'That's the beauty of it, though. The power is with you. And the power has always been with you, Yaa. I've always seen it in you. I saw it when we first met at that rally, and I see it in you with everything you do today, fighting for progress and trying to use your status for good. I think you underestimate yourself. I under-stand why. You were brought up to think you needed them. I didn't understand that then, but I understand now. They made you feel like you weren't enough on your own and that's hard to shake. I'm sorry for how hard I was on you. I'm sorry for the last thing I said to you. I know who you were with me was real.'

Yaa stared at Adric's profile, the slope of his nose, the fullness of his lips, and realised that she recognised his face as home. He still somehow was able to see her in the midst of his own hurt. Unthinkingly, she slid her hand over his on the gearstick and squeezed. Heat immediately rushed through her and made her belly swoop low. She removed her hand in a panic, mortified by her bound-ary crossing. She'd broken his heart and now she thought she could just *hit* on him while he was working, like some kind of pervert? Yaa was contemplating hurling herself out of the moving car when she felt his knuckles graze her cheek gently, sweetly. His eyes were still on the road. She turned his hand over in hers and pressed her lips into his palm.

Yaa's breath hitched as they pulled up in front of the restaurant where she was meeting Kofi. Adric unlocked the doors. Her stomach plummeted as reality crashed down on her, forcing the warmth out of her. They were both quiet for a while as they stared ahead.

Adric cleared his throat. 'Sorry I didn't get you anything for your birthday, by the way. I forgot on account of the whole us not speaking for six years because you shattered my heart into a million tiny pieces to date a tiny-eared prince.'

His voice was straight, but he turned and gave her a small smile as Yaa laughed. She laughed until her eyes filled up with tears, she laughed until her cheeks ached and she shook her head and groaned, wiping her eyes and smearing her make-up happily, messily.

'Oh, man. You're the love of my life.'

Adric didn't say anything. He looked into the bustling, glamorous restaurant and then back out into the road. The air in the car felt heavy, but comfortable. The energy between them hadn't aged. It was as fresh, as vital, as fertile as it had always been and Yaa knew then she didn't want to leave it.

Eventually Adric's voice – now gruffer – broke the silence. 'This was going to be my last ride for the night.'

Yaa looked out into the restaurant. Apparently, they'd been sitting quietly for a while, because she spotted Kofi walk into the foyer. Kofi, who embodied everything that kept her from herself, who had been as imprisoned by expectations and pressure as she was. It was time for them both to be freed. Yaa looked at Adric.

'Then where are we going?'

Adric turned to her. If he was surprised, his face didn't betray it. 'Wherever you want to go.'

Yaa leant in and kissed him. He kissed her back. It was deep, the kind of kiss that reached all the way to the heart and twisted it, the kind that you both find and lose yourself in. She pulled away, swept her thumb across his jaw, and whispered, 'I'm driving this time.'

He passed her the keys.

Siya

SIYA CISSE HELD HER BREATH. Any sudden movement would mean death; not just for her, but for her people. She was their shield, and so had to remain strong. Her arm hooked tighter around the thick branch, fastening her to the trunk as she angled her bow and arrow so it pointed downwards. Her aim was incisive. She felt the presence of her men and women around her, waiting in the shadows of the leafy canopies for her signal, clad all in black so that they melted into the inky night. Siya's hair was wrapped tight under a deep purple scarf that swathed across her face so that only her nose and darkly lined eyes were exposed. She turned to the tree next to her to see Maadi. It was his job to anticipate her every move, and sure enough, when she turned to look over at him his eyes were already waiting for her, bright in the dark. She nodded at him. He yanked his scarf below his mouth before angling his own bow and arrow.

'Fly!'

His voice boomed through the forest just as Siya's arrow swooped down and pierced a man in the back, felling him. Her bow was the Mother, and at her command were all her children, arrows laced with an elixir that subdued its victims. These arrows fell from the trees like lethal fruit, bringing a new season that would rain righteous death, justice from the skies. Below Siya men cried and cursed as they struggled to aim their weapons upwards, chaotically trying to fight what they could not see.

'Who is your commander? Let him come down and fight like a real man!' one brave and stupid waning soul cried, as he struggled to stand. He held up his spear, the one he had intended to use to fight his way into the citadel of Wagadou and kill her people. Siya could see from his attire that he must have been their leader.

Maadi laughed. 'Are you sure you want that?'

Their combat unit ran their drills high up in the mountains, and so they were called The Eagles. They trained at night as well as in the daytime, which meant that their eyes were accustomed to the dark, or more accurately, the dark bowed and weakened for them.

Siya saw the guerrilla chief thump his chest three times, looking up and searching the trees for his opponent. Clearly, he was stronger than his counterparts, who were groaning on the forest floor.

'Show yourself!' he bellowed. 'Are you a panther or a sparrow?' He spat on the ground – the height of disrespect, a direct insult to the ancestors of Wagadou. He dropped his spear and withdrew his dagger. He was demanding one on one, blade to blade combat. He spread his arms wide and hissed like a python; the rallying call of his people.

'Come fight the serpent! Fight Bida!'

From the floor, his soldiers hissed in reply, giving their assent for the fight to continue without them. Emboldened, the terrorist continued: 'I heard this squad of pigeons is led by the greatest warrior of Wagadou. Reveal yourself, my friend!' he sneered. 'Let's see how great you are. Are you a man or a bitch?'

Siya and Maadi locked eyes and grinned. Maadi beat his chest three times – a sign of challenge acceptance – but it was Siya who threw her bow and arrow to the forest floor, leapt from the tree branch and landed on her feet in front of the enemy.

She straightened up from her bent knees, unwrapped the scarf from her head and tied it around her waist. Her thickly locked hair fell down to her back as she unsheathed her favourite dagger – the one she called 'Princess'.

Siya smiled at the oaf. 'A bitch, sir.'

The gang leader looked Siya up and down, rubbed his eyes, and roared with laughter. 'Come, now. I have another dagger for you that you're certain to enjoy a lot more. It doesn't have to be this way.' His men laughed with him.

Siya's smile chilled on her face as her soldiers dropped from the trees behind her using ropes and – under Maadi's direction – began to fight and bind up the Snake Men. The gangster chief looked around, startled, as he observed Siya's army of men and women expertly corral and capture his cronies. He turned back around to see Siya walking towards him. Siya spun Princess between her fingers and caught her by the hilt.

Her opponent straightened up and lifted his dagger, ready for combat, swallowing reality down and clinging to his arrogance. He snarled at Siya. 'The Soninke people are weaker than I thought. Sending a woman to defend their land?' He shook his head in a grotesque pastiche of regret. 'I'm sorry to have to do this. You would have looked so pretty on your back.'

Siya laughed; it was sweet like birdsong or like the sound of a babbling brook after a long and dry expedition. It chimed through the groans and struggles echoing through the forest. She tilted her head. 'So will you. Lifeless.'

Siya watched the blood run down the drain as she washed herself with black soap. The hot spring water, from the cave her quarters were built into, ran over her and rinsed the harshness of the night off her skin. Siya still felt the struggle inside her bones. It had been messier than usual. Tonight's ambush had more men than previous attacks and was more aggressive. The Snake Men were led by the faceless conqueror known as Bida, who sought Wagadou's fertile soil and gold, and Siya could sense he was getting progressively hungrier. When every shady proposition had been rejected and Wagadou had refused to sell her soul to the devil, Bida had declared war. Livestock theft had turned into outright terrorism of the tribes on the outskirts of Wagadou. So, Wagadou folded their cousins in and protected them, but the situation was escalating quickly. The Snake Men had begun kidnapping women and children, and the men of Wagadou left behind with broken hearts had started spying, turning their backs on their ancestral land to swap secrets for their family's safe return. Bida's Snake Men were true to their word. The traitors of Wagadou would indeed be reunited with their families; the Snake Men just failed to mention that it would be in the afterlife.

In the past year, Bida's Snake Men had attacked Wagadou six times. Siya's army had defeated them five times. The first attack was quelled by Siya's father, Khina Cisse, beloved and benevolent chief warrior, Ghana of Wagadou. He died in the bloody battle. Wagadou wailed but Siya channelled her grief into creating a clear war strategy. She used all her rage to power intensive martial training. She made sure all the saltwater of her tears left her body through sweat. Her mother had died when she was young and her father had reared her as a warrior, training her with his men, taking her running on hills and gruff terrains, teaching her how to climb, and to fight; to use fear as fuel. He was the one who taught her to leap from a high distance and land on her feet without injury. To bend her knee in a certain way, lean her weight at a specific angle, strategically empty her mind so she had acute focus on that one goal. He taught her to fly. She could twist nature around herself. Where others used ropes to drop from trees, Siya communed with the wind.

So, when her father's court and advisors ignored Siya's qualifications, aptitude and passion for protecting her people to coronate her uncle, Dyabe Cisse, Siya knew to stay silent and act strategically. Her father's younger brother was a jealous, lazy and power-hungry cad, who, when appointed to his position, proclaimed a motion to form a coalition with Bida. Siya's suspicions were confirmed; Dyabe had betrayed her father. She didn't riot as her uncle wanted her to. He'd have her sectioned and say she was mad with grief. Siya didn't allow herself to be bound by the rules of nature, so there was no reason why she should be suppressed by the rules of a man. Instead, she immediately, diligently, secretly organised a renegade regiment. Through underground messages sent through trusted allies, she called on all who believed in her father's mission to help her save Wagadou. She would not let his death be in vain; she would stop their great nation from bowing to the Serpent that was Bida.

A good number of Wagadou's official army defected to Siya's secret battalion, including Maadi, a young, exemplary soldier who her father had taken a particular shine to as a mentee. It was Maadi who rallied and bolstered the sceptical to Siya's team. He was a trusted soldier, clean in heart and strong in might, known throughout the land for his unswerving integrity and dedication. At thirty-two, he had been tipped to be the youngest officer to take over Khina's command before his untimely death. Dyabe Cisse, knowing Maadi's sharp skill and influence, had planned for Maadi to be his deputy, attempting to cajole him with ill-gotten land, palaces and protection. Dyabe knew that, with Maadi's allegiance, came the loyalty of the bulk of the army; that his trust was the trust of a nation.

Yet, upon the official announcement of Dyabe Cisse's appointment, Maadi went to Siya. His eyes were dark, glinting, full of rage and hurt. She was where he knew she would be; a spot in the forest near a lake where he, her father and Siya used to rest when they went on recreational treks. Silently, his gaze locking on to hers, Maadi drove his spear into the soft soil and bent his knee before her.

'I will do whatever you want me to do, Siya Cisse. You are my chief warrior. I recognise two Cisse commanders. The first is your father, who was like a father to me after I lost mine at a young age.

The second is you. I know of no one better equipped. My allegiance is not to the throne but to Wagadou. You are her only hope. From now, I will be both in front of you, clearing a path, and behind you, watching your back.'

Despite the tightness in his jaw and the angry tension that made his body rigid, Maadi spoke with a measured and tender voice that was steady. She liked the steadiness. He was the only steady thing she had aside from her pursuit for vengeance and justice.

Siya reached out to touch Maadi's cheek. He rose.

For the first time since her father died, Siya allowed a tear to run down her face uninterrupted. She didn't force the tears back, with the self-admonition that it was a weakness she had no time for. Siya found that she did not actually feel weak. Maadi saw all that she was, both a heartbroken daughter and a fearless fighter, and, in his eyes, she saw a space for her strength and softness to meld into each other, her strength buttressing her softness, her softness giving wisdom and direction to her strength. With the two parts of herself not warring each other, she felt some stability. She felt safe to grieve as well as fight.

She cleared her throat and looked him in the eye. 'What I need you to do most is be by my side. Can you do that?'

Maadi inclined his head. 'For as long as my heart beats.' He paused. 'I vow to forever protect my home.'

Siya nodded. 'For Wagadou.'

With Maadi as her deputy and closest advisor, Siya's army grew rapidly. She recruited and trained women too and soon her rebel unit directly rivalled Wagadou's official army in might and surpassed it in expertise. Siya planted spies in Dyabe's forces, and, in the mountains surrounding their land, The Eagles reclaimed and renovated the ancient fortresses etched into the caves, making it their base; a home away from home that became a mini citadel on the border of the city limits. The Eagles' refusal to bend to Bida had shamed Dyabe into recanting his motion to negotiate with the enemy. Aware of how appearing weaker than an armed force with a faceless leader would look, Dyabe chose inaction. He sat back in the belief that Bida's Snake Men would soon squash The Eagles. So far, this plan had not come to fruition. Siya triumphed over Bida at every turn, getting stronger, smarter and quicker.

If the constant warring took its toll on Siya, it didn't show. Only Maadi knew that, after each battle, Siya spent longer and longer washing the fight off of her.

'Commander, they are ready for your address.' Maadi's voice came through her door along with a quick knock.

Siya turned the wooden knob that halted the water and inhaled the mingled scent of black soap and herbal oils deeply as the dirt, grime and fear washed down the drain.

Siya knew she was beautiful. Her skin was sable silk and her body was both flexuous and fierce. She possessed the power to halt a man's heartbeat with a swift kick or soft kiss to the neck, dependent on her mood. Before her father died, she'd had a stream of suitors who considered themselves potential husbands for her. She never considered them at all. Her father raised her to know her power, and so she recognised that every man who sought her wanted to use her solely to bolster their ego. She was known as the Lioness of Wagadou, and they spoke openly of wanting to tame her. They saw her strength as a challenge; did they have what it took to break her down? Besides finding them tedious, Siya knew they would weaken her and slow her down. This feeling intensified after her father's death. Her beauty and the attention it brought, along with becoming a rebellion leader, saw Siya making herself as plain as possible; wearing all black with no jewellery so that her mission was clear. She wanted there to be no misunderstanding: she was a warrior. Her purpose was to fight.

However, a year into her command, Siya had taken to reacquainting herself with herself after battle. The warrior and the woman, the fighter and the femme. The shift happened when, on a rare day of relaxation where they were not strategising, she and Maadi had gone to the market. He was her closest friend now, her tentative confidant. They fought side by side, balanced each other and read each other easily. He had watched her quietly eyeing some colourful gowns in the market. Siya's elegant hands, that in another life had always been intricately patterned with black henna, swept across the jewellery, the lip dyes and the eye paints longingly.

Maadi had said, 'Tell me if I am speaking out of turn, Commander . . .'

Siya smiled as her eyes lingered on a long gold chain with a delicately designed bird of paradise pendant. 'Maadi, please. You can never be out of turn with me. What's on your mind?'

'You are lovely.'

It was blunt and completely devoid of any cloying sentiment. Siya removed her hand from the chain and stared up at Maadi, her smile melting off her face in shock. While it was true Maadi was kind to her, he had always been careful not to say anything that could be interpreted as untoward. They moved around each other with mutual respect, warmth and even companionship, but they never addressed the fact that she was a woman who desired men and he was a man who desired women, or that, when they trained together, her eyes lingered on his bare chest longer than was seemly, or that, when he assisted her stretching to help her ease her aching muscles after a particularly vigorous drill, there was a crackle in the air between them. They never addressed how Siya discovered that Maadi played the kora. How, late one night, when the terrors hunted her down, she'd ventured out onto their balcony and found him plucking a tune, heart-twistingly beautiful, his hands flying over the strings, manipulating them the same way she manipulated nature. She had said she didn't know he could play, and he had said that playing helped him unwind after battle, because it proved there was beauty in the world, that there was hope. He'd lost himself in his explanation before halting with an abrupt stop, embarrassed by too much feeling. They had no time for feeling. Siya had smiled. She'd said it was beautiful. She'd said she liked hearing it; it made her feel at ease. She'd sat down on a lounge chair and listened and then drifted off to sleep. She had woken up in her bed. Ever since, whenever she would hear the faint song of a kora, flowing through the air beneath her door, she would feel her pain loosening and diffusing, creating a space for something more. On those nights, she would rest easy and sleep deeply. They never discussed it.

So, at the market, Siya had blinked at Maadi in shock, rattled by the confrontation of something unsaid. Maadi cleared his throat.

'I say you're lovely as a fact. Irrespective of what I think. It just is. Inside and out. Even when you try to hide it. You're good at a lot of things, Siya, but you've failed at that.'

The corner of his mouth kicked up slightly and Siya laughed and shook her head, hoping to diffuse the rush of blood to her face. 'I miss it, sometimes. My old life. Dressing up with my friends, the courting parties but . . . now I'm a commander. I am not that girl any more. There was a time when I could wrestle a man to the ground and dance in a pretty dress, a time when those two people could co-exist, but . . . that's no longer the case. I need my army to respect me.'

'They respect you for who you are, Commander. Strong and intelligent and passionate.' Maadi's eyes glinted, his voice more forceful than Siya had ever heard it. 'That will always remain true. What matters most is that you feel like you are you at your fullest.'

Siya was stunned into silence as Maadi briskly clipped something about having to get back to their headquarters. Later, hanging on the door handle to her chamber, she found the gold chain with the bird of paradise.

Siya clasped it around her neck the evening after the sixth battle with Bida. It slung down her chest, accentuated by the low cut of her deep purple robe, which hugged her body. There was a slit in the fabric that revealed the round of her thigh and the firm length of her leg. Now, beautifying herself had become part of her post-battle ritual. A woman whose primal power shifted through multiple modes, a sensual assassin. This was when she felt the most herself. Before she entered her war room, she doused herself in perfumes and adorned her locks with golden, woven hair cuffs, letting her softness and strength greet each other as friends.

The six soldiers who formed her cabinet rose as she entered the room, their conversations halting and their triumphant joviality petering out. They respected and liked her, Siya knew, but the nature of her role meant there was some distance between them. She could not sit and drink with them or join in with their bawdy post-battle play. Her mind always had to be one step ahead, seeing beyond.

She assumed her position at the end of the table, with Maadi stood on her right. She saw her cup was already full with forest-fruit wine and raised it.

'I'm proud of you all. Organising an attack during Wagadou's holy festivities was low even for Bida, and I know some of you were sceptical, believing that tonight was a futile mission, that Bida wouldn't attack us again so soon, so I am grateful for your faith in me. I know you would rather be with your families and I am mindful of the sacrifice it takes to fight. I know what you risk. Thank you.'

'To our chief warrior!' One of her cabinet, Kadida, held up her cup and the other soldiers joined her in the toast, cheering. Maadi held up his own cup in Siya's direction and winked at her with a small nod. 'To our queen,' he said quietly.

Siya cleared her throat and put the feeling in her stomach down to the wine she'd hastily consumed and released a small smile. 'I'm honoured to serve you all. Victory is ours. Go home and celebrate what's left of the festivities with your families. That's an order. Tell each of your units the same. We'll meet again tomorrow evening.'

The room emptied. Maadi stayed. He always stayed. They shared the large rock cottage that doubled as The Eagles' main headquarters and had their private quarters next to each other to make administration easier. It made other things more difficult.

Siya took another sip of her wine and raised a brow.

'Insubordination, Sergeant?'

'You said to go home and celebrate with family. I am obeying you, Commander.'

Siya ignored the skitter in her pulse and smiled. 'Sweet, but I know you have a brother and two nephews who worship you.' She glanced at the map spread out on the table before her, marked out, denoting strategy. 'And I have wine, and planning to do.' She turned and rested her back against the table, gently touching his arm. 'You don't have to stay, Maadi. Honestly.'

Maadi's brows furrowed as he moved directly in front of her. Underneath the amber glow of the torches his dark skin gleamed. She wanted to reach out and trace the curves of his lips with her thumb, so elegant with their fullness.

'I don't stay because I have to, Siya.' He stepped closer to her. 'I can see you're worried.'

Siya sighed grimly. Maadi always managed to sear through her cloak and armour.

'My uncle has asked to see me. Tomorrow. Well, he has asked to see the "King of The Eagles". Someone brought me the letter yesterday.' Siya had been keeping up appearances by attending feasts as his niece, reasoning her absences from court as grief. As far as she knew, he had no idea she was the one disrupting his grab for power.

Siya laughed humourlessly. 'He said he wants to thank him for his service in protecting Wagadou. Something he and his army have failed to do every single time. Man to man, face to face. At Red Valley.'

Red Valley held the ancient clearing where duels took place, where men hashed out differences with the traditional martial mode: cane and bare hands. Two men would engage in a debate and, if they could not come to a peaceful agreement, they fought. To the death. As time went on, the debate became a ritualistic performance.

Maadi held deathly still. 'He wants to kill you.'

Siya took another deep sip of wine and shot Maadi a bitter smile. 'Yes. And he'll probably hire his best warrior as a proxy, since my uncle can't fight for oxen shit. If I don't go, he will likely use the opportunity to declare us treasonous terrorists who rejected his offer to work together. He will declare us a threat to Wagadou and wage war against us, detracting attention from Bida. In which case he will try to kill us all. Enough is enough. As long as Bida has Dyabe under his thumb, we will be fighting forever. I have to quell him.' Siya shook her head, looking anywhere but at Maadi's face, her voice brittle with disgust, shame and regret. 'I've been putting these men and women in constant danger for nothing.'

Maadi placed his hand on her shoulder, forcing her to look up at him. 'Siya, you're the reason Wagadou has lasted this long. In *peace*. You protect her. Those men and women fight because they know you are a good leader.'

Siya's eyes glistened in response. Maadi had seen unspeakable things in war, but what he saw in Siya's gaze chilled him to the bone. He shook his head. 'No. Siya . . . you can't go. If anything happens to you—'

Siya gave a grim grin. 'Insubordination again. Don't you trust my skills?'

Maadi inched closer to Siya, his face tense with an emotion she had never seen in him before. Panic? Maadi never panicked. 'Siya, you're the greatest warrior Wagadou has ever seen. You have even surpassed your father when he was your age. Which is why we can't risk losing you. Let someone else go in your stead. Dyabe doesn't even know who you are.'

Siya frowned. This irrationality was odd coming from him. 'Maadi, you know I can't put anyone else in danger like that—'

'We can't lose you.' Maadi's usual still-water voice had turned stormy and gruff and it echoed around the banquet room. He and Siya both seemed startled by it. A few silent seconds passed before Maadi cleared his throat. 'Besides, you need to organise a team to go with you. Medical, someone to keep your weapons, and it's probably too late to . . .' His voice trailed off as he assessed Siya.

Realisation shadowed Maadi's face, and he rubbed his jaw. 'You've organised it. You decided already. You're not asking for my advice.'

Siya swallowed. 'They are meeting me there tomorrow at midday. I'm sorry, Maadi. I trust you more than anyone else in the world. You know that. I just knew you wouldn't agree to this and it is something I need to do. Don't worry. I've been training for this my whole life.'

Maadi quietly regarded her. He took a sip of his own wine. Maadi usually exercised gentle calm when Siya was flying into a passion, often scaling back her strategy into one that kept her from mortal danger as much as was possible. It irritated her sometimes, but she knew it was just to protect her. So she was somewhat surprised when he nodded. 'You're right.'

'I am?' Siya paused and cleared her throat. 'I am.'

Siya could see his mind whirring, thoughts that made his jaw tense up. His gaze drifted to just behind her head, avoiding hers. 'If it's all the same to you, I would like to accompany you.'

Siya looked up at Maadi softly and reached out to squeeze his hand. 'I'd be glad to have you by my side, friend.'

A shadow flitted across Maadi's face and he met her eyes with something that made her breath stagger.

'We are not friends, Commander.' His tone was even, inscrutable.

A stark coolness abated the warmth that had previously flooded through Siya. Of course. Maadi's association with her only went as far as his loyalty to Wagadou and her father.

'You're right. I . . . we are colleagues. Comrades . . .'

Maadi paused as his gaze dropped to the necklace that hung between the curves of her chest. 'That isn't what I meant, Siya.'

She put her cup down on the table after drinking the rest of the wine. A terrible mistake. It only seemed to amplify the rapid beating of her heart and the protest of her body, angry at her for maintaining its distance between her and Maadi. His deep-ochre woven waistcoat was open, exposing the gleaming brown of his taut chest and his matching linen lounge trousers, hung low on his waist. As with his very being, every part of his body was defined and sturdy. Siya tried not to be distracted and fixed her eyes on his, trying to deny the chemistry and biology and attempting to focus on logic.

'We of all people can't afford distraction.'

Maadi shifted closer. 'With all due respect, Siya, I'm not distracted. I'm focused on what matters most.'

Siya's breath hitched. The air between them thickened, becoming increasingly harder to haul down her throat. She'd once had a man twice her size lay a blade across her neck, yet, still, Siya had never felt her heart thump as it did when Maadi looked at her in that moment.

She pushed her voice past the calcified lump of air in her throat. 'Maadi. We're dealing with life and death . . .'

Maadi's eyes were a reflection of the inferno within her. 'Precisely.'

Siya hesitated. Maadi wasn't exactly loquacious, but when he spoke, it was full and heavy with the understanding of her and the world they inhabited. He was right. They had looked demons in the eye and survived. They had shared the void left by someone they loved, and intimately knew how close the afterlife was. They knew that every breath was a gift. And through it all, they had each other. Life was fragile and quick and the only way to slow it down, to give it some semblance of fortitude, was to revel in the heat of it all, the joy of it all.

Siya raised her chin, as she did when addressing her army. 'I have one more order, Sergeant.'

Something like disappointment rose up in Maadi's eyes, but he inclined his head. 'Anything, Commander.'

He stepped back, but Siya reached out to snatch his wrist. 'Kiss me.'

Maadi held her gaze for a sweetly aching eternity and Siya's nerves buckled.

'Unless, of course, you don't . . .'

In a swift, singular motion, Maadi wrapped his hands around Siya's waist and sat her on the table, on the map of Wagadou, on their meticulously marked strategy. Siya's hands rose up to his chest and she felt his heartbeat chasing her pulse. When he gently cupped her face and kissed her, Siya realised that her fear of a broken heart, the thing that scared her more than evil men with daggers and despotic uncles, had led to her suffocating that same heart. She realised this because now she felt she could breathe after holding her breath for so long. Too long. Siya was used to feeling elemental, at one with the wind and in control of nature, but right at that moment she felt at the mercy of all the forces of life flowing through her acutely. Maadi tugged on the belt that kept her gown together and caused it to fall from her body like peel from ripe fruit, as her legs anchored around his waist, her skin pinned to Maadi's, their bodies moving to the rhythm. Their mouths met and answered every question they'd ever had about life's meaning; they discovered themselves to be philosophers, questioning and debating despite knowing, asking just so they could answer again and again and again. Maadi carried Siya to her quarters and their roles as commander and sergeant interchanged smoothly, with authority shared and ceded. Siya let go of thinking and allowed herself to feel, and what she felt was held but not captured, at his mercy but all powerful. She felt loved and loved and loved again.

Maadi stroked Siya's hair as she lay on his chest, his heart beating into her ear and thrumming through her blood, calming her. She smiled into his chest. 'Say what you want to say.'

'How did you know?'

Siya hoisted herself up so she could prop her elbow on a pillow and look down at his moonlit face. She traced the arcs of his lips. 'I can read your quiet.'

His mouth curved against her finger before gently nipping it. 'Siya . . . I'm not good with words. Never have been. I know how to fight and how to strategise. I do it well. But trying to fight the fact that I am in love with you has been my most challenging battle. When your father was alive, I thought it would complicate things. When he died . . . we had other things to focus on. But it was always a losing battle, Siya. I am tired of fighting. I've never been happier to lose. I'm surrendering to it. Surrendering to you.'

Siya hoisted herself up further to whisper her 'I love you' into his mouth before kissing him, pouring all of her adoration into it. She didn't know she was crying until he pulled away to brush a tear away from her cheek.

The corner of his mouth quirked. 'And I promise I will never ask you to marry me.'

Siya snorted. He knew her well.

'But,' Maadi continued, 'I do swear to maintain the vows I made to you. In front of you, clearing a path. Behind you, watching your back. And I want you to know even when I'm not physically by your side, I'll be by your side. Protecting you.'

Siya's heart swelled. 'And you said you weren't good with words.'

Within that night that somehow contained an eternity of daybreak, Siya grew so accustomed to Maadi's heat, to his firm arms securing her and to his whispers against her neck that, when she woke up to find an empty space next to her in bed, she felt bereft. Maadi was the one who usually cooked for them, so she'd suspected he'd gone to fix breakfast. However, upon entry, ready to sneak up behind him and wrap her arms around him, Siya found the kitchen vacant. The atmosphere in their home had shifted the way it did when he wasn't sharing the same air as her. Still, she quashed the sick feeling in her stomach and called his name. No reply. With stilted, ragged breathing and weakened legs, Siya ran to his quarters. His armour was gone. She rushed to every door leading out of their home, only to find them locked from the outside. Her keys were nowhere to be found. She hauled herself at the doors, threw things at them with all her might, tried to pick locks with trembling fingers, but it was to no avail. Siya screamed till her voice was a rasp, running into every room like a madwoman, trying to find anything that might free her. Every tool had disappeared. Maadi had gone to fight Dyabe on her behalf and he'd locked her in because he knew she would never acquiesce to him taking her place.

In that moment she loved him as much as she hated him. Maadi might die. For her. With buckling knees, she staggered to her chamber and picked up her gold bird of paradise pendant, which had been removed the night before, and placed it around her neck. She dressed quickly and wrapped an emerald-green scarf around her hair. She ran to the only other exit she knew: a balcony that looked out on to the hills and steep mountain road. It was high, higher than any of the trees she'd leapt from before. Siya's stomach swirled at the sight of the depth. This was a risk. Still, she saw no other option; either way, this was life or death. She inhaled deeply and climbed onto the stone ledge, just as her eyes snagged on a familiar figure on horseback in the distance, getting smaller and smaller by the second. Siya called Maadi's name, twice, thrice, five times, each time with increased, tearful desperation. He didn't turn around. Siya swore loudly. The man she loved was a stubborn, brave idiot and, if he ended up killed, she would call on all the priestesses in Wagadou to resurrect him just so she could kill him again. She refused to let him break her heart. Shutting her eyes and inhaling deeply, Siya leapt, not thinking of the amount of space below her but of the mission ahead of her.

She was, after all, a girl who knew how to fly.

Nefertiti

MY STILETTOS CLICKED AGAINST THE FLOOR of the basement library. The walls were embedded with shelves from floor to ceiling, carrying texts from every epoque and every genre. I'm a self-taught scholar and so I know that knowledge is power, but my books served more of a purpose than to just feed my mind. They absorbed sound. Though the muted hubbub and music of the club upstairs leaked into the library, no sound ever wafted up from this basement. I eyed the glass box in the middle of the room: it was ten square metres and, crucially, soundproof. I couldn't afford to take any chances. Two of my girls stood guarding it, their weapons concealed expertly within their kalasiris, the two thick straps of the form-fitting sheath dresses covering their chests. Underneath each strap lay a thin spindle of a dagger.

I nodded at them and they opened the door to the glass box. I was immediately met with the stench of stale sweat and the sound of muted whimpering. In the middle of the box was a man tied dexterously to a chair, bare chested in his underwear. There was no mark or bruise on him and not a single drop of blood on the floor. My girls had done well. I hated mess. The man's eyes widened at the sight of me and the whimpering became louder. I bent over so I was at his eye level.

'I see you know who I am, Mr Hemti. I don't usually come down to visit when we have special guests over, because I trust my girls to . . . entertain to my standards. But I made an exception for you.' I held a hand out and, within a second, a carving knife was placed in it. The chair rocked a little as the man squirmed, the muted squeals increasing in volume, and, wordlessly, the girls moved to hold the chair in place, gripping its back.

I smiled straight into Mr Hemti's watery eyes. 'I wanted to give you this gift personally. A souvenir from your visit.' I deftly sliced into his thigh and carved out the image of a sun disc. It couldn't have taken me more than a minute and the pain couldn't have been more than that of an intricate tattoo, but Hemti squealed like a mad boar. I rolled my eyes. Men were so dramatic. I handed the knife back and retreated a little so blood wouldn't drop on my shoe.

'Ungag him,' I commanded.

My guards ripped the tape from Hemti's mouth, and he spat out the cloth that was stuffed into it. 'Please! I have a family! I am an honourable man. I have a wife and baby son! Please, I'll do anything . . . I have money! Land! Anything you want, you can have it.'

I let him go on while I watched him impassively for a few seconds before I held a palm up, shushing him. I chuckled lightly. 'I know you have a family. How do you think my girls knew exactly where to find you? It was your wife who sent for us, Mr Hemti.' His eyes widened and he shook his head.

'No! No—'

'A beautiful woman, strong and smart. She told us that you beat her. We saw the bruises, the marks. She said that she's lost two babies. Yes. You're a real family man.'

He started shaking now, spitting as he begged. 'I'll stop. You don't know how disrespectful she can be sometimes, she— Please don't kill me. Please. I won't lay a finger on her again!'

I raised my hand again and kept my voice soft and genial. I hated rough noise.

'Mr Hemti, please, I'm not going to kill you. I'm not a brute like you. And I know you won't lay a finger on her again.'

Relief flitted across his pathetic, sweaty face as his body sagged, panting. I was used to seeing the faces of desperate men and, as I expected, along with the relief, I saw the old menace beginning to take the place of fear.

'Thank you. Thank you—'

I continued cheerily: 'You won't lay a finger on her again because you won't be able to.'

His brows furrowed in terrified confusion as I continued. 'Everything,' I ran my eyes across him, 'on your body that you used to hurt your wife shall be removed. I think that's reasonable.' I smiled widely as dark realisation flooded through him and he began to tremble. 'I'm sure you can understand, Mr Hemti.'

I nodded at my girls and they gagged him again, muffling his screams. 'Ladies, will you please take our guest to the abattoir?'

'Yes, madam.'

I tilted my head apologetically at Hemti's pale, damp face. 'It's just a funny little nickname we like to call it. Now, I hope you'll excuse me, Mr Hemti. I have a club to run and a show to put on. If you breathe a word of what happened to you here to anyone, your tongue will be cut out. Your wife and child are in a secure location with plenty of money to tide them over, so don't worry about them. However, I assure you that if you try to look for them, I will know about it. You don't want that to happen, Mr Hemti.'

I stopped on my way out of the box and turned around.

'Oh. Where are my manners? Welcome to House of Aten.'

'Ladies . . . are you ready?'

Ma Isis's voice, both smoky and smooth, resounded around the dim din of the room. It echoed around and mingled with the aroma of luxury and liquor, love and lust.

Whoops and cheers beckoned me from where I stood backstage, behind the curtains. Ma Isis stood on the other side, the crowd surrounding her. She tutted, disappointed at the response to her call and placed a hand on an audacious hip. The light focused on her, all white and gold, bangles and anklets chiming, heralding my arrival.

'Is that the best you can do? I'm disappointed. I don't like to be disappointed. She cannot come out to that.'

Ma Isis's cadence tipped and lilted, up and down like a reverse lullaby that sought to coax you awake. Her voice rose like a sunrise.

'Come on. You know who we're here for.' She clapped her hands together and bells sounded.

Nefertiti

'The one you've been waiting for all night. The queen of the House of Aten. She is the Great of Praises, she is the . . .'

Ma Isis's voice hummed low and the hollers of the crowd increased, building to a roar. I knew Ma Isis would smile into the mic as she glided across the platform, her kaftan billowing behind her. She would leave a waft of lily, myrrh and cardamom in her trail; her very own perfume mix that I sometimes let her sell in back of house. 'Mama Isis's Love Potion'. I loved Ma Isis as if she'd birthed me, but she often had a mind of her own when it came to making extra cash – no, I had to focus. I wasn't House Mother right now, owner of the largest, most (in)famous bar, club, home, sanctuary in Thebes City, Kemet, I was . . .

' . . . Lady of Grace . . .', with each name there was a roll of the drum, a thrum of the bass, and Ma Isis fell into a rolling, rousing brassy melody:

' . . . Sweet of Love, Lady of All Women, Akhen's Beloved, *Our* Beloved . . .' She floated around the stage, preparing it for me.

'The one and only, Queen Nefertiti.'

Spotlight.

I opened my eyes and, thus, gave the music permission to enter. The melody is my lover, but sometimes she can be a little reckless, a little careless. I have to prepare for her, teach her patience. She can't have me on her terms. It's got to be on mine. Always on mine. The plucks of the bass reached deep through me and twined around my spine so tight it made it jerk. My hips then moved accordingly, smooth with the motion, left and then right, my heart falling right into the beat. I settled into my skin.

I sang, something like silk over gold. I knew how I sounded, and, if I didn't know, then I would have felt it, and if I didn't feel it, then I would have seen it all over their faces. I had them in my palm. They were rapt, all eyes on me. I was home.

To most of the people of Thebes, Kemet, House of Aten was a place of disrepute. My personal favourite review came from the *Thebes Telegraph*. According to this article, the House of Aten was a

'cesspit full of rough and wild women reigned over by the criminal queen known as Nefertiti Aten, a former singer and widow of the notorious gangster Akhen Aten. Under Akhen's management, the lounge was a gentleman's club that was a hub for anti-government activity. With Nefertiti's ascension to his throne, the House has become a cabaret lounge where women, and women only, have the privilege of becoming guerrillas, indulging their vices while organising protests and civil disruption. More and more women are now sporting the sun disc tattoo – the infamous insignia of the club. The government posits that House of Aten has evolved into a dangerous misandrist cult and directly contributes to societal unrest and decay. The problem is, how can it be shut down when nobody can get close to Nefertiti? The elusive crime boss is untouchable. She fears no one and nothing.'

I always got a thrill when I read that part.

It continued:

> 'Though they do not hide their illegal activity,
> the brave officers of The Duat have found it near
> impossible to trace crimes back to the women of
> the House of Aten. The policing force successfully
> removed the threat of Akhen; it is undoubtedly
> clear now that his wife poses a far bigger threat.
> House of Aten is far from neutralised, it is embold-
> ened. Nefertiti is an elegant thug and an incisive
> assassin. She tidies up after herself so well that she
> does not need to hide her face. She wants you to
> know her. The women who work at House of Aten
> revere her and will forever protect her. She is the
> goddess of the underworld, and as long as she has
> the loyalty of her faithful, who can stop her?'

I had it pinned to the wall of my office. The piece was almost
sycophantic. I nearly got 'elegant thug' tattooed on my arm. The
journalist did get a couple of things wrong, though. I wasn't a
'former singer'. Though club business took up most of my time
these days, every once in a while, like tonight, I took to the stage. It
was a gift for my people. They saved me as much as I saved them.
We were family.

However, in that moment the women were not looking at me as
if I was their sister or the owner of their favourite club. They looked

at me as if they either wanted to be me or be with me or sometimes both at the same time. I sang and I danced, the beauty of my movement filled them with painful yearning and then soothed it away. I smoothed a hand across my form, snug in my shimmering bead-net dress comprised of faience and black-and-gold cylinder beads, and tilted my chin up, pushing up against my deep-blue headdress, bejewelled with turquoise and a ruby that matched my lipstick. House of Aten was my kingdom.

Just before Akhen died, he kissed the inside of my wrist, as he always did – he said he liked feeling my pulse against his lips – and told me to run the business as I saw fit. He knew how I grew up and what I had seen on the streets; he wanted me to provide a home and haven for those who were like me, and had lived through what I had lived through. He told me to ignore the vultures who would try to slip into his place, who thought I would need a man to feel seen. Akhen was the only man I ever loved. He knew who I was, not just who I was to him. Before my husband left me, he said, 'Thank you for letting me love you. Thank you for loving me back. Thank you for staying. I know it was hard, sometimes. I hope now you live free.'

And so I lived free, turning the House into a home for women only, a place for lost women to find themselves. I continued to protect the streets of Thebes that Akhen and I had ruled over together when he was alive, as equals, side by side. We fought against an oppressive government – the Isfet – and disrupted their peace. Akhen was a great man, but he was still a man. I no longer had to compensate for his blind spots. My husband often got seduced by the lure of quick money to bolster our work, and this usually meant bad business. It ended up getting him killed.

The House of Aten was far from holy, but it protected those who needed protection: the downtrodden and the abused. The Isfet portrayed us as the underworld, when it was them who were corrupt and would rob the poor and suppress the powerless to gain control. The wealth of the state was contingent on suffering and imprisonment. House of Aten was freedom. We were the deciders of our own destinies.

In the audience I saw that many had decided that their destiny was to be entwined with mine, at least for tonight. It was the magic of me on stage that called to them, I knew, because the reality of me, the flesh and blood and bone me who had to deal with flesh and blood and bone to keep us safe and the Isfet at bay, would eventually scare them away. Our circumstances were very delicate. They enjoyed the glamour but not the gore, not knowing that the gore was what gave the glamour its gleam.

I have a scar across my back from when they tried to kill me. Jagged, deep. The women loved to trace it softly and ask me how I got it, but they didn't like it when I came home carrying the scent of blood. The women who surrounded me liked the power I had but didn't want to know how it was kept. They didn't want to know how many men's bones I had to break to build the fences that protected them. They wanted to be with a queen, but no queen can be a queen without also being a warrior. I couldn't hide it from them and so I stopped trying to. Relationships were out of the question. I retained my power by my distance . . . emotionally, anyway.

It was time for me to choose someone for the night. My gaze roamed, swam through the wanting and waiting women, and landed on her. The eyes were crystalline and black, piercing right through me, and making my soul stand still in shock. Her hair was neatly shorn at the edges, but soft and cloud-like on top, highlighting the cheekbones I wanted to slice my tongue on. The neckline of her black jumpsuit plunged to a depth I wanted to dive into. More than all of this, though, I saw she wasn't flustered. She didn't preen under my attention, even as I raised my arm and twirled my hand in her direction, singing to her and dancing directly towards her. She didn't perform for my affection as the other girls often did. She stayed staid, with the corner of her mouth lifting ever so slightly, and she lifted her wine glass to her lips and sipped in challenge.

I needed to know her.

'What do you mean she *won't* come?'

Bastet shrugged, and shook her head, her mass of glossy curls emphasising her bemusement with a slight shimmy. 'I told her that you wanted her to come to your booth, and she said "I'm happy where I am, thank you", and stayed put. She's very beautiful, by the way.'

I was sat in my booth in my corner of the bar, all plush velvet and mahogany. It was divided from the main room by wine-hued Chantilly-lace curtains, intricately decorated enough for me to be private when I wanted to be but thin enough for me to see everything on the other side.

I raised my brow. 'I *know* she's beautiful, Baz.' I paused. 'Do you think it's because she wants you? Because you can say so, you know—'

Bastet was my closest friend, right hand and majordomo of House of Aten. She was also feline-fierce and fine, with sharp hazel eyes, a permanently sly smile and an edge that provided just the right balance of sex and danger, encapsulated with the ouroboros tattoo that climbed up her right arm. She targeted and pounced. She purred and made her women purr, and then she slinked away.

Bastet rolled her eyes and laughed. 'Neffi,' she was the only person who could call me that and not fear death, 'I know what I got and who I am, but I think we both know that there has never been a time where I have called a woman over for you and she hasn't come.' She shot me a smirk with a wink and picked up my glass and took a sip of my drink.

I took my drink back from her. 'No drinking on the job. Was she with someone?'

Bastet grinned. 'Look at you. You're just not used to this, are you? No, she wasn't with anyone else. Not that I know of. She wasn't really talking to anyone either. Just . . . observing. Taking in the atmosphere. It's a good night tonight. I mean, it's a good night every night, but tonight? Whew. You killed it.'

I shook my head, preoccupied. 'Something feels strange.'

Bastet raised her brow. 'Why, because she doesn't want you? Neffi, come on . . .'

'Can you ask the bargirls if they've seen her around here before?'

Bastet's sharp brows knitted in confusion, before she froze. Her eyes flashed. 'You don't think—'

I took another sip of my drink. 'I don't know.'

With her teasing sister mode deactivated and the ferocious guardian in her engaged, Bastet nodded and slipped out of the booth. 'Five minutes.'

Bastet returned in three. The look on her face was equal parts grim and livid, hackles up. I could see the hunter in her come alive. Bastet was from the streets, and though I was reared by them, she was nursed by them. It was why I needed her by my side.

'The girls say they've never seen her before. She's asking them questions.'

I downed my drink. 'All right.'

Bastet checked that the curtain was drawn in tight, then she sat down close next to me and lowered her voice. 'What do you want me to do? I can deal with this.'

'Baz, please calm down.'

Bastet hissed. 'Neffi, there is a pig in our home and you want me to calm down?! Remember what The Duat have taken from us. From you . . .'

The Duat were the guardians of Isfet, and they were the ones who enforced their evil. Of course, they didn't see it in precisely that way – they called themselves 'the policing force of Thebes, restoring order and maintaining peace'. I placed a hand on Bastet's to steady her, but also to steady myself.

'I remember. Of course, I do. I live with it every day. Without him.'

Bastet put her hand over mine, her breathing slowing. 'Sorry, Neffi. I just—'

'I know. But we don't *know* if she's one of The Duat yet. We have to be smart. I'll deal with it. Don't worry. Just . . . cast an eye out. Watch. Make sure she's alone. I'll handle this.'

Bastet nodded. 'If you need me to rally the troops, just give me the signal.'

'Always.'

'I'm not used to working this hard for what I want.'

I smiled in a way I knew disoriented. The lady blinked several times before she smiled back – fully, no coyness, no demureness. It brought her cheeks higher, lifted her face in a way that made her more stunning. My heart rate lifted with it, bizarrely, even with the knowledge that she might be an enemy. She gestured to the empty chair at her table. I sat and put my drink down.

'I trusted you would come over.'

She was confident. Despite myself, I liked it.

'So you're saying I'm predictable.'

She shook her head and laughed, and it was surprisingly sweet sounding, bubbly, at odds with her sophistication. 'I'm saying that you're probably used to having your way.' Her voice dropped. 'I don't want to be something that you're used to.'

She was very good. 'What's your name?'

'Ma'at.' Her eyes flickered as if she'd said something wrong or given too much away. Her confidence had faltered. 'Friends call me Mattie,' she added.

I nodded and took her hand, shook it, let my thumb stroke the back of it. 'Hi Mattie. I'm—'

She leant in closer and wafted her scent in my direction: mellow, honeyed. 'Nefertiti Ay. Everyone knows who you are.'

I allowed a finger to circle a spot on her wrist. I felt her pulse quicken. 'Everyone knows parts of who I am. And, actually, it's Nefertiti Aten. Nefertiti Ay was a girl. I haven't gone by that name in years. And even then, very few people here know me by that name. Most of them are dead or feds.' I looked up from her wrist and directly into her eyes.

Ma'at's smile froze on her face and I saw her swallow tightly. I kept my voice jovial, and switched so I was holding her wrist gently, but firmly. I caught Bastet's eye from across the room, as she was speaking to a dancer. She raised a brow in question and I gently shook my head. I had this. I looked back at Ma'at. She was still trying to hold it together, trying to play seductive again, hide the panic in her eye. I flashed her a grin.

'You're new to this, aren't you, Mattie? I can tell. What, did they just upgrade you to the undercover unit? And you were excited for your first case to be me, weren't you? It's glamorous and I'm meant to be such a charming bitch, so you could have fun with it too.'

She let out a little choked laugh, ever the consummate professional. 'I have no idea what you're talking about. You're clearly a little paranoid . . . tense. I can help with that—'

I continued, 'I get why they chose you. Dedicated.' Something shifted in her eye, not defeat but adaptation. She was trying to figure out a way out of this.

'You also have the look.' I lowered my voice and tilted my head. 'You're gorgeous. And you're smart. You made me come to you.

146

That was a smooth move. See, usually when they send a pig in here – once in a while, but they do – she's obvious. Garish fashion sense, too flirtatious, sloppy. You, though? You have taste—'

I reached over to take a sip of her drink and grinned. 'You're professional too, so you wanted to keep a clear head, go teetotal for the night. I respect that. It's unfortunate that you slipped up and told me your real name. You're pissed at yourself because it was such a silly, rookie mistake. I can tell it's your real name because you regretted saying it as soon as it left your mouth. *Ma'at.* Then you decided to lean into it, by telling me your nickname. It's pretty. *Mattie.* Both names are.'

Ma'at nodded slowly, and something slipped from her face, revealing an even more devastating beauty. She wasn't scared of me. She smiled. 'Thank you. So . . . what now? You kill me?'

Her voice was so warm and so soft against my ears and, at that moment, I felt something cold and hard and sharp against my thigh. I glanced under the table to see that Ma'at was holding a tiny hunting blade to my flesh. I laughed in surprise and genuine delight.

'How did you slip that in here? They didn't pat you down?'

'Oh, they did.'

She was, truly, a worthy opponent. I had to give her that. We both knew she wasn't going to do a thing; she couldn't. She was surrounded. She was technically in an unsafe, hostile territory. I could gut her if I wanted to. She'd put my family in danger. This was what made the blade against my thigh fascinating; it was a statement. She wasn't afraid of me. She wanted me to know that she was dangerous too. It was sweet, really. She was playing with me.

I smiled. 'Don't be crude, Mattie. Of course we're not going to kill you. There's no need for all this. You'll just go back to your bosses and say you couldn't get in. Ouch, by the way.'

She'd pressed the blade a titch too hard, so that it pierced the flesh a little, a minuscule prick I felt across my whole body. It was the opposite of painful.

She cleared her throat. 'Oh, I'm sorry. I . . . that was an accident.'

In a swift, slick move, she flipped the blade shut and slipped it somewhere into her jumpsuit. She lowered her hand back under the table, against my thigh and stroked a finger across the soft plump. She brought up a smear of blood on her fingertip, dipped it into her mouth. Her face was impassive and something sharp and hot ran through me. She was playing with herself too, seeing how far she could push this with me, seeing how far she could withstand our physicality without compromising the reality of it all.

I manually had to remind myself that she was my enemy.

I nodded and leant closer to her. 'I could like you. It's a real shame you are who you are.'

'I could say the same about you. Fighting the people who try to keep our city safe—'

I couldn't help but laugh loudly at this. 'Are you talking about The Duat? Wow. Your face when you said that. Like you really believed it—'

Her face was steely.

Ma'at leant closer too, about to say something when the doors to the Main Room opened with a bang that caused the dancers to swing to a stop. The music was drowned out by the sound of raw screams. I could smell blood. Jolted, I leapt up to see two of my guards carrying a girl whose brown skin was turning grey, whose clothes were so stained with blood that they were turning stiff.

I swore and immediately called to Baz for help; she was my right hand, quick and incisive in these situations and usually by my side within seconds. Actually, she was usually already at the scene. But as I got closer, she was nowhere to be found. Confused, I called for her again, craning my neck to look around the lounge. 'Has anyone seen Bastet?!'

The girls' screams turned to whimpers. They turned to me, wide-eyed and shuddering as I pushed past the crowds that had gathered to see who they were carrying. I frowned. Incidents were not a regular occurrence, but they were not rare either. My girls were trained for emergencies, so it was odd to see them this shaken.

'Look, I know this is frightening, but I need someone to answer m—'

An arm, decorated with an ouroboros tattoo and smattered with blood, drooped towards the floor. My knees buckled and a scream leapt from my throat. I looked desperately into the frantic faces of the girls, needing an answer.

'She went to go and ch-check a disturbance, outside. A man was attacking a woman. He drew a gun,' one of them stuttered out.

I never lost my composure. I had seen everything under the sun and everything below earth. Horrors embedded within horrors. I had skills to deal with these scenarios. I could patch up, stitch, balm, extract, treat – but seeing my best friend bleeding to death immobilised me.

The sounds of alarm blended into a cacophony. Somebody was ordering the patrons out, commanding the guards to stand by the door to keep The Duat out, but I couldn't make out who. I couldn't breathe. Bastet's eyes were vacant, her skin damp, her breathing slow and jagged.

They were asking me what to do. I knew what to do – of course I did – but I couldn't extricate any solution from the viscous swamp my mind had regressed to. All the panic and fear I'd been impervious to all these years flooded through me.

'I need jugs of water, towels and a bucket. Now. Place her down over there, in that booth. Quickly. She's losing blood.' The foreign voice again. I turned to see Ma'at commanding the girls, her face focused. They looked at me in question. I didn't trust her, but she was right. I swallowed, forcing my voice out.

'Do as she says. We don't have time.'

Ma'at turned to me and grabbed my arms. 'Look at me. We need to take her to the hospit—'

This shook me out of my shock and I tore my arms from her grip. 'What? Of course we can't take her to the hospital! They're controlled by the— we can't call anyone. They'll let her die to get to me. They'll—'

My voice was shrill and Ma'at grabbed my arms again and rubbed them. 'It's okay. I'm sorry. That was a stupid suggestion. Look, I can treat her, I'm trained—'

Of course she was. All The Duat had basic medical training. I pushed her to the side, sniffing, wiping away the tears, anger warring against fear. 'No. You should leave— can somebody get my kit?'

I knelt by the booth and brushed my best friend's brow with a napkin. She was whimpering, rapidly losing consciousness. 'Nef—'

'Shh, don't speak. Everything will be okay.' I tore her dress open and bit down to stop my scream at the sight of the wound. My stomach turned. I felt faint. My kit appeared but my hands were trembling. My eyes blurred.

Bastet's blood was seeping into the velvet of the chair, making it deeper, richer. I could hear the labour of each breath. She was leaving me. I felt a hand over my own, gently pulling me up and away. I couldn't fight it even if I wanted to. I was limp. Ma'at moved past me, took my kit, and knelt before the dying body.

'How are you feeling?'

Ma'at's voice was level as she looked at me from across the kitchen, eyes glistening. She was shell-shocked too. Somehow, she had saved Bastet's life. Swiftly, incisively, commanding my girls with expertise. It had been a deep flesh wound and Bastet was still hanging on by a thread, but she was alive, and would pull through. Ma'at had helped me back to my quarters, where I washed the terror from my skin, and poured myself the strongest drink I could find in the cabinet.

I shook my head at Ma'at. 'If you weren't there she would have died. I should have been in control. I should have been able to save her.'

Ma'at walked across the room and held my hand. 'You cannot do this to yourself. You were in shock.'

I stepped back, battling between my caution and the trust planted by the fact that she had saved my best friend's life. When I opened my mouth, it was clear that trust was winning. 'Ma'at, a man killed my mother in front of my eyes at fifteen as she tried to protect me. The Duat did nothing, said it was our fault. I started singing at men's clubs at sixteen to survive. Most of the men who frequented there were from The Duat. I've looked Osiris in the eye and survived many times. The Duat poisoned my husband. I shouldn't have been shocked. I should have been stronger. What was all of it for if I'm not stronger because of it?'

Ma'at's voice was soft. 'Nefertiti. You may be stronger than most, but you are human. Not a goddess. You are allowed to feel.'

I looked at her suspiciously. 'I expect you'll tell your superiors about this?'

Ma'at moved so she was leaning against the counter next to me. 'No. But you should know there are some good people there. I didn't know about all of this. I'm sure if I explained what happened, we could catch the man that—'

I laughed humourlessly and rubbed my forehead. 'Bless you. You don't get it, do you? They will never catch that man, Ma'at. They *are* those men. House of Aten are the ones who catch those men. The few women they have on the force are part of their performance. You are their pawns. Tell me, Ma'at, how many women are there on the force?'

She was silent. I nodded.

'And I know your accent. I hear it now. You're from Aaru. A sweet mountain city, where all the Isfet live. I bet you grew up smart and strong and thought you'd come down to the valleys to show us how it's done. They told you we were corrupt, and you believed them because it served you to believe them, otherwise you would have to question why you were up there and we were down here, so you wouldn't come to the conclusion that you need us down here to keep you up there.'

Ma'at wore no make-up or pretence. The honesty suited her. Her skin glowed in the warm lighting of the kitchen, silken, deep.

She nodded. 'You're right.'

We were both quiet for a moment, eyeing each other. I was so very tired. I sighed.

'Ma'at, I do bad things to stop bad people. It's the only way to get them to stop doing bad things to good people. Do you really not know what your people do?'

She shook her head so heavily that I couldn't believe it was a lie even if I wanted to.

'Well, that's pathetic.'

'It is. I'm sorry.' She looked as if her universe had just inverted.

I cleared my throat. 'I am grateful to you for today. Truly. You saved my best friend's life. But this . . . let's not do this. I don't want to be some kind of fantasy. My life is not a game. You don't need to pretend to be interested or care.'

'I think you already know that I'm a bad actress.' A small smile crept up onto her face, and I surprised myself by smiling back.

I paused and leant back against the counter. She pulled out a part of me that wanted to be honest. I'd spent so long with my heart shuttered. The exertion it took to protect it exhausted me. 'There's a part of my soul that is callused. To defeat monsters sometimes you have to become one. You know what I did an hour before I met you? Ordered the excision and castration of a man.'

Ma'at looked unperturbed. 'What did he do?'

'What?'

She shrugged. 'What did he do to make you do that?'

'Beat babies out of his wife.'

Ma'at nodded. 'So, he deserved it. Nefertiti, I am on the side of justice. That's why I joined The Duat. If The Duat isn't enacting justice then maybe I need to think about what side I'm on.'

I held still as she continued. 'And . . . I don't think you have a callused soul, just one that carries the pain of others. It's a strong one.'

I swallowed, trying to keep the tears at bay. In a bid to self-distract, I turned to grab some more liquor from the cupboard. As I did so, the silk blush of my robe skimmed her body and I poured quickly hoping she hadn't felt my weakening. I offered her some. She nodded and I raised a brow. 'No longer on the clock?'

She laughed humourlessly, and it was deeper than before, raspier, sugar and grit. 'The clock is destroyed. I don't know what time is any more.'

I held my glass to hers and we clinked. 'Welcome to House of Aten, where the sun never sets.'

Ma'at took a sip of liquor, winced, but kept my gaze. Her eyes pierced through me as they had when I'd been on stage, and I felt like the spotlight was on me now in a different way, shining through my skin so that my soul was exposed to her. I scared myself by not minding it. She ran a finger from my forehead, to my nose, to my lips, a soft trail that made me feel delicate. She traced the shape of my lips and I felt myself relax.

When she whispered, her breath was laced with alcohol, and I inhaled deeply, tipsy with her proximity. 'So when do you get to rest, Nefertiti?'

Ma'at held my face and my eyes closed, automatically; she kissed my lids gently and I saw stars. That night she offered herself up as a shield so I could be soft, be myself, be loved like a precious thing. She embraced all of me, kissed my jagged scar. That night House of Aten became home to a new freedom.

It was funny that I believed that I was her fantasy without it ever occurring to me that she was mine.

When an intruder entered my room the next morning, bypassing the gated security, I blamed myself. I should have known. It was Mattie's partner. When the Duat officer dragged me from my bed and hurled me against the wall and told me to put my hands up and not to move, I didn't move, but I did chuckle. I looked at Mattie as she pointed her gun at me, still in my robe, smelling like my soap, my cream, me. It was poetic, really. I had done this to myself.

'Well done,' the officer said to Mattie. 'This must have been difficult for you.'

'Oh, you have no idea,' she said. 'Don't worry.' Her gaze didn't move from mine, heavy and inscrutable, when only a few hours ago it had been soft with lust. 'I have this handled.'

The officer whistled low, impressed. 'You sure? Let me do it. Please. I told them the mission was aborted, like you told me to, so this can just be our victory. But *please* let me do it. I've been dying to kill this bitch. Do we have to do it with a gun? She's so creative. No reason we shouldn't be too.' The officer was a chatterbox. I couldn't help but roll my eyes. I had six guns in my quarters and not one of them was accessible to me right then. Typical. Even if I had grabbed the knife under my pillow, it would have been useless. I should have killed her when I had the chance. Last night had felt real, and safe, and sweet, and that is exactly why I should have known it was a lie. People like me, with power like mine, do not get to have real, and safe, and sweet. I deserved this. I was weak.

Mattie looked me in the eye, in the same way she did last night, those same fingers that had caressed me curled around the trigger.

'I said I have this handled.'

'Ugh. You get to do all the fun shit.'

I closed my eyes. I saw Akhen's face. Bastet's face. All the girls' faces.

And then I saw stars.

The bang resonated through me . . . without a bullet.

I opened my eyes again to see the officer bleeding over my pristine wood flooring. It would be a bitch to get out.

Mattie was out of breath. She looked up at me with wide, wild, beautiful eyes and her gun still pointed.

'Do we have people to clean this up or is this the kind of thing we do ourselves?

Naleli

I WAS HOT. Like, *sweltering* hot. Not the kind of hot that the guys described other girls in the school as. Not the kind of hot that made boys' eyes heavy and their voices drop a number of octaves. No, I was hot as in baking, the long sleeves of my shirt soaking up the sun and trapping all the warmth between the material and my skin. The skinny jeans that clung to my legs were quickly becoming a device of self-flagellation. Was I really sacrificing myself to the gods of adolescent social acceptance? I was a heathen! Why was I at an end-of-school pool party that encompassed everything I had spent my entire school life apostatising?

Alas, my 'best friend', Letsha, had dragged me here because she said it would be 'fun', and she had a new swimsuit she wanted to 'try out' and 'you can't just *read* your life away, Naleli'. Thanks to her, I was now going to *die* of heatstroke. It was summer in Lesotho, mid-November, and the sun was beating down with that

157

specific kind of ferocity that only happened a few days before heavy rainfall, as if it was determined to fight back the inevitability of the clouds.

'You know you could just, like . . . take your clothes off, right?' Letsha said, as she tilted her chin into the air and let out a curling plume of smoke from her mouth, her voice tight and muted from the inhalation of a pretty fat-looking blunt. She was sat on the squat brick wall next to me, considerably cooler in the black cut-out one-piece swimsuit that displayed all her soft curves.

I'd only worn the ridiculous hot pink bikini my mother bought to shut her up and it was safely hidden under my shirt and jeans, where it would stay until I got home.

'Naleli, you can't keep hiding,' my mother had pleaded. 'Wear it just in case?'

Just in case what? Just in case my skin magics its way to being one colour? Just in case my peers suddenly become less ignorant and dickhead-like?

I watched the newly freed final-year students of Maloti Valley Secondary dip their legs into the cool water or lie together on blankets on the neat turf, not having to think twice about their bodies or what they were doing with them, tangling themselves up with each other as if trying to compensate for the inevitable separation that graduation would bring. I was fine where I was, sat on the brick wall observing, under the cover of a tree. On the wide patio in front of the glass doors of the rondavel-inspired mansion, the royalty of Maloti Valley were glowing and gorgeous as they flexed their bodies beneath the sun, basking in its rays.

I looked away from their glow to roll my eyes at my best friend. 'You're funny.'

Letsha turned to me and lifted her shades so they sat on her intricate blonde-and-black cornrows, which fed into waist-length plaits.

'I'm serious.'

'Letsha, please, I came here. For *you*. Isn't that enough?'

On the patio across from us, Keeya and her ladies-in-waiting preened unashamedly. Keeya looked like an angel on celestial rumspringa in her tiny white bikini. She swung her long, glossy pressed hair and extended her phone towards the sky. At first, she took selfies alone, and then, when satisfied, she magnanimously allowed her friends to bask in her glow (with glinting lipgloss and screeches of 'Eesh, Lindelani, can't you see you're blocking my light?').

To their left was the chief of the bunch, Khosi. Khosi Nkoli, who threw this party, Khosi Nkoli, who was Captain of the track team, Khosi Nkoli, who *could*, in theory, be described as a snack. Khosi Nkoli (Head Boy), who was in an extended situationship with Keeya (Head Girl), because *of course* he would be one half of a tense will-they-won't-they relationship with all the peaks and lows of a glossy American TV show, where thirty-year-olds play seventeen-year-olds. On the school website, Head Boy and Girl were described as individuals who were voted in according to 'dedication to school spirit and who would best represent the interests of the student body to faculty'. In actuality, the Head Boy and Head Girl mandate was decided by how many people wanted to bang them and Khosi and Keeya were easily coronated Most Bangable.

Letsha smirked, following my eyeline to the couple. 'Yeah, sure. Let's pretend it was for me.'

'What?'

Letsha ignored me. '*Anyway*. High collars, long-sleeves . . . it would be cool if that's what you wanted to wear, but I know that it isn't. I see the clothes you stare at in stores . . .'

'I just think they'd look good on *you*!' I interrupted.

Khosi was sipping from a plastic cup, his tall, athletic and theoretically bangable body glistening under the bright sunlight in his lemon-yellow swim shorts. His body was all hard ridges and angular definition, but his face was soft; he stood in the midst of his court looking slightly disorientated. Keeya yanked at his elbow and forced a shimmering (was that body glitter?) arm through it as he regaled his crew with a story. Khosi chuckled but then reached up to run a hand across his head and, in doing so, extricated himself from Keeya. His eyes drifted across his kingdom lazily and caught mine. I almost fell off the wall. His eyebrows furrowed in surprise before they rose up in tandem with the corners of his mouth, hauling my heartbeat up with it.

'Why not *you*?' Letsha asked quietly.

The prickling sensation that I felt beneath my shirt was becoming distinctly sharp, the heat coming up from deep below the surface of my skin. 'You know why.'

Khosi and I had been friends in another life. As eight-year-olds, back when my mother worked in his mother's salon, we would play together after school in the heat of hot combs and steamers. At ten we developed a secret handshake that necessitated advanced dexterity. At twelve we would sit together as he read his comic books and I read my novels and we would take turns explaining the wonders of our worlds to each other, bringing each other in, merging them and creating our own universe. At thirteen it was clear that hormones and puberty had re-shifted our world, pushing us into a new epoque: The Teen Age. Khosi grew taller as his muscles got tauter and his voice got deeper. My evolution, however, saw pale pinkish patches grow on my deep brown skin. First on my face, then on my arms, until it was almost everywhere, impossible to hide. I had cried back then, scrubbing at my skin until reality sank in. Khosi never said a word about it. His smile remained at the same wattage whenever he saw me, and it was somehow a balm for the sting of the comments other kids made (though Letsha always ensured they never made them again). There was also our basic social shifting; I was book clubs, he was sports clubs. Girls wanted to be with him and girls rarely talked to me. Boys wanted to be him and did not seem interested in me. His membership of the track team gave him a pre-set clique with the athletes, and Keeya, as netball captain, was very ready to be his match.

For a little while, Khosi and I were still living in the fantasy that our friendship could survive this social schism, that it could defy nature. I was actively ignored by the people he called his friends, but he never noticed, blinded by the fact that, because he was beloved, he assumed that everybody's default was to be kind, not knowing that their kindness was dependent on whether they saw you as *their* kind. He never saw that people either ignored my existence or stared at me with hostility, as if I possessed a power to detract from their attractiveness via proximity. The ease with which he interacted with everybody was proof to me that his charisma had been provided by a magical elixir, drunk on his thirteenth birthday, called 'Prince Charming'. That *had* to be the case. It isn't normal to get along with everybody the way Khosi does, not without magical aid. The elixir was composed of this: a non-threatening amount of intelligence that was enough to keep him from being a fool but not enough to have him branded a geek, some friendliness (but not enough to suggest that everybody was on his level, because you cannot inherently be a prince if everybody is equal), and, of course, an aspirational quality. What were Popular Boys made from if not Old Spice, honey and all things money?

At fifteen we had started to drift apart, but we still texted, still hung out when we could, still trying to deny the cracks. Then came his sixteenth birthday party. As soon as I walked into his house I got a sick feeling in my stomach, a turgid lump that had threatened to pull me back to the door. Even the security of Letsha by my side didn't abate the sense that I was in foreign and unwelcoming territory. Feral eyes snapped my way, watching me warily, gazes made even crazier by the effects of smuggled fluorescent alcopops. I was wearing a white strappy top and a denim skirt borrowed from Letsha (to my mother's delight), but suddenly felt naked. My heart pounded in my ears, drowning out the pulsating sound of an Usher song. I was about to turn to Letsha to inform her that this was a supremely bad idea and we should leave *immediately*, but she was already throwing a flirtatious smile at a cute guy, and, really, all it took was a smile from Letsha for a boy to fall. I couldn't deny my best friend fun just because of my discomfort, so I gestured at her to go, and after ensuring I was sure, she left, her hips swaying a little as she approached her prey. Without Letsha I was even more vulnerable. She was cool, too cool for even Maloti Valley Royalty. It was a widely known fact that she was a jurisdiction of her own, and now I was on *my* own without the protection of toleration-by-association. Quickly slipping into survival mode, I spotted a nook in the far corner of the room that I could nestle into, but as soon as I took a step towards it, my face smashed against a warm, firm chest, thwarting my carefully laid plans. I looked up to see the bright grin of the owner, eyes sparkling into mine.

'Yo, Leli! You're here!' Khosi's voice was sunshine.

He wound his arms around me in a hug and my nose buried into his shoulder, allowing direct access to his warm, sweet woodsy scent. A foreign tingle had whirred through my body. *Interesting.* I made a note to analyse that later. He released me and I felt a little lightheaded. Dehydration plus allergies maybe. I cleared my throat.

'Um, well, I wasn't going to. But then I felt bad because we both know my presence makes or breaks a party.'

Khosi nodded, his smile widening. 'That's true. Ain't no party without Naleli Labello. Actually . . .' He stepped back, curved his hands around his mouth and bellowed: 'Everybody out! Naleli's here! You can all go home! You're not needed!'

Laughing, I pounced on him, dragging his hands down from his mouth. 'Stop! Idiot.'

He grinned and ran his eyes across me. 'Seriously, you're the main reason I threw this party. Had to figure out some way to get you to dance with me. It's so hard to get you to hang these days.'

It was true that every time Khosi had asked me to chill in those days I'd declined, but it was only because he always wanted to hang in areas where his friends would be at. His friends who would ask me, 'Were you born that way? Or did it like . . . *grow?*' or 'Do the white parts of your skin like . . . itch?', and even, 'Do you call yourself black? Like *can* you call yourself black?' As if vitiligo was a mutation that was somehow beyond common biology and *sense* and erased my ancestors. I had decided to make an exception for his birthday.

I made another decision to evade the hard truth with a softer one, tilting my head to the side.

'Eh, Khosi, you think I'm one of your little cheerleaders following you around? Because of your two chin hairs and the fact that your voice has a little bass now?'

Khosi threw his head back and bellowed, 'Come on—'

'No, *you* come on, chief. I have a picture of you wearing Mrs Majoro's church wig with your hand on your hip. You can't do your smooth boy shit with me. I *know* you—'

Khosi held a sassy hand out and stopped me in my tracks. 'First of all, I slayed in that wig. Second of all, you know I could never think that. You lead, I follow. That's the reason I was wearing the wig in the first place. It was *your* idea to steal it and I would have done anything to make you laugh. It was also *your* idea to choreograph that dance we used to do to "Khona".' He paused and tucked his lip between his teeth, eyes gleaming with an idea. I instantly started shaking my head, my blood running cold as I held a single warning finger up.

'*Khosi*. No. Nope. I am *not*—'

But he was already calling to his boy in charge of the bluetooth, impervious to the curious looks of his peers, who wondered at the cross-species interaction. Popular and plebeian. Normal and abnormal. The first hits of the drum resounded through the room.

'Turn it up!' Khosi yelled out. I wanted to be annoyed, but my scowl had barely assembled when my smile broke through. Such was Khosi's power. His shoulders were bouncing to the beat as he backed his way to the centre of his cleared-out living room, arms outstretched in front of him, hands rhythmically beckoning me.

'You know I can't dance without you, Leli.'

His face weakened my resolve. We, of course, had drawn in an audience. Letsha had pushed her man to the side and was looking at me with wide, gleeful eyes as she nodded and mouthed a 'do it', fortified by the knowledge of the many dances I'd made us do in her room in front of YouTube. I exhaled heavily.

'This is your birthday present for the next ten years.'

Khosi's smile broadened as I stood next to him and started on the intricate legwork. The room exploded into whoops and hollers as Khosi joined in, muscle memory aiding us as we fell into step, hopping and twisting and bending, arms swishing sharply through the air. We were in a years-old private conversation that felt timeless, our vocabulary complex, layered, energy gaining momentum. This was us running around in synthetic curly wigs. This was us racing each other in his family pool (ironically, I always won). My self-awareness fell away and I felt easy in my skin, free within it. Khosi was a little clumsier than me, slower, and eventually he stopped, letting me finish the dance on my own. I fell into centre stage. I finished to raucous applause; his cheers the loudest, his smile the widest. I'd forgotten we were being watched. He bowed before me.

I laughed. 'Why did you put yourself through that? You know I'm the better dancer.'

His shoulder twitched. 'I told you. Anything to make you laugh.'

The force of Khosi's gaze pushed words back into my throat. I swallowed.

'Khosi! We run out of ice, man!' The sound of his boy's voice made us both jump.

Khosi's eyes stayed fastened to my face as he called out, 'There's some more in the outside freezer! In the garage.'

'Where's that?' the voice intruded again.

Khosi swore under his breath and shook his head. 'Idiots.' He swept his thumb over my racing pulse and dipped his head to ensure I was looking him in the eye. 'Don't move.'

'Too out of breath from being the Beyoncé of this party to move.'

Khosi laughed as he backed away from me, eyes dancing into mine. His bottom lip tucked into his teeth in a way that made me acutely aware of every single part of my body, before he put two hands together in prayer and lightly jogged towards the back door.

I hadn't realised how stilted my breath had been till I'd released a heavy exhale, the thrills I'd been trying to ignore rushing to the surface and making me hot all over. The butterflies in my belly told me that my affection for Khosi had undergone a metamorphosis. Who'd have thought having a gigantic crush on the boy who once asked me if *Titanic* was based on a Shakespeare play would be my destiny.

'That was cute.'

Though I only vaguely recognised the voice, it was enough to dissolve my smile and sour my sweet dreaming. I turned around to see Keeya, head at a tilt, her lips a glossy curve. Letsha had spotted the scene from across the room and was already striding towards us. I shook my head surreptitiously. Having a bodyguard would only make me look weak. I returned Keeya's fake smile.

'What was, Keeya?'

The sparkly eyeshadow she was wearing only made the dark glint in her eye more pronounced.

'That little dance, sis. It was cute.'

She reached out to play with a single one of my braids, like a cat toying with a mouse, and flicked her eyes across me. 'I can make you cuter, though. I brought my make-up bag with me. We can do a quick make-over!'

I narrowed my eyes at her. Was she drunk or just mad? 'What? No, I don't want a—'

Keeya reached out to tilt my chin up, her eyes on the brink between cutesy ice-skating rink and snowy abyss. 'It's just that you would be so pretty without—'

My stomach twisted, and I manoeuvred my face out of her grip. Her face feigned apology and she released that saccharine smile again. 'Look, all I'm saying is I think that we're the same shade. Ish. Well, your brown bits are the same shade, obviously.' She laughed and the shards lacerated through the remnants of my good mood.

'So, I can help cover up all those bits on your face. Make it all one colour, eh? So people won't stare when you guys are together.'

I stepped back from her, ignoring the warning sting in my eyes. 'Khosi and I aren't—'

Her smile shrank and she became steely. 'No. You aren't. And you could never be. All this is charity. He's being nice to a girl his mother made him invite. We both know Khosi is a sweet guy. He wanted you to be comfortable. But I want to remind you to not get too comfortable.' She moved closer to me and put a hand on my shoulder. I shrugged it off. She laughed.

'Look,' she continued, 'even if he thinks he likes you, don't you think, eventually, he'll get tired of people staring at you like you're a freak? This is for your sake, sis. Eventually he'll want to be with someone normal. You deserve to be with someone . . . like you.'

I gritted my teeth, wishing my tears would defy gravity. 'Fuck you, Keeya.'

She grinned. 'I'm just trying to help.'

I pushed past her. As soon as Letsha saw my glistening eyes, she wanted to pull Keeya's tracks out. The only thing that abated the murderous look in her eye was my desperate pleas. 'Please, Letsha. Can we just *go*?'

We'd just made it out of the doorway when Khosi appeared and snatched at my wrist, gaze wide and concerned.

'Hey, whoa—, Leli, what's up? What happened?'

My tears got heavier at the sight of him. The ground was finally shifting beneath us, separating us and our universes. Keeya might have been a mean little witch, but she had a point. Our friendship wasn't sustainable. He might not have known it, and why would he? He was King of the Jungle. He had no known predators. I, on the other hand, had started developing whatever the opposite of camouflage was and it was only growing more conspicuous every day.

'You know what, Khosi? I think it's best for us to give this up. We were friends as kids. Let's leave it at that. You don't have to try any more.'

He shook his head. 'What? *Naleli*—'

I snatched my wrist from his grip. 'No. Khosi, *look* at me. Do you see me? Like, really see me? Do you know what your friends see when they look at me?'

He frowned. 'I don't care what they think. What you look like doesn't matter to me—'

I laughed humourlessly, the tears falling more aggressively. 'Thank you *so* much for being able to look past my hideousness.'

'Come on. That's not what I meant—'

I shook my head. 'It doesn't even matter. You see what you want to see, Khosi. You want to believe that everything is cute and fine and sunny because that's what works for you—'

Annoyance flitted over his face. 'Leli, I know you think my friends don't like you, but have you ever thought that maybe it's because you push them away? You don't even try! You think you're better than them—'

Letsha gasped and only bit her tongue because I gripped hard on her wrist. My heart cracked, but I hardened my voice, tilted my chin up.

'I *am* better than them. They're a bunch of shallow dicks.'

Khosi stepped back a little, his pretty face collapsing. 'Is that what you think of me, Leli?'

I swallowed. 'I don't know. But I think we should stay away from each other from now on.'

Which we did. For the next two years we moved around each other like strangers, barely acknowledging each other until I received the mass text invite from him for his birthday party. We were eighteen, about to go out into the world, a new world where the factions in school meant nothing. I'd held still, staring at the screen, struck with déjà vu. The last text I had got from him had been a personal invite to his sixteenth birthday party:

Leli. My sixteenth ain't gonna be sweet without you. Please come.

I was here, at his house, of my own volition. Why? Was it the same reason I took both debate club and Model UN? Masochism? It didn't matter now, because he was smiling at me and, like a fool, I found myself smiling back as I sweated through my shirt and jeans. A damp dummy.

'Um, Letsha, I'm gonna get myself a drink. I need to cool off. You want anything?'

Letsha raised a brow as she clocked where I was looking. 'No, I'm good. You go get yours, sis.'

Her wink was unnecessary.

I wasn't long at the punch table when I felt a presence beside me and I smelt his scent. I looked up to see him pouring himself a drink, despite the fact that I was pretty sure he'd had a full cup five minutes earlier.

He turned to me, shot a tentative smile. 'I'm really glad you came. I wasn't sure you were going to.'

I shrugged. 'Letsha's idea.'

Had he gotten *taller*? Why did he smell so good? Was the heat interacting with his natural musk? Had I really just thought the words 'natural musk'? Clearly the heatstroke was reaching fatal levels.

He nodded. 'Of course,' he rubbed the back of his neck awkwardly. 'Uh. I saw online that you got a scholarship for Government and Politics. Don't forget me when you're Prime Minister.'

'I won't. Gonna push for a law that says, if you throw a pool party, you have to get in the pool. So, you're retroactively going to jail.'

Khosi laughed. 'I want to. It's just that nobody wants to get in with me.' He paused, and cleared his throat. 'Look, Naleli—'

I shook my head and laughed awkwardly. 'Nope. You really don't have to—'

He twitched his head to the side of the garden table and we moved a little away from the people who had suddenly also found themselves thirsty, pouring their punch slowly while we talked.

Khosi levelled his gaze at me, ensuring that I was looking him in the eye. 'Yes, I really have to. I haven't stopped thinking about it for two years. You were right: I was selfish. I didn't want to see the truth because it would have . . . disrupted things for me too much. I didn't want to accept that all my friends are dickheads. I regretted it, like . . . immediately, but after a while I was just too ashamed to try to talk to you. And when I said that what you look like doesn't matter to me—'

My stomach dropped at the memory. 'We don't have to rehash—'

'What I *meant* to say is that you're beautiful. Inside and out. You've always been beautiful to me. You don't need me to tell you that, but I just want you to know it. I've always looked up to you. You're so sure of yourself. You know who you are. And I'm sorry I was too weak to chase after you. And I'm sorry that I'm too late.'

I took a sip of my rum and coke, barely cooled by the melting ice I'd stuck in it. I thought maybe it would control the emotions tumbling about inside of me. No such luck. I looked out to the empty pool and then up at the sloping mountains, hoping it would calm my frantic heartbeat. Again, my attempts at repressing my feelings proved futile. I looked up at him, finally. His eyes were glinting, face open, jaw tight. I took a deep breath.

'Um, for what it's worth, I never thought you were a shallow dick. I've always thought you were a deep dick.'

Khosi threw his head back and guffawed in the way I hadn't realised I'd missed. 'Thank you. That's worth a lot.'

I cleared my throat. ' . . . and, um, for the record I *was* trying to push you away. I was scared that eventually you would push me away. Thought it would hurt less if I beat you to it. I was wrong.'

'I would never push you away, Naleli.' His voice was quiet and raw and held my breath to ransom.

Our eyes stayed fastened on each other as a sweet silence fell between us, accented with muted hip-hop and laughter and—

'There you are, babe.' *Keeya.*

172

Keeya made like she was about to put her arm through Khosi's, but he pushed his hand swiftly into the pocket of his shorts, holding his arm tight to his side. Keeya's lips parted and she started blinking rapidly, as if not quite realising what had just happened. It was a decisive move, the statement clear. They were not together – for real. Clearly unused to the lack of control, she turned her gaze to me, eyes narrowed in the same lethal way they had been two years ago, clearly hoping to garner power back by usurping me.

'Cute outfit, Naleli.'

I tilted my head to the side, my armour already on. 'Aw. You think, Keeya?'

She nodded. 'Yeah. Like you really tried. It took a lot of guts for you to come here, and just making it to the party alone is just, like . . . so confident, you know? We couldn't expect you to wear a swimsuit too.' She put a hand on her tiny hip. 'I can imagine it's super daunting with your . . . condition.'

Khosi was looking at Keeya as if seeing her for the first time, disgust strewn over his face. 'Keeya, that's enough. What the hell is wrong with—'

I shook my head and laughed. 'Keeya . . . how does it feel to be *so* terrified of me all the time.'

She froze and released a hard cough of a laugh. 'Excuse me?'

I shrugged. 'I'm just saying. If I knew that I had the superpower of making mean girls feel threatened, I would have shown up to more things.'

Keeya stuttered and had just gathered herself together enough

173

to enquire if I was 'fucking mad, you cow-looking bitch', when I looked up at Khosi and asked, 'Hey, do you want to go for a swim?'

Keeya stopped squawking long enough for her jaw to drop. Though Khosi's brows creased in confusion, his eyes lit up. 'What?'

'I *said*,' I lifted the bottom of my shirt, pulled it over my braids and threw it on the floor, revealing the hot pink bikini that I'd been hiding, 'I'm going for a swim. You coming?' My jeans were next to be peeled off and the feeling of fresh air kissing my skin was euphoric. It almost beat the high of making Keeya lose her shit.

Khosi eyes quickly flitted across my body before he met my gaze, the corner of his mouth tweaking upwards in assent.

And so, with Khosi behind me, in my hot pink bikini with the pale and brown of my skin exposed and shining, I walked past a gawping, speechless Keeya to the pool. Conversations petered out and gave way to hushed murmurs, eyes swivelling in my direction. I pushed their attention out and pulled focus on to the singular feeling of being whole in my skin – full up inside of it.

I jumped in. I didn't even notice when Khosi joined me. I hadn't been in a pool – *this* pool – since I was twelve, and I relished the cool chlorine familiarity, enveloping my skin, all of it, the sun glowing down on the patchwork of my back, my shoulders, caressing it. It was feeding me, I was elemental with it – part of nature and gloriously natural. I splashed and twirled and bumped into Khosi, who was watching me, smiling, starry eyes brighter than ever. For a few seconds the only sound was our laughter and hip-hop playing from the speakers.

Then, I heard a hoarse voice echo through the compound:

'THAT'S MY BEST FRIEND! BADDEST BITCH IN MALOTI VALLEY. TIDDIES SITTING IN THAT PINK BIKINI, AYYYYY!' The proclamation was punctuated by a large splash. Letsha's head popped up a few seconds later as she raised both fists and yelped in triumph. 'WOOP!'

A moment later her hollers were joined by applause, cheers and more splashes as people ran into the pool giggling, dancing and plashing, pulled out of their pool-side mannequin posing and into animation. The music was louder, the chatter was wilder, the laughter more uproarious.

I floated to the edge of the pool furthest away from the speakers, and leant against it, spreading my arms out on the ledge. I closed my eyes and raised my face up at the sky, braids dripping, wondering how I'd gone so long without feeling as free as this. When I brought my head forward, I found myself face to face with Khosi and I wondered how I went so long without being looked at like this.

'Ain't no party without Naleli Labello,' he whispered, his eyes glinting into mine and a soft smile curved into his lips.

'I lead,' I reminded him softly, pulling him in until our faces were just inches apart, 'you follow.'

Zhinu

'LET'S GO THROUGH IT ONE MORE TIME, ZHINU.'

Zhinu didn't even have a chance to sigh before her mother continued. 'The jet departs at 11 a.m. The breakfast show is at 7 a.m., but we're only an hour away from the airport and your segment is fifteen minutes. There is time for a three-minute performance with some leeway for delays or runs.'

Zhinu's mother didn't look up from her phone as her manicured nails click-clacked on the gleaming oblong of wires, glass, cobalt and lithium. Her mother changed the world with each finger swipe, each tap; she conjured action from rock and sand. The white light lit up her face in the dark, making the deep red paint on her lips brighter and emphasising the chic, silver streaks in her sleekly bobbed hair. She already looked ageless thanks to genetics, but injections also helped. The glow from her phone gave her an ethereal, goddess-like quality that jarred with her brisk, business-like husky tone, which

177

she'd acquired from years of smoking Vogues. Zhinu used to tell her to stop, and her mother would release a raspy cackle before chiding, 'Who is the mother here? Me or you? Little girl, your voice works in this world because it is sweet and soulful. My voice works because I sound like a man. A man the men in power want to have sex with. It helps me get things done. And you need my voice to work for your voice to work and for you to be successful. Don't you want to be successful? Sing those songs, make your father proud, and all you need to do is pass me my cigarettes. Be a dear and do that.'

She continued tapping away as the car moved.

'We'll do hair and make-up at the hotel. I decided that tonight.' Her mother's long false lashes still didn't flutter up. 'I booked the girl who did your face tonight at the award show. I liked her. She didn't talk too much. I hate when they talk too much. I hate when you talk back to them. Why do you need to be their friend? What are you going to gossip about, *boys*? Will you invite her to your wedding? They just want to use you for what you have! Leeches. Always maintain a cool distance, Zhinu. You are their empress and empresses do not gossip with silly market women. Besides, I don't trust the beauty people at the station. They always age you . . .'

Zhinu was sure not a single breath had been taken. She often wondered if breathing was something her mother pantomimed so that people wouldn't ask too many questions concerning her immortality.

' . . . Hey, Bingwen. You remember last time? They emphasised Zhinu's laugh lines. I keep telling her about those laugh lines! No need to smile that wide. You're a popstar not a clown, I said!'

Zhinu's mother didn't glance up as she called to her personal assistant, who was sat in the passenger seat of the sleek, tinted saloon car. Zhinu saw the back of Bingwen's designer haircut (a ridiculous low-fade dyed blond, quaffed at the top, while his edges remained dark) bob up and down.

'Oh, absolutely.' His voice dripped with thick derision. 'It was dreadful. She looked older than you!'

Bingwen's primary purpose was to echo Zhinu's mother's thoughts with just a little added acid. Zhinu's mother was shrewd enough to know she had to be at least a little careful with her delivery; she acknowledged her dual role of manager and pastoral carer to that extent, at least. So, yes, while she always kept a sword pointed to Zhinu's back to keep her moving, she also pressed the flat of the blade against her child's head to cool her when she had a fever and used it to gently brush hair from her face and tell her that everything would be okay. 'As long as you do as I say, Little Star.'

Bingwen was her conduit, through which she could deliver the messages she knew would sound too harsh coming from her own mouth. Bingwen relished this role. The contempt with which he spoke might not have been audible to the untrained ear, but Zhinu was a musician, and had been so since birth, so she could detect a key that was even very slightly off, or a pipa that was just a little out of tune, or, in this case, the bitterness of a wannabe star with no discernible talent and an unhealthy obsession with fame. Bingwen was her mother's lapdog. He started as her hairstylist and rose through the ranks by unrelentingly sucking up to her. Zhinu's mother's vanity made the seduction easy, and it was clear that Bingwen was who she wished her daughter was. It was clear mainly because she often said it out loud. She joked (lamented) that 'if only it were possible to pour Bingwen's soul into Zhinu's body . . .' Zhinu's mother would then laugh. Bingwen would laugh louder still – too loud, deafeningly loud – with the kind of unhinged raucousness that usually came with grief-fuelled wailing, yearning. They would laugh while Zhinu would remain still, silently nauseated, marvelling at the ease with which they referred to this actual nightmare as if it were a wistful dream. And they never wondered about what would happen to Zhinu's usurped soul.

Zhinu had often made intimations of wanting her own assistant, but her mother had swatted her away. 'You have me, Zhinu. What else do you need? I know best. I know you better than you know yourself.'

The crystals that dotted Zhinu's near-sheer, skin-tight gown began to feel heavy on her skin. As if she could feel each and every one pressing their weight into her. 'Pressure creates diamonds, Little Star! Suck it up,' her mother would say . . . Oh no. She could now hear her mother's voice inside her head. Zhinu adjusted herself in her seat and looked out of the tinted window of their chauffeured car, into the falling dusk. She didn't recognise the town, but it was gorgeous. Rural blended into the urban, and towering, elegant ginkgo trees lined the streets like flirtatious lashes, giving way to bright, yellow, glowing windows and glittering storefronts that were stacked, multi-coloured, seductive. From the outside, all anyone would see looking into the car window was a gleaming black pane that shut them out. Zhinu leant her forehead against the cool glass and saw a strange warping of reality, the world as it was but muted, less vivid. It was as if she were tasting food with a numbed tongue.

It was late, and they were just leaving an awards ceremony where Zhinu had been nominated for Most Popular Potential Idol, which – what did that even mean? She was the best at *not* being a superstar yet? Well, apparently she wasn't even the best at that, because she hadn't won. Her mother was angry about that. In fact, she was so incensed that she had insisted that they skip the after-party to make some sort of point. 'Create mystery around yourself,' she said, as if mystery was what someone who had the potential to be a potential idol needed. 'Make them *thirst* for you. Overexposure cheapens.'

Her mother had owned a haberdashery before she had started managing Zhinu full-time, but she spoke like a PR exec. who'd hatched from a high-rise in the city, craving black coffee and nicotine from their first breath. Zhinu had no idea if her mother knew anything about what she was talking about or if she merely just willed everything she said to be true. Either way, it was somewhat working. Zhinu had gone from singing in local pageants to award shows in just three years. Still, Zhinu wished she was at the after-party; she didn't care that she hadn't won. What was the point of sucking it in, pushing it out and singing songs that rhymed 'kiss me' with 'miss me', written by forty-seven-year-old men who leered at both her and her mother, if she couldn't even get wasted with her peers? She might have even made friends. Years of home schooling and music classes, in which her mother pitted her against everybody else, had made her social life sparse. She had hoped at least that, by the time her (mother's) dreams were within reach, she would be able to connect with someone, anyone. However, by now she'd acquired a reputation for being an ice queen. She kept herself to herself at industry parties, because she found that, when she tried to interact with people, her mother interjected. Her mother maintained that it was important to remain aloof, that cliques were for the weak, and that the more isolated you were, the more powerful you were. She was of the notion that having people around you sapped at your essence and diffused your energy.

Zhinu wondered if her mother had created this philosophy when Zhinu's father had died. Her mother and father had met young, in a small village, and so much of her was in him and him in her. Her father brought out a tenderness and a playfulness in her mother that withered in his absence. Their friends soon fell away from her after he died. She became a bare bones version of herself and her sharp tongue, which had been sweetened with love, lashed like a blade. She couldn't help it. Softness reminded her of her lost love. Perhaps believing that solitude was the source of her power was a survival mechanism, maybe it comforted her? Maybe isolation was a gift she felt she was bestowing on her daughter – she wanted Zhinu to avoid the hurt she had endured. All Zhinu knew was that she missed her father, and who her mother had been when she was with him.

It took a few moments for Zhinu to notice that the world had come to a stop. She turned from the window and was welcomed back to reality with her mother's colourful cursing at the hapless chauffeur – together with Bingwen's ad libs – and angry honks outside the car that indicated that it had stopped moving.

'Did you not think to check if the car was up to standard before deciding to drive it?'

The poor driver pleaded with Zhinu's mother as he held his phone to his ear. 'I'm so sorry, madam. I am arranging an alternative mode of transport right away. This has never happened before . . .'

'And it shall never happen again! I will see to it that you're fired!'

Bingwen jumped in: 'You are carrying precious cargo . . .' Zhinu knew he was referring to himself and her mother. ' . . . not a truck full of slaughter-house chickens! I should have known by your suit that this would be a shit-show. How could I expect someone who can't even get his uniform tailored to be competent?'

Zhinu rolled her eyes. 'Bingwen, settle down. Don't be a dick. Your shirt literally has a torn-up hem and holes in it. I can see your entire nipple.'

Bingwen turned around and slowly lifted the sunglasses he was wearing for reasons unbeknownst to anyone. 'Are you slut shaming me?'

'I'm style shaming you.'

'It's actually the reclamation of peasant identity and it's not only subversive but it's extremely chic. I'm glad the traditional princess look works for you, but some of us like to dress outside the box . . .'

'I'm sure the box is grateful.'

Bingwen made a sound that could only be described as a hiss.

'Enough!' Zhinu's mother was usually entertained by their bickering – she thought it denoted some sort of sibling intimacy rather than actual pulsing hatred – but at that moment she was panicked by their predicament. 'Zhinu, what has gotten into you? We don't have time for this! We are stuck in a village in the middle of nowhere and we have things to do tomorrow!' She tapped (slapped) the driver's shoulder. 'Could you make yourself useful and tell us precisely how long a replacement vehicle will take?'

The driver stuttered while her mother screeched at him to speak up, until Zhinu interjected and smiled at the driver. This seemed to calm him a little.

'Sir, it's okay. We just need to know so we can plan our night.'

The driver looked at Zhinu and only Zhinu, his eyes clinging on to her as if she was his life raft. 'Two hours, madam.'

Zhinu could have sworn the screech her mother released was succeeded by the sound of wings flapping frantically outside the car.

'You mean we're STUCK in this village?'

Zhinu's mother wrapped her lilac fur coat around her tighter, as if to shield herself from the curse of a town with no Starbucks in her immediate eyeline. It was summer – too hot for such an outfit – but her mother always dared and defied nature. She was a microclimate unto herself. 'And we can't even call a taxi because it's unsafe! Do they even have taxis here?'

Zhinu tapped on her phone and in a few seconds sourced their precise location. 'Okay, Mother, it isn't a village, it's a town. And from what I've seen from the window, it's pretty. It's actually quite close to where we're going tomorrow. I think it would probably be easier for us to stay here for what's left of the night and make an early start tomorrow. There will be someone here from the agency to pick us up tomorrow, right?' She turned to the chauffeur and nodded at him hopefully. He nodded briskly back.

'Yes, ma'am. Of course!'

Zhinu smiled and turned to her mother, trying not to relish this detour from routine too much. This was an adventure for her. 'See? Breathe, Mama.'

Her mother glared. Zhinu couldn't help but laugh at her mother's dramatics, and her mother glared even harder.

'Glad to see you find this amusing, Zhinu. Fine, we will stay here if we must. Bingwen, find the most expensive hotel. God help me if it's a Marriott.'

They soon discovered that the town was a premium staycation destination. Zhinu's mother balked at the term 'staycation'. With all the hotels booked up, the only place with any availability was an inn called The Magpie Lodge. To Zhinu, it was a sweet boutique hotel. Her mother referred to it as 'a shack hardly fit for animals'. At this point, Zhinu genuinely thought her mother might faint. This only made Zhinu like it more. It was only a seven-minute drive from where their chauffeured car had broken down (her mother had insisted on a taxi) and it was nestled on a narrow street built into the neighbouring forest. It seemed like a world away from the cities Zhinu was so used to staying in. Its grey bricks were illuminated by bamboo torches that lined and lit up the gravel path like noble guards. The encaustic tile roof was an inky celestial blue that melted into the sky. It was beautiful, delicate. She felt a sudden lightness come over her, a weightlessness that made her feel buoyant, despite the grumbles of her companions. Everything in her life was regimented, ordered and pre-ordained. This felt like a getaway.

*   *   *

185

There was no one at the front desk. The glossy rosewood was guarded by two blown glass magpies at each end, who watched on regally as Bingwen frantically tapped the bell to get someone's attention and Zhinu's mother demanded to know whether anybody in the empty lobby knew who they were.

Zhinu watched the two of them in amusement for a few moments before she decided to make her entertainment experience interactive.

Zhinu schooled her face to reflect her mother's irritation. 'Yeah, this is ridiculous! Why are we being treated like peasants?' Her mother looked at her with what looked like a glimmer of pride as Zhinu continued, 'I mean, where is the red carpet for the once nominated Most Popular Potential Idol? What's next? People not recognising me as "shopping girl number two" from the Korean medicated anti-dandruff shampoo commercial? I'm Shopping Girl Number *Two*, damn it!' Zhinu slapped the desk for emphasis.

Bingwen stopped tapping the bell to look at Zhinu with disgust. Her mother sighed heavily and rubbed the bridge of her nose in tiny circles.

'Zhinu, for once in your life will you just grow up—'

'Oh my God! Shopping Girl Number Two? It couldn't be!' The deep voice belonged to neither Bingwen, Zhinu or her mother.

The three guests turned to see a man walking towards the front desk from a side door in the lobby, the door swinging behind him. Blood rushed to Zhinu's face, pinking her cheeks. He was tall and was wearing a green flannel shirt, with sleeves rolled up to reveal sinewy forearms, thrown over a white tank top that was a little smudged with dirt. It fit close enough to his shape for Zhinu's eyes to linger for longer than was appropriate. His half smile revealed a dimple in his right cheek that seemed deep enough to trip and fall into. His face was high angles and steep edges softened by a pillowy mouth. He situated himself behind the desk and looked directly at her. The look threatened to ruin her entire life as she knew it.

'If I knew Shopping Girl Number Two was here, I would have dressed more formally.' His smile widened and Zhinu's skin prickled. She nodded.

'Thank you. I appreciate that. I worked on that hair swish for three months. Do you know how many times strands got stuck in my lipgloss? I also had to get the frustrated scratching just right.'

The guy's head tilted slightly, as if taking her in differently, his dark eyes flashing across her crystal dress. 'Dedication to your craft. I respect that.'

The air in the lobby became still and voltaic and Zhinu suddenly became very aware of every inch of herself. Her mother cleared her throat.

The guy tore his gaze from Zhinu and smiled at her mother. 'Welcome to The Magpie Lodge. I am the owner, Zhou Niulang, and you must be our booking for the family deluxe suite. I'll just draw up your information and your keys will be with you right away.'

Niulang tapped at the computer beside him as Bingwen stepped away from the desk and whispered 'Keys?' He rubbed his forehead. 'I'm freaking out. We don't even have electronic locks. God help us.'

Zhinu smiled. 'Nobody wants to steal your raggedy V-necks, Bingwen.'

Zhinu's mother rolled her eyes. 'Kids, I am exhausted. Not this again. And, Zhinu, the gall of you to attack Bingwen's style when you were just making gooey eyes at a man dressed like a *farmer*.'

Bingwen cackled and Zhinu wanted to die.

'Hardly a farmer, madam.' Niulang's voice piped up. 'I only own one cow. Taurus. Which is why I'm dressed the way I'm dressed; I was milking her, and she prefers me casual. Sweet girl. A little moody sometimes . . .'

Zhinu choked on air and her mother glared.

' . . . I wasn't expecting guests this late. Apologies. Room 7.' He handed the keys to Zhinu and shot her a tiny, incubated and almost imperceptible smile that was clearly just for her.

Zhinu's mother released a strong and hefty 'Hmm', before she nodded twice and gestured at Niulang to pick up their bags. 'It's late. The quicker I sleep, the quicker this nightmare will be over.'

Zhinu's heart dropped at the thought of the night being over. Her body revolted against the idea. She hoped it would never end.

Zhinu's first kiss had been with a boy from her dance school. She was fourteen and it had been sloppy. He told everyone he'd felt her right breast the next day. Zhinu had always found the specificity of his lie fascinating. Why only the one breast? Why the right one in particular? At the time, it was the bigger one, though, so objectively it was an intelligent choice. Perhaps he found a dual breast squeeze too unrealistic. Either way, somehow it got back to her mother. She, of course, was livid. 'Only when you're eighteen and it must be someone who is rich. You can't afford distraction for anything less.'

This rich man hadn't magically shown up when she was eighteen. Zhinu's mother had moulded Zhinu's life so everything was focused on her ascent to stardom, so there was no time for anything else. Now, she was twenty-three and the only person she'd ever shared a bed with was her mother. She was still sharing a bed with her mother. Zhinu shifted so her mother's elbow removed itself from her back. Bingwen snored from his single bed in the corner of the room. Since there was obviously no mini bar, both of them had gone to the small bar in the inn and attempted to buy a bottle from Niulang. He'd given it to them for free. The two of them had had three shots of whiskey and an Ambien each and were knocked out pretty quickly, thankfully. Zhinu, meanwhile, was wide awake.

It was a warm night, and even in the crop top and cycling shorts Zhinu had procured from her overnight bag, Zhinu felt suffocated. The window was open but the stuffiness only became more oppressive with every second that passed. Bingwen snorted. Zhinu's mother stirred, sighed and then whacked Zhinu in the face. Zhinu removed her mother's hand and climbed out of bed. She slipped on a hoodie for decency's sake, put on her sneakers and slipped out of the room in search of something she couldn't identify yet.

That was a lie. Zhinu knew what she was looking for. She knew what she was looking for because, when she saw the empty front desk, her heart plummeted, her cheeks became hot and she had the profound, heavy sense that she was, in fact, a clown rather than a popstar. Why would he even be there? There was no reason he would want to wait up to talk to her at – she glanced up at the clock behind the desk – 1 a.m. Shit, 1 a.m.? She had to be up in four hours! The right thing to do was to go back to bed and stuff her ears with cotton wool, and yet, her body balked at the very idea of sleep.

The growl of her stomach gave her an excuse to delay the inevitable, and also reminded Zhinu that there had been a vending machine in the bar area. Zhinu followed where her ravenous body pulled her, with the idea of filling herself up with something fried and beige and salty and pre-packaged sending a delicious thrill through her. Her mother had her on everything steamed, lean, clean and green. It was somewhat anti-climactic then that, when stood in front of the glowing, humming machine, Zhinu remembered that she had no money on her. Returning to the room sort of defeated the purpose. Continuing along with her rebellious mood, Zhinu kicked the machine. The packet of tempura seaweed she'd been targeting shimmied but didn't budge. She slapped the glass. It flirtatiously wiggled and moved a little closer to the edge. Zhinu's hand smarted but the exhilaration that shot through her balmed the sting. She laughed; it bubbled over and out of her. She kicked the machine again and started hitting at it with both hands simultaneously. This time she didn't even care if the bag moved, all she felt was the vibration within her veins and a new power moving through her. She felt like a superhero after the first mutant bite. In an instant she was pounding the glass with her fists, kicking it in a flurry and finding herself releasing sounds that were guttural and primal. It felt good to be using her voice in a way that wasn't sweet or controlled. She was euphoric and furious, feral and free . . .

'Are you okay?'

Fuck.

Zhinu's arms dropped to her side. She held still, save for her panting. She turned around and dabbed at her eyes, which she'd just noticed were watering, to see Niulang stood in the doorway, staring at her with gentle curiosity. He'd had a shower – she could distinctly smell the soap and shampoo on him – and his hair was now ruffled. He'd changed into sweatpants and switched his vest for a clean one. He looked quite delectable. Zhinu brushed some of her hair out of her face and cleared her throat, stood straight and forced a beam on her face. 'Yeah! Yes. Thank you. Um. Sorry I just . . . I . . .' Nothing she said would make sense of what he had just witnessed. Nothing would make him think she was a normal person. At the very least she'd just exposed herself as an incompetent thief. She sighed. 'I was hungry.'

Niulang walked towards her, his gaze fastening her to the spot and making her breath heavier. Shit. He was going to throw them out of the inn. Her mother was going to murder her. Bingwen would feast on her remains.

'What do you want?' he asked.

Zhinu swallowed. 'What?'

Niulang pointed to the vending machine.

Zhinu cleared her throat. 'Oh!' She pointed at her target. 'Those please. Thank you.'

Niulang approached the machine, kicked twice and hit the side of it in an intricate, expert pattern. Two packets of snacks dropped down. He passed her one and grinned.

'There's a technique to it.'

Zhinu laughed, and with it, all her tensed muscles relaxed. 'Oh. See, I was doing bang, bang, bang . . .'

'That's where you went wrong. It's bang, bang, *bang.*' Niulang tapped the side of his head. 'It's a science. Don't feel bad about it.' His eyes skipped across her. 'Zhinu, right?'

Her name sounded good in his mouth.

'Um. Yes.'

'Niulang,' he said, as if her mind hadn't clung to it the minute she'd heard it. 'Do you want a drink? I know a great bar around here. The bartender is kind of a dick, but you can just ignore him.'

Zhinu bit back her smile. 'Um, I really should get back to . . .' What? The bed she shared with her mother?

'I would love a drink. Thank you.'

In approximately eight seconds, Niulang had hopped behind the bar and poured both of them a finger of baiju. Zhinu sat on the bar stool and relished the burn from her first sip; the fire in her chest felt appropriate, made her adjust into the moment more. It was a surprisingly delightful accompaniment to the tempura seaweed.

'I was angry.' Zhinu twisted her tumbler around on the coaster before looking up at Niulang. He was a stranger. She had nothing to lose. 'That thing you walked in on? Was me being angry.'

Niulang nodded. 'What were you angry about?'

'That's the thing. I don't even know. Everything? Nothing. I didn't even know I was angry until then. I'm not usually angry.'

Niulang took a sip from his drink. 'So, what did you think of it? Would you try it again?'

Zhinu laughed and nodded. 'You know, I think I would. It felt

amazing just to be able to feel it. I haven't had space to feel in a while.'
She paused. 'I'm sorry for doing that to your vending machine.'

Niulang shrugged. 'It's okay. No damage done. You've actually opened my eyes to a new use for it. Snacks and outrage. I should try it sometime.'

'Yeah? What do you have to be angry about?'

Niulang laughed, and it was deep and round, nutritious and delicious, and it filled Zhinu's stomach till she felt she had no need for the tempura seaweed.

He rubbed the back of his head. 'Uh. Let's see. The fact that my dear father died on me two years ago and left me this place while I was in the middle of my degree? The fact that, because I'm the eldest child, it became my responsibility and I had to drop out to run it so my little sister could go to university? The fact that it saps at my social life so my only friend is a cow that gets constipated far too often for my liking?'

Zhinu snorted and slapped her hand across her mouth. 'I'm sorry, I wasn't laughing at . . .'

Niulang shook his head. 'Don't be. She's a great kisser, so I forgive her.'

Zhinu giggled and took another sip of her drink, and soon her thoughts melted her smile away.

'I'm sorry about your dad. Mine died when I was twelve years old. He was a classical musician and could play nearly every instrument. He could sing too. He taught me everything I know. As pathetic as it sounds, he was my best friend. My mother used to joke that she was jealous, but I think she loved it. She didn't know how to be close to me, so she let him do it. But then he went and . . .' Zhinu shrugged and pushed back her tears. 'Then he went.'

Niulang nodded. He didn't say anything for a while. He allowed the seconds to stretch before her. Eventually he said, 'So as well as being an incredibly successful medicated dandruff commercial star, you're also a singer?'

It was exactly what she needed. He pulled another smile out of Zhinu. 'Yes.'

'Oh no. You're famous, aren't you?'

Zhinu laughed. 'In parts. Not enough, according to my mother.'

Niulang groaned. 'Of course you're a star. I mean, *look* at you. I thought you were coming from a wedding or something. My little sister is always making fun of me for not being current. I'm sorry for not knowing.'

Zhinu tried to tame the butterflies that rioted in her stomach when he'd said '*look* at you'. Zhinu liked the idea of being looked at by Niulang, more than any audience she'd performed for.

'Oh God. Please don't be sorry. I'm grateful! It feels good for someone to be interested in me for me rather than . . .wait, I didn't mean to say interested, I meant . . .'

'But I am interested.'

The room around them contracted, darkened, till all she saw was him.

He smiled. 'So what kind of songs do you sing? I should look you up . . .'

'Please don't.' Zhinu thought about her last music video. It involved her dressed up as a mermaid and seducing men at sea.

Her shell bra was made from rhinestones, her face so covered in make-up she hardly recognised herself. The song was called 'Lost at Sea'. It was written by men who wanted to have sex with her, and it was *about* men having sex with her. 'I don't sing the kind of stuff I want to sing.'

'Which is?'

'My own songs. Apparently, they're not the right sound for my look. How are *my* songs not right for *my* look? And it's all decided by these gross old men, or beasts, actually, who are paid to make me marketable. And I have to be nice to them because at least it brings me closer to the point where I might be able to sing my own songs. It's like I have to kiss a troll for a key to the castle. You know, I've never even played one of my songs in front of an audience before?'

'Well, that's unacceptable.' He straightened up, slapped the bar and went to the storage room. Zhinu strained her torso over the bar, trying to see what he was doing. 'Niulang?'

After a few moments of rustling and rummaging, Niulang reappeared with a guitar in his hand. He beckoned her to follow him.

'Come with me.'

'Meet Taurus.'

They were outside in the sweet softness of the summer night, among the chirrups of the crickets. The cow was kept towards the back of the inn, in a field that faced a forest. Niulang had clicked his tongue twice and the animal had lugged towards them almost immediately.

Zhinu laughed and leant over the fence to pat the soft fur on Taurus's large head. 'She's stunning. Why is she up at this time?'

Niulang reached over to tickle Taurus under the chin. 'She prefers the night. Ever since she was little. Hence the name.' The cow blinked her long lashes coquettishly at Niulang.

Zhinu raised a brow at him. 'You sure you were joking about the kissing thing?'

Niulang straightened, grinned and passed her the guitar he'd acquired from the storage room. 'We sometimes have musicians play at the weekends, open mics, that sort of thing, so we keep a few instruments in storage. I thought that Taurus and I would make a wonderful audience for your first show as a singer-songwriter.'

Zhinu laughed and shook her head. 'Sweet. But absolutely not.'

'Why not? You have a song in mind. I can see it in your face.'

Zhinu opened and shut her mouth. She looked at Taurus for help, but she almost looked as expectant as Niulang in the dim of the outdoor lights. 'I . . . it's not finished. It doesn't have a bridge, yet.'

Niulang shrugged. 'So?'

Zhinu tried to protest again, but her fingers were already brushing against the guitar, wanting to do what they were accustomed to doing.

'What if she boos me?' Zhinu asked, as she put the strap around her and started tuning up.

Niulang looked horrified at the thought. 'Who, Taurus? She would never do that. She might *moo* you, though.'

Zhinu laughed. 'Wow. That was terrible.'

But it had worked, because she found her nerves receding and the pounding in her ears fading. Niulang turned and leant his elbows on the fence, and Taurus's head peered over to watch. Zhinu closed her eyes. She listened to the babbling brook in the distance, the chorus of crickets, and the sound of Niulang's deep breathing. She felt she had a whole orchestra behind her.

And so she sang. The song wove itself around the guitar strings as her voice rose up from her soul to the heavens. It was a song about pain and anger and yearning, and as she sang, the bridge danced from her tongue, flew into the sky, with words of hope and triumph and love. Of a strength she didn't know she had. She switched up the chorus to mimic it.

When Zhinu opened her eyes, she realised tears had fallen from them. Niulang's eyes were glistening, all playfulness had vanished from his face as he took her in. Zhinu's stomach flipped, as she removed the guitar from her neck and propped it against the fence.

'Was it bad? It's really the first draft of—'

'Zhinu, that was . . . you are . . .' Niulang shook his head, as if trying to force the words to fall into proper formation. 'It was beautiful. You are beautiful.'

It was around 4 a.m., and the birds had started to chirp, as if responding to Zhinu's song. Though the sun had barely shown its face, Zhinu felt her own glow within her. For the first time she felt like she didn't need to look outward to seek guidance, to know what to do, to measure what she wanted. She knew what she wanted. Niulang stepped closer to her, and the heat in her burnt with increased ferocity. Then, her chest was against his, his arm was around her waist and her hand was stroking across his chest. She enjoyed feeling her power over him; the rapid movement of his ribcage. Her palm roamed across his heart and pressed against it. Their noses bumped and grazed each other, and, for a moment, Zhinu relished the stillness of just being; without her mother's voice, without pressure, without expectations. She felt almighty and in possession of her destiny. She curved her hand around the back of his neck and stood on her tiptoes to kiss him. He kissed her back immediately, eagerly, as if he'd been waiting for her, as if he was welcoming her home.

The kiss became more voracious, indulgent, his hands traversed and caressed her, both satiating and worsening her hunger. She jumped up and curled her legs around his waist, needing to be as close to him as was possible. Niulang sat her down on the fence. When they pulled apart for breath (*why* did they need to be mortal?), Niulang gently pushed some hair out of her face and smiled at her tenderly.

'You're a much better kisser than Taurus. She uses far too much tongue.'

Zhinu snorted and her eyes drifted away from him as she noticed that Taurus had wandered off, bored and probably jealous. She turned back to him and traced his profile with a finger.

'Hey. Thank you.'

He gently leant into the pressure of her finger. 'For what?'

'Letting me sing my song to you. It felt good.' Zhinu smiled. '*Really* good. I felt like a star. For real.'

Niulang looked at her with glinting eyes. 'I mean . . . you are one,

Zhinu. Your soul is bright. I knew it as soon as I saw you. Lit my whole world up.' He paused as realisation flitted across his face, '. . . and you're leaving in an hour.'

Zhinu wasn't about to let disappointment sour the moment. She had gone through too much to let something as mundane as time impede on her happiness. She reached out to capture his chin and whisper against his lips. 'So we better make the most of it. Any special requests?'

Niulang's eyes darkened in a way that made Zhinu's blood stir with something molten and ravenous. 'An encore.'

'Song or a kiss?'

Niulang pulled away and put the guitar between them. He leant forward and pecked at the space between her jaw and her neck, making her heartbeat speed up as he smiled against her skin. 'I'm a groupie. I'm here for both.'

Zhinu laughed. She brought the sun up with her song.

'Are you on drugs?'

Zhinu stared at her mother in the reflection of the vanity mirror as she applied her lipgloss.

'Mother, just because I decided to do my own make-up today doesn't mean I am on drugs.'

Her mother shook her head and squinted at her daughter. 'It's not just that. You seem different. Why were you already up and showered and dressed this morning? Why were you staring out the car window and smiling on the way here like an idiot?'

Zhinu bit her lip as memories of that morning flitted across her mind. 'I'm just excited about my job, Mother. I thought that was what you wanted?'

Bingwen was sat on the green-room couch and Zhinu saw him slide his head to the side as he analysed her. Today he was wearing lens-less glasses. 'Definitely not weed. Is it a special kind of shroom?'

Zhinu laughed. 'Bingwen, I've always thought of you as the evil big brother I never had.'

The smirk dropped from Bingwen's face. He looked genuinely frightened. 'Oh my God. She is having a mental break. Should I call someone?'

'Zhinu? You're up next!'

A production assistant with a clipboard peered into the green room with the five-minute call.

Zhinu turned and gave her bewildered mother a kiss on her cheek. 'I love you. And I'm grateful for the opportunities you've opened up for me.'

As Zhinu walked out of the green room, she heard her mother cry, 'Bingwen, what am I going to do? I can't afford rehab!'

'Thank you so much for talking to us this morning, Zhinu!'

The presenter's voice was eerily sing-songy, contrived and artificial. 'And now, here at Channel 77, we're pleased to have Zhinu performing her latest single, "Lost at . . ."'

Zhinu leant into her microphone. 'Actually, I'm not performing that song.'

The smile that was fixed on the presenter's face jarred slightly with this revelation. Auto-cue couldn't help her now. 'Oh . . .'

Zhinu

Zhinu turned and took the guitar from her band and beamed, ignoring the distant sound of her mother's squawk. She adjusted the instrument against her, closed her eyes and inhaled, hearing the crickets, hearing the birds, hearing Niulang. She opened them again and smiled at the camera. 'This song is called Magpie.'

Thisbe

THE MUSIC THROBBED THROUGH THE WALLS of Thisbe's dorm room, permeating the stuffing of the pillow folded over her head. Loud and unrelenting, it filled her room, filled her ears, filled her head. She growled into her mattress. There was a chance that the music could have been described as 'good', but what does 'good' have to do with any-fucking-thing when it is three in the morning and you have a seminar on the feudal system in less than six hours. Not forgetting the fact that she'd have to walk twenty minutes to get there in *winter*. In the *North*. Surely, she couldn't start her collegiate life with homicide. Her parents would be so disappointed. Also, murder had the potential to derail her plans for being the next Michelle LaVaughn Robinson Obama.

There had been a mix-up in Thisbe's residence application and, instead of the modern all-girls block close to the library she had signed up for, she'd been placed in a remote co-ed in an ancient hall with paper thin walls – and worse, there was a crack in her wall that the superintendents still hadn't fixed. They had said they'd sort it in a week. This was why, though Thisbe hadn't met her (clearly dickhead) neighbour a month into the term, she knew exactly who he was. '*Pyramus*', she would hear them moan, late at night, cushioned among giggles. '*Py* (bang) *Ra* (bang) *Mus (*bang)! Open up, you fuckboi-dickhead-mother-fucker!' she would hear screamed outside of her door, at almost any time, really, from highly irate and clearly heart-broken voices. Thisbe would hear the click and creak of his door yawning open and, within minutes, no – seconds, no – milliseconds, the growls and curses would turn into mews and sweet concessions, the anger would subside and the storm would pass, calmed by a low, level voice. Reasonable, considered, smoothing away all perceived indiscretions and hiccups. *Babe, baby, boo.*

He was like some kind of Bad Bitch Whisperer. And they were all bad bitches, have no doubt. Once one of his visitors banged on her door, and Thisbe had the privilege of seeing Pyramus's type. Immaculate, Rihanna-lite, edgy. Tight abs revealed under a cut-up Wu Tang shirt. An artistically decorated face, cheekbones that cast a shadow. A sleek, cropped haircut that Thisbe lacked the face shape or patience to sport. Many ear piercings. Tall. The girl had looked down at Thisbe through inky, feathery lashes and raised her eyebrows at Thisbe's Global Gyaldem T-shirt (a large conference for young black women who seek to speak truth to power), headscarf and bleary eyes before smiling sweetly. 'Oh. Wrong room. Sorry.' Because apparently it was inconceivable that Thisbe could have been one of his guests.

She banged on the wall between them. Three fisted pounds

against the cracked plaster usually did it. For some reason, this time it took six. Within a few moments, the music reduced to a decibel that wasn't quite so deafening, followed by the usual 'My bad!', except this time the 'My bad' sounded choked for some reason, the 'My bad' sounded *bad*. Thisbe thought to say something, but couldn't think of what to say and, besides, he was a stranger and, besides, how could she presume she could detect his moods just because she was used to hearing his insincere apologies through the wall after he had *kept her up*. And not in the way he usually kept girls up either, this was far from pleasurable. Not that she, personally, would have liked to have been kept up by him in that way. Although she did take a sneak peek at his Insta-Twitter-Book or whatever, just by the by, because he'd come up on the side as a 'suggested friend' (no, thank you), and he *was* handsome, if you liked that sort of thing. That sort of thing being, like, a sloping wicked-looking smile and the build of someone who only had to go to the gym twice a year to build physique. Smooth, buttery cinnamon skin like he was poured into form. His short black curls looked well acquainted with shea butter, like they had coffee together once or twice a week. Fulsome lips, somehow looking they were sculpted with a chisel and stuffed with angel-wing down. However, Thisbe was an evolved woman and therefore *that* sort of thing did not move her, she was only attracted to men when they met her on a certain holistic, spiritual, multi-dimensional level and even then—

She heard four loud bangs on her door. Thisbe swore under her breath . . . and then promptly became short of it. In a well-rehearsed minute, she leapt out of bed, slammed the light on, threw her headscarf off of the Senegalese twists piled high on her head, switched her T-shirt to a tank top, dabbed some lip balm (with a soft sheen) on her lips, gargled some mouthwash and spat it out of her window.

She opened her door and smiled at the person on the other side of it.

'Hey, Kazeem.'

Pyramus

Kazeem was a prick. Pyramus had it on good authority that Kazeem was fucking Kyla Reynolds, two floors down. Kyla Reynolds had grown up in Suffolk, wore Barbour jackets and, once, when Pyramus had put on his 'Netflix and Chill' playlist, she had asked why his taste had to be so 'typical', just as Usher's 'Can U Handle It?' started playing. She proceeded to ask if he could switch to something more 'interesting', such as Mumford and Sons, which sounded like the name of an artisanal butchers in Kensington. But that was besides the point – Kazeem was a dog, and now he had taken to drunkenly stumbling into Pyramus's neighbour's room – what was her name? Phoebe? Nah, it was Thisbe. On one of the few times he'd seen her, he'd noticed she was wearing a gold chain with a T on it. It was late, and she was rushing somewhere, holding books, and he was ambling somewhere, holding booze. So anyway, he'd noticed Kazeem had decided to start stumbling into Thisbe's room on indiscriminate days of the week.

Everybody thought Kazeem Kamais was a good guy because he

wore these bullshit glasses and studied medicine and owned a weird amount of knitwear for somebody who wasn't a thirty-six-year-old Lit professor, but really he was a dick, and the worst kind because he was a dishonest dick. Pyramus knew he was also a dick, but at least he was a truthful one. He never played girls. They knew what it was and what he was (in)capable of. It was boring, really: a mother who died during his formative adolescent years and a father who thought grieving should be a private, stoic process, which, in the end, made him seek controlled affection and attention (not too much: he wouldn't know how to handle it). While he held women in deep reverence and respect and truly (on God) thought they were the superior sex, he was unable to form a lasting attachment to them, because: *loss*. It was textbook, and he knew this because he took a psych module and there was literally a chapter on his abandonment issues. He had highlighted it and the girl next to him had noticed and asked him about it. They had two great weekends together. She said he had great hands, soft but sturdy.

Women came to him for a good time, and he did his utmost to deliver. It was a mutually beneficial agreement, and any misunderstandings occurred only because, well, let's be real, sometimes women liked to look beneath and behind words to try to find something that they would actually like to hear. He didn't blame them, and he got it, but it did tend to complicate something that should have remained uncomplicated. Still. He actually *liked* women. Kazeem, on the other hand, was the kind of asshole who secretly hated them while he pretended to be this woke god who went to the black feminist bookclub, and tweeted 'black women' over and over again (nothing else, just 'black women'). That was enough to cement his status as the Good Guy. He was going to be a doctor, after all, so why go through the stress of trying not to be an asshole? It didn't matter how evolved they were – girls always harboured a primitive desire to date a doctor.

Anyway, Pyramus knew that his neighbour, Thisbe, had a 9 a.m. lecture in the morning, because he always woke up to the sound of her listening to some kind of women's empowering mantra every Tuesday: *'You are a queen. You are Lorde, Angelou, Simone, Walker, Hooks, Davis, Morrison, Knowles, Fenty, Robinson-Obama. You will shake the world, you will move the earth, you will be audacious with your essence, you will take up all the space, you will not stay in your lane, you will build new roads—'*

Pyramus felt like a bad bitch by proxy now – a powerful, independent woman who don't take no shit – he even found himself snapping when one of his boys called one of his tings 'female'. He felt empowered by Thisbe's lectures, his world view shifting, but the main point was, if *he* knew that Thisbe had an early morning lecture the next day (he hadn't thought his music would wake her, and he felt bad about that: he swore it was at a respectable decibel), then why didn't Kazeem? Pyramus didn't know Thisbe, but he knew that she deserved better than Kazeem.

Pyramus put his headphones on, stuck on his own DJ mix and flopped back in bed. He preferred the music to fill up his room, surround him and envelop him, but this would do. He had only put it on to drown out yet another argument he had with his father over fuck-knows-what-maybe-everything. Through his headphones,

Thisbe

Pyramus heard Kazeem drunkenly stumbling around the room. Kazeem was a dick.

Thisbe

Last night Kazeem had dropped in again. They'd had a fight. Actually, it was less of a fight and more of an awakening. Last night, when Thisbe had broached the question of why Kazeem only ever wanted to see her in the dark, unannounced, when in public all he did was nod at her and maybe discreetly grab her ass, Kazeem had said: 'I want to keep us special, for now. Too much outside pressure will dilute what we have.' Thisbe didn't quite bite, because, what, did Kazeem think he was some kind of Hollywood heart throb whose marketability relied on his romantic accessibility? Thisbe wasn't a dummy. Thisbe knew that she was rounder than the girls that preened around Kazeem and the ones that he flirted with in public. She knew that she was plump in thigh and thick in the hips, plush, dimpled. In the dark, Kazeem squeezed and caressed and sank into it. In public he preferred girls that he could run up to and lift and swing, girls he could fit his arms around easily, covering them completely. Thisbe had a sharp mind and a cushy body, and she couldn't help but notice that Kazeem had no problem being openly affectionate with girls who were closer to the opposite. She found that they nodded more to the things he said, like 'we need to redefine what it means to be black'. One time, Thisbe had questioned why they needed to redefine their blackness and asked him why they couldn't just *be*. He'd said that 'being is too passive', and when she started to question him further, he'd got his back up, tripping over and tangling his words, because Kazeem wasn't used to being questioned. He muttered something about a previously non-existent morning lecture and ducked out.

Thisbe decided she wanted to know why she was only his type when he was a couple of drinks in. She wanted to know if there was something about the light of the day that turned her into an ogre. She could see that Kazeem was startled by his powers of charm running out of juice, and she saw his defensiveness curdle into fury before his mouth even opened. He'd said that she was exaggerating, being extra, and besides, he'd said, throwing his shirt back on, 'you're acting pretty dramatic considering we aren't actually fucking'.

When he said it, Thisbe had felt something akin to relief. Ever since they'd begun fooling around, she wondered when he would get bored, when he would throw her virginity in her face. She'd said she wasn't ready and he'd said it was cool, but clearly it was only cool as long as she was grateful that he deigned to bless her with his mediocre feeling-up techniques. A clumsy tit squeeze. An oddly administered ass-smack. Thisbe often wondered why he kept coming back to her when there was no sex involved, but it was clear to her now. Kazeem thought it was a virtuous act for him to partake in sexual activities with her while adhering to her boundaries, and, as a treat, he also got to hold it over her, keep it in his arsenal for when the rose tint on her spectacles faded and she wasn't dazzled by the paltry performance of his affection. He must have known that day would eventually come, which was why the poisonous comeback was already fully prepped on his tongue. He thought she should have been *grateful*. Thisbe was a late bloomer; she had her first kiss at nineteen and wouldn't insult herself by calling the awkward drinks she'd had at the student union bar 'dates'. With Kazeem she'd enjoyed being desired more than the acts of desire themselves, but was it worth being desired as a guilty pleasure? Like, *shit*, had she been so starved? Clearly, because she was settling for the bare bones of romance, the scraps and crumbs. She deserved something hearty and healthy and filling, she deserved something that would overflow out of cupped hands, she deserved to be scooped up and loved on. She wasn't going to be anybody's dirty little secret. Last night, she had told him to get out, and he'd said 'what?', with the kind of incredulity that made her stomach turn. The *arrogance*. She'd pushed him out of the door, and out of her life. She felt *shame* that she'd allowed herself to be treated this way, that she'd let his stupid, empty words smooth over the sharpness of her mind, but, mostly, she felt rage: pure, unbridled, potent.

Last night, when Pyramus played his music – rap, mostly female artists – so full of braggadocio, belief in their innate sauce and power, sex appeal, right to be revered and *fuck* anyone who doesn't, Thisbe let him. It was a salve.

Pyramus

R&B mingled with the sound of rampant banging on Thisbe's door. Pyramus had found Thisbe's playlist a welcome accompaniment to his coursework and pot noodles until Kazeem decided to add some cacophonous percussion. Pyramus had doctored his pot ramen with herbs, spices, bits of rotisserie chicken, humming along to Thisbe's trippy, spacey R&B while he poured boiling water into a plastic cup, stirring with all the panache of a Michelin chef, narrating his non-existent cooking show: *'Now, you gotta add a little more water than you need, just to make sure it's more soupy, but remember to correlate it with the amount of seasoning you use.'* He was proud of his culinary skills, and he really wanted to enjoy it, but the incessant knocking was increasing in fervour, breaking through the R&B and cutting through the umami of a crushed up cube of Maggi.

'Come on, babe. Don't move mad. I'm sorry, Thisbe. Let me in.'

Pyramus rolled his eyes. Kazeem was pissed because of his loss of access – he'd heard the whole thing the night before; excellent show from Thisbe – and the rejection was driving him crazy. He wanted to be wanted by Thisbe, and Pyramus could guarantee that, if Thisbe opted to take him back, he would revert to his old ways in a week.

'I know you're in there, Thisbe. Let's work this out. I miss you and I know you miss me.'

Fuck's sake. He couldn't hear any more of this.

Pyramus put his noodles down, and went out into the corridor, not bothering to throw on a shirt. This needed to be over quickly.

'She's not in,' he said.

Kazeem looked Pyramus up and down. 'Do I look like a prick?'

Pyramus grinned. 'You really want me to answer that, man? I mean, I can. But I just wanna make sure.'

Kazeem faltered and cleared his throat. 'This is between me and her.'

'Really? Right now it looks like it's between you and her door.'

Kazeem kissed his teeth and went to bang on the door again when Pyramus intercepted him with a swift step, standing between the door and him. Pyramus sighed. He hated when his dinner was interrupted.

Kazeem blinked. 'What are you doing, man? You can't be smashing her . . . wait— *are you?*' His laugh was vicious and laced with venom. 'That would explain so much.'

Pyramus locked his hands in front of him and relaxed his shoulders. Kazeem was a couple of inches taller than him, but he'd never seen anyone so small.

'I said she's not in.' Pyramus's voice didn't raise in tone or decibel, it stayed low, like a tiger in the grass. 'But you're welcome to try and knock again.'

Pyramus didn't budge from in front of the door.

Kazeem rolled his tongue in his mouth and sniffed. He nodded as if leaving was a decision that he made out of choice rather than coercion. 'Fuck it. Have at her, man.'

He backed away, and Pyramus waited until he was sure Kazeem was gone before he went back to his noodles. He noticed that the R&B was now playing quieter. 'I Wanna Be Down' was playing now – that was Brandy, right? It was a perfect song. Why hadn't he noticed that before? Four bites into his noodles, he heard a soft knock against his wall.

'Hey . . . um. I don't know if you can hear this . . . but thanks.' It was Thisbe.

The sound of her voice speaking directly to him made Pyramus weirdly nervous.

He cleared his throat. 'It's okay. He's a dick.' Pyramus paused. 'This playlist is sick, by the way. Is it yours?'

'Yeah. You're not the only one with taste.'

Pyramus smiled at the thin line that ran through the plaster of his wall.

Thisbe

A few days after Pyramus had dealt with Kazeem, Thisbe's mother bustled into her room with bags stuffed full of Tupperware filled to the brim with baked sweet goods, rice and chicken. Mama Thiz was talking without inhaling, switching between topics, as she swished around Thisbe's room, leaving trails of floral perfume behind her.

'So, I've got this great new pink lipstick that is far too funky for me, but I think will look great on your complexion, also, candles are a health and safety hazard, don't risk your life and the life of others just because you want your room to smell like peonies. Why don't you buy actual peonies? Maybe we can buy a plant for you in town? By the way, how long have the lifts been out in your building? Should be illegal. I thought I was going to pass out on the stairwell but then this handsome young man helped me with my bags. He was actually on his way down, but insisted on helping me up. So lovely. Anyway, turned out he's your neighbour! Arms like a ship labourer.'

'Wow. Ma, *what*?'

'You don't think he's handsome?'

'He obviously is, but—'

'Why did you never mention him?'

'Why would I?'

Her mother raised a brow and shrugged. 'I don't know. When I said you are my daughter, he said, "Ah, I see where Thisbe gets her good looks from," and I just thought, wow. A young man with taste and the good sense to flirt with the mother of the girl who he very obviously has a crush on—'

Thisbe laughed out loud. 'Right. Okay, Ma. I know you think that everybody must have a crush on me because you made me, and I don't mean to insult your work, but I assure you, in this instance, this is not the case.'

She was glad Pyramus wasn't in his room. He probably would have laughed too. He actually had a great laugh; she had heard it occasionally. It was warm and strong enough to hoist her spirits up when she was feeling low.

Pyramus thought she had 'good looks'? This, coupled with his actions the other night, slightly threw her for a loop. Though she rolled her eyes at Kazeem's incessant texts, she had to admit that she was kind of freaked out when he showed up at her door. Pyramus had defused the situation with such swiftness, and Kazeem hadn't come near her since. She had surreptitiously peeked through the peep-hole of her door to see the event unfold, and noted that Pyramus was bizarrely topless while warding Kazeem off. It was a good thing Thisbe was a woman of heightened discernment and taste or the sight of him might have been slightly distracting. Despite her resentment that it took another man to ward Kazeem away, she was grateful, and so had said thank you. It had been sweet but – *really*? He thought she had good looks?

Pyramus

Pyramus was halfway out of the halls when he realised he'd forgotten his headphones. He doubled back. Just as he entered his room, he heard the muffled voices of Thisbe and her mother. He couldn't have been sure, but—

Ship labourer?!

A *handsome* ship labourer.

He smiled to himself.

He walked to the gym with a new swagger that morning, matured.

Thisbe

He was upset. Thisbe could tell. Even without hearing him on the phone before he started up his playlist of furious music.

'Why can't you be a dad for once? Why do I have to beg to see you? You leave the country with your new girlfriend and I gotta find out through an Auntie on Facebook?'

Thisbe

Pyramus

Pyramus had no idea why his face was wet. He knew his music was too loud. He was an asshole. He switched to his headphones and let the music directly smudge out his thoughts.

Thisbe

Knock and stay? Or knock and go. Knock and stay, right? That's what a normal, rational human being would do. It wasn't a big deal. She would knock and stay. Obviously. Why was her heartbeat knocking against her ribcage like that? Ew. What was wrong with her?

Pyramus

Pyramus thought he heard a knock at his door. He took a while to get up, but opened it to see a bag full of Tupperware so deliciously fragrant that his stomach growled. There was a message on a pink post-it note attached to it.

Hey. My mother gave me far too much food. Thought you might like some.

P.S. You single? I have a fifty-five-year-old woman who wants to take you out on a date. Thisbe xx

Thisbe

Had she really put two kisses? Desperate. Might as well have dropped to her knees in front of him. She flopped onto her bed and shut her eyes, hoping to erase the embarrassment.

Then there was a rap on her wall that was too purposeful for her to ignore.

She bolted upright.

'Thanks, Thisbe. The food is delicious.'

While her name sounded good coming from his mouth, he'd very politely and graciously ignored the ill-advised quasi-flirtatious part of her note.

'You're welcome.'

Thisbe dropped back down on her bed and pulled her pillow over her face.

Pyramus

Why were his hands sweating? He'd never been more conscious of the fact that his hands had sweat glands till this very moment. He flexed them before knocking, as if he needed to prepare himself for what he was about to do. His instincts were correct, but he was still ill-prepared. In fairness, he wasn't sure if anything could have prepared him. When she opened the door, Pyramus became acutely aware that his memory had not done justice to Thisbe's face. In passing he saw her as cute, pretty, but now, up close, he saw that she was staggering, soul destroying and also restoring. Her eyes were round and bright, and he wanted to be guided by their light, her smile was soft and plush, as she bit into it. She was wearing gold hoops, that glinted like little halos in her ears in the white fluorescent of the industrial lights of the hallway. Her white crop top read 'Cuz I'm black, bitch' in stark black letters, and hovered over a cute belly button piercing, she wore grey jersey short-shorts that accentuated a soft, dimpled curvy body and her braids came down to a waist that gently dipped. She made the pace of his heartbeat quicken.

'Hi,' she said, and he realised he hadn't spoken yet. Without a barrier, the melodiousness of her voice had a new clarity.

He nodded. 'Hey. Uh, I'm—'

'I know who you are.'

He smiled and rubbed the back of his neck. 'Is that a good thing or a bad thing?'

Her shoulder twitched. 'I haven't made up my mind.'

Her smile was wicked and should have had some kind of governmental guidelines on it. It was potent, illicit, and it went straight to his head.

'I thought it would be easier to talk face to face. Are you the fifty-five-year-old woman who wants to take me on a date? Because you look really, really good for your age.'

Thisbe's smile broadened. She nodded. 'Thank you so much. It's definitely not because of beauty sleep. You know, because your music keeps me up at night?'

Touché. Pyramus rubbed the back of his neck again and hung his head, releasing a sheepish smile. 'Yeah . . . I'm really, genuinely

219

sorry about that. Music is how I forget about the world. Problem is sometimes I . . . forget about the world.'

He wondered if Thisbe would like to share the world with him one day—

'I get it. You're lucky I like your music.' That smile again. Her eyes flicked down shyly and she bit her lip. Pyramus was losing his mind. He cleared his throat. 'Do you want to take some of this food down to the canteen and eat with me?'

She paused for three excruciating seconds.

'I'll get my hoodie.'

The crack in the wall was plastered over two weeks later, and the music no longer leaked through gaps, conversations no longer travelling without permission. They aggregated their favourite songs from that period into an ever-growing playlist that went from being untitled to, eventually, months later, being christened 'Love Your Neighbour' by Pyramus. Thisbe had laughed at the name. 'Funny.'

'What's funny?' Pyramus said. 'It's accurate. We're neighbours. And . . . I'm in love with you.'

It was the first time either of them had said it. She said it back.

The playlist was a haphazard harmonious mash-up of who they were; 'I Wanna Be Down', 'Can U Handle It?' Conversations happened with nothing between them, no walls, no pretence, punctuated with laughter, melodies swirling and smoothing over them, perfuming their words with extra sweetness. Pyramus's hands were a conduit of affection and desire, and when they were outside, he would reach out for her hand to curl confidently around his. Her body unfurled around him, she felt at ease, loved on. He massaged her belly, kissed the dimples in her thighs.

The first time they had an argument, Pyramus had walked out. He'd snapped at her while they were discussing his father, agitated by how suddenly he felt able to open up to her, by his own vulnerability. Thisbe had been sure it was the end; she knew what he was like with commitment, knew he ran scared when things got deep. She knew he locked himself into himself so securely that girls had to bang against his door. She refused to be that girl. Maybe he was more comfortable with a wall between him and love. Thisbe was not. So this was it. Thisbe had logged on to her music streaming account to cry to a soundtrack. She saw that a new addition had been made to their playlist: Jodeci, 'My Heart Belongs To U'.

A few minutes later, Pyramus knocked on her door.

'I am an idiot.'

'You are.'

They talked it out, kissed it out. She smirked against his lips and asked him to do a sing-along serenade if he was really about it. She said: 'I'm talking old school R&B, fists clenched, begging *on your knees* in the rain, babe. I want a *performance*.' Pyramus grumbled into her neck and pretended to be embarrassed for three seconds before he leapt off the bed, shirtless, using a bottle of deodorant as a mic. Their playlist filled their room, filled their ears, filled their hearts.

Thisbe laughed, curved her hands around her mouth, cheering from her front-row seat on the bed.

'Turn it up!' she yelled.

New Tales

Tiara

Tiara's Top Tips

- When you bump into an ex-boyfriend in public, perform the 'Say Hello and Go'. Make it cute and graceful. That way you're the bigger person. Shake their hand, maybe give them a kiss on the cheek and a trite, flat 'How you been! Long time!' and leave.

- While I am on the subject, unfollow and mute all ex-boyfriends, and if they just so happen to be a famous heart-throb, definitely do not Google their name at 10 p.m. on a Friday night out of morbid curiosity because you might learn that they are currently in your city after being away in LA for nineteen months (not that anybody is counting) for an award ceremony.

I squinted at my laptop screen. I wasn't sure this was precisely what the magazine meant when they asked for some quick bullet-point tips for publicity for my memoirs (*Tiara's Top Tips*, based on an advice Twitter account that unceremoniously blew up). My agent had dubbed it an 'Eat Slay Love'-type memoir, encapsulating both the zeitgeist and the young millennial black girl. The idea of having to be all that kind of exhausted me.

I wound my finger around the elastic hanging from my £2 lacy knickers and tore it off.

I was sat cross-legged in bed in an over-sized shirt, phone open on Instagram, laptop open on Word. A spaced out, two-inch-long chunk of writing blinked at me from the blank screen. I had been shovelling dry granola into my mouth – my stress comfort food of choice – the evidence of which was present on my keyboard. I tried to blow it off. This was pathetic. Why was I so stressed out? Yes, the man I thought I was going to marry was back in the country after nearly two years, but why was I letting that small, inconsequential fact distract me from my work? I couldn't believe I was letting my ex-boyfriend risk the security of my bag. Money before honeys. No. Men weren't honeys. Scratch that. Fees before The D. Contracts before Phone Contacts. Those were all terrible and I cannot believe someone is paying me to write. I opened up Instagram to distract myself.

I'd unfollowed him, but that didn't stop his page being the first to come up when I tapped the search bar. My phone was kind of old (it had all my writing notes on it: I was attached and a luddite), so sometimes bulky apps made it jam. This meant that, often, when I tapped the search bar, the screen would freeze and black out, and I would be forced to take a second to look at my own frazzled reflection judging me; 'Really, Tiara? This again?'

Nevertheless, I persisted. I would find my thumb dancing and hovering over a digital mosaic of his life, a life I was once a part of – a life I now observed through a screen – carefully navigating my trail, lest I slip up and like a picture, lest I slip up and let him know I give a shit about what he's up to. Which, technically, I don't. It'd been a while since I'd scrolled through the sunny LA life he'd curated for himself since he'd moved. The past year and a half I'd done well to mentally disassociate from him. It was a clean break, a new me. There was no relapse. I was determined to tuck that part of my life in cutely, only untucking it if I needed to access something significant from it; like, who was the person I drunkenly and successfully performed all parts of 'Aaron Burr, Sir' to? Oh yeah, him. Sometimes I wanted to access a light memory from those days, but it forced me to untuck the heavy ones too. The memories that included fiery touches and hot breaths on neck. When we hooked up that night after I performed 'Aaron Burr, Sir', giddy on cheap wine and each other, I remember it was different from the other times. It was a confirmation that we had transitioned from 'seeing each other' to 'being with each other'. It was slower, sweeter. We relished each other.

And now he was someone else, relishing someone else. I was three scrolls down on his page when I saw her, smiling next to him in a beaming selfie. Riley Dawn. Riley Dawn didn't even sound like it was a real name. Riley Dawn was the name of a high-school nemesis in a movie. Riley Dawn had to be called by her first name and surname at all times to maintain a sense of careful detachment lest I attempt to humanise her. Riley Dawn had to remain Riley Dawn to avoid making the mistake of seeing her as more than the woman potentially fucking the only guy who I had ever truly – wait, Riley Dawn was definitely wearing at least BB-cream in that #nomake-upselfie, #naturalbeauty selfie. No one's skin is that flawless. Her eyebrows are definitely micro-bladed. She did *not* wake up like dis. I'm not sure anyone ever just wakes up like dis?

Riley Dawn played his love interest in his latest blockbuster summer movie: *Rough & Reckless*. He and Riley Dawn had sex while he was driving a car at like 150 mph. In the movie. Or maybe even in real life. Who knew? It was all so predictable. Of course he'd start fucking his beautiful co-star. Riley Dawn was working on a lipgloss line. E! News told me that her last public romantic liaison was with Drake.

You know what? Who cares! Clearly, I'd moved on. I was good. I'd learnt the art of the thirst-trap, which had upped my Instagram likes by, like, 20 per cent at least. I mean, I'd turned a Twitter account I had into a *book deal*. I'd found purpose! I had progressed. It was ridiculous, that I, Tiaraoluwa Ajayi, should be sitting bottomless on my bed at 10 p.m. on a Friday night looking through pictures of him hiking with his adorable dog.

Shit. I love dogs.

Aside from the obvious evisceration of my heart, the break-up wasn't actually as hard as it could have been, because my guy, *the* guy, went to LA shortly after we broke up. And when I say shortly, I mean two months after the door slammed and the tears poured. When I say shortly, I mean my stomach hadn't untwisted itself yet and the branding of his lips on my body could still be traced. Shortly, like I could still run my fingers across my skin and they would dip into the indents his fingertips had left. I would put my hands on my hips and my fingers would slip into the shape of his. The spaces where he had been were still warm.

Tiara's Top Tips

- If you're going to break up with someone, ensure that you do it right before one of you leaves the country. Distance is key to moving on.

Although, in my case, I guess him leaving was technically the reason we broke up. The memory is imprinted on the lining of my mind and replays every time I'm reminded of him, my own personal movie reel of torment. He'd just got a role in a network TV show filming in LA; it was his big break and I was over the moon for him.

'Come with me, Tiara,' he said, brimming over with excitement. He was already there in his mind, eating acai bowls al fresco. 'It'll be perfect, TiTi. Think about it: me and you taking on LA. We can pretend to be Idris Elba and Naomi Campbell's cousins. Nobody will ask questions. Isn't Hollywood like the perfect place to start your writing career?'

Despite my feelings for him and how tempting the idea of pretending to be related to a supermodel was, I knew it wasn't for me.

'Babe, it's a place where every coffee shop is full of wannabe writers. It is literally a *farm* for writers. On top of that, are you forgetting that I'm a black woman? It's twice as hard for me. Seye, if I go, it needs to be on my own terms. I'm at the beginning of my career and I'm still figuring it out. We can make it work long distance—'

I was sat cross-legged on my bed while he paced in front of me, topless and in his sweats. It almost dissolved my resolve.

'This is precisely the right time to go. There's nothing at stake, nothing to lose.'

I could tell by the way his face fell that he knew he'd made a mistake as soon as he'd said it. I was a writer's assistant then, *aka* a coffee and admin. bitch, fetching teas and hoping that somebody would be able to see in the tea leaves that I had the capacity to write an award-winning episode. I was a long way from my dreams, but I felt them inching closer – I thought he could feel that too. My heart dropped into my stomach.

'My career and my dreams are nothing to lose?'

He sighed and pinched the bridge of his nose. 'TiTi, that's not what I mean, I just— you're the most talented person I know. You're so smart, and I just feel like it's wasted here. It's time for you to take charge of your future—'

'As long as it's in line with what you want?'

'You loved LA when we visited! Said you could move there. And now suddenly it's a problem because I've got an opportunity there and you haven't? Does this relationship only work when our careers are at the same stage?'

I felt like somebody had kicked me in the stomach. Tears sprang into my eyes. It was the first time he'd ever made me cry.

'You're being a dick.'

Regret shadowed his face. 'I know. I'm sorry—'

'Your wins are my wins. I couldn't be prouder of you. And sure, I said, *maybe* one day I could move there. But not like this . . . not living off my boyfriend while I flounder around—'

'TiTi, I want to do that for you. You know I don't care about that.'

'Okay, but I do, Seye! This is how I'm taking charge of my future!'

I was trying to slow my breathing, trying to ignore the fact that the fragments of my world were swilling in the air, torn from each other, jagged edged. I still hoped I could pluck them from suspension, put them together again, despite knowing the truth, feeling it. Seye swallowed and sat next to me, defeated.

'We don't fight. We don't do this. What the hell is happening to us, Tiara?'

I turned to face him, feeling as if an anvil was pressed into my chest. 'I don't know.'

He exhaled deeply and looked at me with gleaming eyes. 'Isn't this relationship enough for you?'

I stared at him in disbelief. 'Don't do that. Don't you dare make this about my love for you, because you know—'

He shook his head, eyes flashing with annoyance. 'Apparently, I don't know shit, T. Because I thought it was me and you against the world. This is what we agreed. You with writing, me with acting. We were gonna be on our Bey & Jay shit—'

'Jay cheated.'

'Bey & Jay pre the first *On The Run* tour.' Damn. I'd really taught him well. 'The point is I thought we were gonna take it on together—'

'Seye, we still can! We're a team. We can do Facetime, visits—' I could hear the desperation in my voice fighting against the descending reality that was thickening the air. I could barely breathe. He gave me a look that made all the floating fragments of my world crash to the floor.

'Tiara, I don't know when I'm going to come back. Or if I'm going to come back. And you don't know when you want to move to LA. Or if you want to.' He paused and leant his elbows on his knees, burying his face into his hands. For a moment we both just sat there in the stillness of our sadness, the inevitability of our demise sinking into our bones. It was summer and the sun was setting, orange light softly beaming into the dark of my room, 'Right Here' by SWV flowing through an open window, mingling with the taut air. I would have laughed at the irony if I hadn't been crying. Eventually Seye lifted his head from his hands. His eyes were bloodshot, and when he spoke, his voice was croaked.

'TiTi, who else am I gonna do this with? My family didn't think I could do this, but you always did. You read lines with me. You're the one who told me to go for it. I really don't want to do this without you by my side.'

Something in me snapped and melted. I climbed up on his lap and wrapped myself around him, legs clamped around his waist, arms winding themselves around his neck as he buried his face into mine, his arms anchoring me to him as he breathed me in. We stayed like this for a minute or an hour, clinging to each other while the world as we knew it disintegrated around us.

I leant my forehead against his. 'I love you.'

'I love you too.'

'—and I know you've convinced yourself that this move would be for us, but it's for you. And that's okay. This is your moment. We can make long distance work. This is worth it.'

Seye opened and shut his mouth before he straightened up, his arms loosening their hold on me. 'I . . . I don't think I can do that, T.'

My throat tightened. I suddenly felt an odd sensation of intense nothingness. It was as if the hurt was too immense, my heart too broken, and so my whole body was pulling me into self-protection mode, stopping me from fully feeling the brunt of the love of my life telling me that he didn't think I was worth it.

'Right.'

I climbed off his lap. He wasn't prepared to do long distance but I was supposed to be prepared to leave everything I knew behind to be a budget Real Housewife. We sat silently next to each other for a few moments, before Seye lifted my limp hand to his lips and kissed it. Then he walked away.

Two years dissolved into nothing. Dissipated into the air. Thanos snap. Dust. It was the last time we spoke to each other.

I'd seen he was doing well. His recurring gig as the wise-quipping mate of some super rich teens living in New York got upgraded to series regular. He played the son of a fraudulent *African* politician. The part of Africa wasn't ever really stated, but, according to the guy who played his dad, whatever country he was from boasted an impressive accent that was a mixture of Zimbabwean, Nigerian and some alien colony that only communicated in guttural grunts. He shone with what he was given, eking out depth from what was initially a two-dimensional character. It's what landed him *Rough & Reckless*, a movie that tripled his star power, playing a rogue ex-cop with a need for speed and women with unfathomable hip-to-waist ratios. Somehow, he even managed to make *that* watchable.

Tiara's Top Tips

- Try not to fall in love with someone passionately dedicated to their craft, because after they've broken up with you, you will still be impressed by them. You may find yourself unable to distinguish between your feelings of professional admiration and feelings of a deep and irrevocable love.

My phone rang and the name of my best friend, Kameela, replaced the picture of Riley Dawn and Kourtney Kardashian doing kissy faces at each other. As usual, she seemed to sense when I needed saving from myself.

'You okay?'

I swallowed some of the granola that was in my mouth. 'I'm fine! Look, I knew he would come back eventually. It's cool!'

'Are you stress-eating granola?'

I picked a raisin from between molars, reached out for the quarter glass of stale wine from my bedside table to wash it down.

'No.'

'Are you watching the award ceremony tonight? I'm watching it with Malik. Seye's category is coming up soon.'

Tiara's Top Tips

- Never hang out with your boyfriend and invite along his best friend and your best friend. Never go to Afropunk Paris together, never go to see Frank Ocean together and definitely don't go to Nando's together. Never encourage your best friend and your boyfriend's best friend to get together, because they could end up, selfishly, having a stable and loving relationship, meaning all your lives are entangled forever, long after you have broken up.

'I don't know. Do you know if Riley Dawn is with him? By the way, can we talk about how stupid the name Riley Dawn is?'

'So stupid. Surname as a first name and first name as a surname? Ridiculous. But anyway, why would she be with him? The award isn't for *Rough & Reckless*.'

'They're obviously dating. I mean, Instagram posts from the same location? Please.'

'They are literally colleagues, Tiaraoluwa. Look, don't you

think your projection on to Riley Dawn is really about something else . . .'

I hated when she full-named me. 'Don't shrink me! I am not your patient. Did you know that Seye has a dog now? Called Huck! Like, from *Scandal*. Can you believe that? I got him into *Scandal*. He's a Boxer. Riley also has a dog called Dougie – so stupid – and there's a picture of Dougie and Huck together on her Instagram, hashtagged *RuffAndReckless*. Get it? I mean, really, the whole thing is just such a performance. Has the movie ended or what? I can't even tell.'

'Sis . . . I don't know about all that, but if, hypothetically, Seye was single and he apologised, would you even consider taking him back?'

I chewed slowly and tried to ignore how my heart flipped at the idea. 'I mean, that scenario is highly unlikely, but maybe. I thought I was going to marry the guy, Kam. Those feelings don't just disappear. But that's not gonna happen. You know why? Riley Dawn. Hey Malik! You there?'

'Hey sis!' My best friend's boyfriend responded immediately. I knew I was on speakerphone.

'Is Seye dating Riley Dawn?'

'I don't know. I mean. He's a movie star. He's probably drowning in pu—'

The rest of his words got muffled. It sounded like Kameela had thrown a pillow at him. I'd been chucking granola into my mouth and Malik's sentence made me choke on an oat cluster.

'Wow.' I beat my chest with a closed fist and coughed. '*Wow.*'

Kameela's voice was thinner and further away from the phone.

'Thanks, Mal. Really nice.' Malik's defiant claim that it was a joke was followed by another muted thump of a pillow.

I got up to go to the kitchen to get a refill of granola. 'I just thought he was a man with discernment. You know what? It doesn't matter. I am happy. I have a popping career and also a popping butt. Have you seen it recently?'

'Out of this world, babe,' Kameela affirmed. 'But this is precisely why I think you should watch the award ceremony. It might be closure for you. You were there from the very beginning of his career, so this is your moment too, in a way.'

I sighed. Maybe she was right. The first time we'd met was when he was auditioning for the role of the wisecracking, streetwise best friend of the white main character in what would be a failed pilot. I was a production assistant at the time. When I went down to reception and called his name from the list, he'd done a double take. In the lift, the air had shifted between us. Upon noting that I was only an assistant, the other high-cheekboned men would often render me invisible. But Seye had looked me in the eye, said hello, shook my hand and asked my name.

'What do you reckon my chances are then, Tiara? Any tips?' His voice rolled low and deep into the silence of the lift.

I looked pointedly at my sheet with its list of 6ft something handsome black men, aged 18–25. 'I don't know. Everyone brings so many different qualities to the table.'

He laughed. 'Yeah, but I feel like my crooked front tooth will actually bring a lot of depth to the character.'

I smiled. He was joking, but I liked his slightly crooked front tooth. Made his good looks interesting, made his smile more endearing. I cleared my throat and decided to give him real advice.

'Okay, listen. I'm sure you don't want to play a 2D character that only exists to say, "Yo. That's messed up", when the main character is in a predicament, but this is a stepping stone, right?'

Seye raised an offended brow. 'Excuse me? It's my dream to play Jamal, funny and cool, with dreams of becoming a rapper.' His voice was deadpan as he quoted the character description verbatim. His face broke open in a half smile. 'That was convincing, right?'

He was easy, self-effacing, and despite myself, I was drawn to him. I kept my laugh in check, though, not wanting to gas him. He was still an actor.

The lift pinged open and I led him through the maze of glass-walled meeting rooms.

'Oscar worthy. Anyway, my point is, you should think about what this is a stepping stone to. Think of your dream role and let that fuel you. That's what gets me through. Do you think I want to be fetching lunch and making tea for producers named Hugh who don't know my name, stare at my tits and don't say thank you?'

'You spit in it, right?'

'Obviously. But what gets me through, aside from spitting in their tea, is thinking of where I wanna be.'

'And where's that?'

'I want to make my own stuff. Being part of the machine that makes the thing is great, but I want to be the generator.'

He was silent for a few moments and looked at me in a way that made blood rush to my face and my stomach dip. I cleared my throat and gestured to the audition room. 'Um. Good luck.'

He slapped his script on his hand and nodded. 'Thank you.'

I nodded back and walked away. I'd barely moved when I felt a tap on my shoulder. I turned around to see him looking slightly, sweetly nervous, at odds with the confident demeanour I'd seen earlier. Man, I really didn't have time to coach people through audition jitters today.

'Everything okay?'

'Hey, sorry, real quick. Do you think I have what it takes for the other role?'

I frowned. 'What other role?'

'The guy who's going to ask for your number after his audition so he can fetch you lunch and maybe, if he's lucky, sit and eat it with you?'

'Man. That was . . .'

He looked embarrassed. 'Yeah. I know. Too late now. If you're gonna reject me could you do it softly so I don't weep through my audition?'

I smiled. 'I . . . reckon you have potential.'

I decided to watch the award show. I said goodbye to Kameela and switched on the TV just as they were about to announce his category. I found that my hands were prickling, that my heart was punching hard against my chest, which was odd, because it obviously made no material difference to me whether he won or n— oh my God, he won. He won. *Seye Ojo.* I heard that right, didn't I? My phone buzzed. It was Kameela with a series of exclamation marks. I definitely heard that right. I sat back on my sofa as my eyes blurred, laughing giddily, waiting for him to accept, when the presenter's chirpy voice announced that 'Unfortunately, Seye's not able to be with us this evening, but his mother will be accepting the award on his behalf—'

I didn't hear the rest over the cacophony of my frantic thoughts. Why would he miss his first British award show? Also, why would he even be in this country if he wasn't going to show up? Was he okay? I was about to pick up my phone to call Malik and find out if he had any valuable information to give me when his mother's voice drew my focus back to the TV.

'My son has always been brave. Always dreamt bigger than I dreamt for him. I didn't always support him the way I should have, because I was scared. Scared that the world would reject him. I thought I was protecting him. But my son has always taken risks for the things he loves and that is why I admire him. It's the reason why I am accepting the award this evening on his behalf instead of him. He's taking a risk of the heart. He'll kill me for saying that. Anyway, he would like to thank—'

Wait, what? Has he eloped to Las Vegas with Riley Dawn or something? We always joked about doing that as a political stance against the capitalistic circus surrounding weddings. In their case, it would just be a press gimmick to cement themselves as a 'quirky' Hollywood couple. Tacky. My heart dropped and I felt panic rising up in me when there was a knock on my door. This was alarming for many reasons, not limited to but including: I lived on the fifth floor, you needed a key to get into my building and it was nearly midnight. I really hoped it wasn't my neighbour who listened to

Eminem on repeat for hours, because that much commitment to aggressive white man rap scared me a little.

Not bothering to pull on any bottoms to complement my baggy shirt, I paused the TV and crept to the door, grabbing a bread knife from the kitchen just in case I needed protection.

'Who is it?' I called, before even looking into the peephole.

'It's me.' I dropped the knife. I held still; the wind completely knocked out of me. There was a gruff clearing of the throat. 'Sorry, I mean it's Seye. Someone let me in on the ground floor. I got your address from Kam. Don't be mad at her. I basically begged and she dragged me to hell before she gave it to me.' He paused, 'Now that I'm saying all this out loud, though, I'm hearing how creepy it is for me to be standing outside your door at midnight with no forewarning.'

I looked at my mirror by the door. This is not how I expected our reunion to go. I was meant to look glamorous, not hair tied up in a headscarf with eyeliner-smudged eyes and a large faded T-shirt covered in granola. It was meant to be at an industry event where I was wearing a dress that accentuated my ass. I'd have to make do. This was casual chic, right?

After a few moments of silence, he said, 'You're right. I should go. I'm sorry. It's just . . . it's just I was on the way to the ceremony with my mum and she kept asking me what was wrong. She said there was something off about me. And I didn't know what to tell her, T. Like this should have been one of my proudest moments. Being recognised in my hometown . . . but I felt like something was missing. Someone. Mum knew, though. She said part of the reason she came round to me acting is when you went to see her and said that her lack of support was hurting me. I didn't know you did that, T. I know this is mad, but the award honestly doesn't mean anything without—'

I opened the door and felt my breath hitch. He was leaning against the door frame in a clearly expensive tux, shirt rumpled and his bow-tie untied around the neck. Facial hair looked good on him, and his skin glowed deeply from the LA sun, like the rays had decided to take up residence in him, saw something in his skin that was worthy of its glory. He looked up and let out a small crooked smile that caused my repressed feelings to form a wave that almost broke the dam I had built to stop them. Almost.

'Hey, TiTi.'

I wanted to punch him. And then kiss him. Scream at him. Push him in the chest. And then kiss him again. He was looking at me and into me in, I suspect, much the same way I was looking at him and into him, and I didn't have time to lock him out of me. Even if I did there was no point, he knew all the secret passageways, the alternative routes in.

He swallowed hard and looked very serious, as if he were about to say something devastatingly profound.

'You're wearing my shirt.'

I glanced down, swore internally. 'I forgot who it belonged to.' This was both the truth and a lie. I always knew it was his, but he had been such a part of my life at one point that knowing it was his and knowing it was mine was the same thing.

Seye smiled. 'Really? Because it's the Shroom Shirt.'

The Shroom Shirt. The shirt that Seye wore when we went on a hike in California with Malik and Kameela, and Malik had had the genius idea of us going on another kind of group trip. Kameela refused, offered to be our guardian. Seye and I did not take kindly to drugs. At the height of his high, Seye had announced he was hot and proceeded to get tangled up taking his shirt off, screaming at me to come and save him; in my altered state, it was the funniest thing I had seen in the world. I'd collapsed laughing, giddy with the fact that this sweet, gorgeous fool was mine.

I snorted and quickly cleared my throat. 'Come in.'

I surreptitiously kicked the felled knife out of sight with a socked foot. Seye took his shoes off at the door and released a low whistle as he cast an eye around my flat. On one hand, it was bizarre and disorienting seeing him, in the flesh, in his rumpled tux, smelling like whatever aftershave he was the face of, in the space I had curated for myself. On the other, it felt like he'd always been there. He turned to me.

'This place is amazing, Tiara. You did it. I knew you would. I've pre-ordered your book and—'

'You never said goodbye to me.' Pressurised by time and deeply repressed hurt, the dam broke, and the sentence exploded from me with tears.

Seye's eyes shone. 'Tiara—'

'No.' I walked to my kitchen and he followed me as I poured myself a glass of wine to the brim and leant against the counter. 'Do you know how messed up that is? I texted and called after we broke up and you didn't respond once. You left me to try and figure out if I had just imagined that what we had was real or not. If you ever even really loved me or not. Then you show up at my door in a tux like black James Bond after having all the sex with all the Riley

Dawns and expect everything to be cool? Fuck that . . . and fuck you!'
I gulped down some of the wine in my rage.

Seye took the glass of wine from me and set it down, gaze glinting. 'I deserve that. This isn't an excuse, but . . . I didn't say goodbye
because how the hell could I say goodbye to *you*, Tiara? I couldn't. I
still haven't. I was a prick and you were right. I should have known
you were not the kind of person who would want to move without
a plan, to not be able to support yourself on your own. But I was so
focused on what I wanted I forgot that was the reason I fell for you. I
was selfish. I am so sorry and— wait, who is having sex with Riley?'

'You . . . are?'

Seye laughed. 'What? No. That's the homie. She actually told
me I needed to get a grip and try and win the love of my life back.'

I forced my pulse to slow, reality combatting hope. 'Seye, I am
not moving to LA anytime soon.'

'Actually . . .' his voice dropped and he moved closer to me. I'd
missed the tenor of his closeness, how it made my whole body hum.
'I just landed a role for a play here. Six-week run. And after that I
was thinking I might stick around for a little bit. Figure out how I
can be transatlantic. Look, if you tell me you never want to see me
again, I understand. I know it will take time. But if you'll let me,
I'll do whatever it takes to be in your life again. You're part of my
generator. Does that sound weird? It's true, though.'

I held his gaze for a few moments. 'You know, my top tip for
bumping into your ex is "Say Hello and Go", but I think for you, I
need you to say goodbye and go. You owe me a proper goodbye.'

Seye's shoulders dropped. He was quiet for a while before he nodded and rubbed at his chin. He stepped back, 'You're right. Tiara, I—'

Reaching forward, I tugged him towards me by his shirt. His gaze shifted along with the air between us, drawing us closer. I took his features in close-up, high definition, technicolour, for my viewing only; full, bossy mouth, the curve of his nose. I dragged my thumb across his lips.

'How would you have said goodbye to me?'

He swallowed hard as his eyes took my face in, flaming. 'I would have said that leaving you was the hardest thing I have ever had to do.' His arms were curving around my waist, mine were winding around his neck. '. . . and that I would miss you so much it would nearly drive me insane.' He lifted me up and sat me on the counter. 'But then I'd give up, because I'd realise that it ain't possible for me to ever say goodbye to you, Tiara. That I won't ever want to.'

Tiara's Top Tips

- When the man you are in love with pisses off his agent, publicist and producers to abscond from his first award ceremony and tell you that he has never stopped loving you, and he isn't dating Riley (who is really quite a lovely girl), tell him the audition process to be back in your life starts tomorrow. You tell him you think he has potential.

And you throw out all your granola.

Orin

I AM ON WHAT IS POSSIBLY THE WORST first date of my life. On paper, it should be ideal. I'm at an open mic/DJ night Upstairs At The Ritzy in Brixton on a Friday night, the lights are dim, the bar is cosy, I see some familiar faces in the crowd. He is a friend of a friend, works in finance and is good looking enough for me to allow my friends to set me up with him. However, the problem is, he works in finance and is good looking enough for me to allow my friends to set me up with him. His head is so far up his ass he should be submitted to scientists as an anatomical wonder. He's talking about how brave I am to be in a field that is high input and low return, and while music photography is a novel profession – he's dabbled in photography himself, had I seen the series of pictures he took while on a firm retreat in the Alps last winter? It's such a *shame* for my law degree to go to waste. I smile and bite down the slight tingle of homicidal thoughts and tell him to pull out his phone and open his music app.

After navigating my way out of a podcast called 'Money Matters: It's A Man's World' (I give myself props for not walking out right then), I go to a Top Ten 'Urban' playlist and tell him that I have worked with six of the top artists. He chokes on his gin and tonic and tells me that he has never heard of them. He swiftly changes the subject and starts talking about how the gin he ordered – the most expensive on the menu – tastes like cat piss, and it's nothing compared to the gin he tried while touring a distillery in the Cotswolds, where, by the way, he used to summer with his family. They had a country home there. I take a large gulp of rosé, hoping it might sweeten the acetic taste of him using 'summer' as a verb.

His name is Raphael Adeniyi Akinyemi.

'It's funny,' he says, assuring me that the following sentence will be so aggressively bleak it may make part of my soul die, 'that my name is Raphael, you know, like the angel, when I can be such a demon.' He winks at me and my stomach turns.

'And I know,' he continues, 'you're thinking that Raphael may be a weird name for someone whose parents were born in Nigeria, but I think it's, like, cool that I stand apart like that, you know? My parents call me Adeniyi at home, but I may drop it. Thinking of dropping Yemi from my surname too, though. Raphael Akin sounds so much more dynamic, you know?'

I lean back on my chair, resting my elbow against the back of it, having given up any attempt at feigning interest, as I understand now that I am a third wheel on Raphael Akin's date with himself. Or, more accurately, I am an audience to Raphael Akin's date with himself. I decide that looking at it from this angle is the best way to salvage the evening; this is *immersive* entertainment, The Modern Narcissus. An afrobeat song comes on while we wait for the acts and I start to shimmy, my waist immediately called by the beat, I find comfort in the song. Raphael chuckles and says, 'Look at you go! Shout out to Burna Boy, innit!' It is, in fact, Wizkid that is playing. My small moment of solace is unceremoniously shat on. I hear a sharp choke of what sounds like laughter and my eyes drift to the other side of Raphael, where a guy sits, trying and failing to cover up a smirk with a beer bottle that is lifted to his lips, eyes unashamedly glinting in my direction. I raise a brow as a question and he only smiles wider. A dick, clearly, who thinks the possession of a sexy smile is enough to distract from the rudeness of openly eavesdropping.

I'm grateful when the band starts setting up, eager for the sound of a white boy doing an acoustic folksy cover of Lil Wayne's 'Lollipop' to distract me.

'Do you know what my favourite sound is?' Raphael Akin asks.

I smile widely. 'Is it the dulcet sound of your own baritone?'

This time, the guy on the other side of us snorts. Raphael Akin doesn't seem to notice.

'No, I was going to say the banjo. Although I was in an all-male a cappella group at my college. We were called the Knightingales – with a K. They used to call me Lancelot. I was kind of a player.'

I clamp my jaw down on itself to keep my tongue in check, and the guy on the other side catches my eye and mimics a fascinated look. He is an asshole and, unfortunately, very cute. He's sat back in his chair in a thin and loose wide-necked white T-shirt, jeans and a simple, fine gold chain that stands at stark contrast to the chino slacks and button-down shirt with a tiny embroidered man on a horse that my companion wears. The more I look, the more I think that it is a very good white T-shirt. It really takes exquisite taste for someone to choose the perfect white T-shirt to make them look good; it is truly a barometer of style. Though the shirt is loose, it is clear that it hangs on a well-built torso . . . and here I am checking out another guy while on a date. My eyes snap up to see his are already fastened to me, full of something that elicits a tweak of warmth to dive into the pit of my belly. Was he just checking me out?

The sweet heat that rushes through me is quickly dissipated when a girl sits down next to him, all shiny hair, statement heels and a cloud of heavily scented floral perfume. Our gaze splits as he turns to her and, in greeting, she plants a long, complicated kiss on him that involves so much tongue movement that it leaves the confines of their mouths. The slimy, writhing tangle of pink looks like a living, breathing entity. Her hand trails down his chest and stops just above his belt. 'So sorry, babe,' she husks, 'the shoot ran late!'

I smile. The guy's date sits down and kicks her bare, shiny legs up as she crosses them. She is wearing an anklet. This guy's date is wearing an anklet. It would then follow that I am not his type and he isn't my type. I really cannot fantasise about a guy who hooks up with a girl who wears anklets with what seems to be butterfly charms on them; my imagination simply does not have the ambit for it. I sit back in my seat, somewhat comforted by this knowledge, while Raphael talks about the multi-media crime novel he's working on: 'What if, while you're reading on an electronic device, instead of describing the car chase, there's a clip of a car-chase? I'd like to call the idea Novies. It's a novel and a movie in one.'

I wonder if I'm getting wine breath. I contemplate asking someone on our row if they have a stick of gum or cyanide.

The night takes an interesting turn when the MC announces that the next performer will be none other than the date of Hot T-shirt Guy. The urbane ease I saw in his face slips away with a swiftness.

'Wait— what?' Hot T-Shirt Guy asks quietly, with a stiff smile.

His date's perfectly puffed lips spread into a grin. 'Yeah! I wanted to surprise you!' She bops his nose with her finger, and proceeds to ascend the dingy stage, her heels and bodycon making her look like a diva doing community theatre as punishment. She takes the mic and flicks her hair and I flick a gaze to Hot T-Shirt Guy to see that his face is now comically frozen in a grim smile that barely conceals his utter terror. She clears her throat and taps the mic. It squeals in apprehension.

'Hey, guys!' She says it in the same exact tenor one might use to begin a YouTube beauty tutorial. She's fascinating. I like her. 'So, I'm Lissa. You can follow me on Lissa Underscore Loves on IG, by the way! Anyway, I'm going to be doing a Taylor Swift cover. Do you know any of her songs?' She turns to the bemused ankh wearing neo-soul specialising band, who stare at her as if she has spontaneously sprouted a second head. She frowns but is unperturbed.

'Really? Weird. This song's a classic. Anyway,' she waves her hand, 'it's fine. I'll just do it a cappella and you guys can catch up. Also, I'm giving it a fun twist, I have a little spoken word I prepared to go right in the middle!'

It is then I know that I am in love.

If it were possible for Hot T-Shirt Guy to go pale, I have no doubt that he would straight up look like someone who belonged in a Stephenie Meyer novel. As it is, his jaw is tight, and his eyes look arrested in a state of shock and horror. Well, this is wonderful.

The superstar-model has a singing voice that sounds like what candyfloss would sound like if it were a sentient character in a cartoon, with accents of drowning cat. It is so beautifully terrible. I'm having a great time, she's even managed to drown out Raphael. Her long lashes flutter as she focuses on her date, serenading him as he sits rigid on his chair, unblinking. I bop my head along to the song, and when she breaks into her spoken-word verse, which involves the line 'peng boy, don't play me like a toy', I click my hands in the air. 'Say it, sister!'

Hot T-Shirt Guy glares at me. I grin.

'Shout out spoken word!' Raphael says.

'Do you wanna get out of here?' Raphael's brazenness is staggering.

It's the interval and we're in the smoking area, where I am drinking my second glass of rosé and, judging by Raphael's increased proximity to me, where he thinks we're going to make out.

' . . . I don't live far from here, only Clapham, and I actually have a bottle of gin from that distillery. I can expand your palate. I don't have any of that fake wine you've been drinking all night. I mean, rosé? What are you, a Real Housewife? Haha. Nah, I'm joking. That ain't your vibe. Clearly. I mean, would it kill you to wear a dress on a date?' I am wearing fitted cargo pants, a black strappy crop top, an oversized button-down shirt that slips off my shoulder, sneakers and red lipstick, and he wishes he had such flawless drip. 'Haha, I'm kidding. Anyway, yeah, I can call an uber and—'

I hold a finger to my temple and release a long, loaded sigh as I try to gather what is left of my fast dwindling patience. 'Oh, man. Raphael, do you think this date is going well?'

He frowns, confused. The sheer unbridled hubris is almost endearing. 'I think it's vibsey, yeah.'

I know I should be more tactful, but rosé has eroded the ability to temper my words and my jaw is aching from keeping my laughter repressed, and his use of 'vibsey' has pushed me to the edge. So I shake my head, smile, and say, 'Lancelot is a super shit nickname to make up for yourself if you want to pretend that you were a player in university. When he proposed to Guinevere, she rejected him and he fled to a monastery where he died of grief. You might have known that I knew that if you bothered to ask me any questions, because then you might have found out that I took a history module in Ancient Mythologies. That, however, would require you to be less enamoured by the sound of your own voice, which seems to be physically impossible for you. Also *Novies*? I mean . . . objectively? That is not a thing that makes sense. I'm just telling you as someone who – okay, not exactly someone who cares about you, but somebody who cares about the state of our culture, that that idea is an abomination and an insult to the concept of both novels and movies.'

Raphael blinks at me, and, in a flash, I see the shock of rejection bypass self-reflection and sidle into something snide. 'Whatever, dude.' *Dude?*

The corner of Raphael's lip turns up in an ugly snarl that makes him look like an evil Disney prince. Finally, something zesty. Ironically, I might actually fancy him now.

'This date was a favour anyway. It was obvious from the beginning that you were intimidated by me. Plus,' he runs his eyes across me, 'why would I want to date someone whose dress sense is a cross between a stripper and a thug? You seem confused, love.'

This makes me laugh hard, because though I adore the idea of a stripper and thug aesthetic, I *know* that someone who's a walking complex racial allegory fit for a Jordan Peele movie isn't calling *me* confused.

I gather myself up and open my mouth to say just that, when a cool, low, bemused voice says, 'You're joking, right?'

Raphael and I both look towards the direction of the voice to see Hot T-Shirt Guy, leaning over the balcony, beer in hand, smirk on his face.

Raphael scowls. 'Excuse me?'

Hot T-Shirt Guy laughs and straightens up, rubbing the stubble on his chin. He shrugs. 'Sorry, it's just genuinely amazing to me that you have the audacity to say that she's intimidated by you. Like . . . of what, man? A store brand Carlton Banks?'

My hand flies to my mouth and covers my elegant gasp and snort combo while Raphael splutters 'Mind your fucking business, dude', and when this fails to get the response he desires, he says 'Man, fuck off, *nigga!*'

Our part of the balcony falls into a stunned silence that is more confounded than awkward. Hot T-Shirt Guy's eyes are bright with delight, but he fixes his face to look grave.

He flattens a hand across his heart as if stabbed, and says, with Sidney Poitier gravitas, '*Wow.* That hurts, brother.'

I clear my throat to disguise my laugh and shake my head, pulling out my own imitation of intense disappointment. 'Yeah. No need for that kind of language . . . dude.'

Raphael looks mortified. He is blinking a hell of a lot. He turns to me and opens his mouth before realising – probably by the exaggerated devastated look on my face – that there is nothing to be salvaged here nor is there any way to save face. He storms back into the bar, leaving a plume of Ralph Lauren cologne behind him.

A few more moments of confused quiet passes before laughter breaks free from both Hot T-Shirt Guy and me, bubbling over as we double over, our chuckles and wheezes and huffs layering over each other in giddy camaraderie.

'Oh my God,' I squeal. 'Did that just happen? That was kind of incredible, right? I have never seen a black man say nigga like it was a slur.'

Hot T-Shirt Guy's shoulders judder as he nods, his chuckles rolling and infectious. 'That was one of the best things I've ever seen. I am so serious. Also why did he *act* like he was saying a slur? Why did he say it like that? Nah, that was awesome. He has stage presence. Fuck a cappella, he should have been in a drama troupe.'

'Oh, actually he was. Well, an improv troupe. You missed that part because you were on a bathroom break and not able to shamelessly eavesdrop. It was all male and called Fried Whiskey.'

He stares at me evenly. 'Are you fucking with me?'

'How could I possibly make something so dark up?'

He twitches his shoulder in a shrug. 'I don't know. I don't know you.'

I raise my brows. 'Oh, okay, but you're comfortable enough to interrupt what would have been a sublime drag? By the way, you didn't have to do that. I had him.'

Hot T-Shirt Guy turns to me fully, resting against the balcony railing, his beer hanging over the bustling street below. It's a mid-summer evening and the air is cushy and thick as it tucks us into the night with a lullaby of car honks, bus wheezes and weekend chatter. The breeze is scented with fried chicken, cigarette smoke and a pungency that is derived from the sublime blend of sweet weed and sour alcohol. For the first time in the entire night I feel utterly relaxed.

'Oh, I have no doubt,' Hot T-Shirt Guy says, with a dangerously sloping smile. 'I mean "the dulcet sound of your own baritone"?' He releases a low whistle, 'Jheeze. Artful.'

I'm a sucker for a man who can quote literary genius. I bow. 'Thank you so much.'

He laughs. 'Nah, for real, I'm sorry for butting in. It was rude. It was just like an immediate automatic reaction to the sound of his voice. I mean his tone . . . like my whole body reacted to it, you know?'

I move closer and lean against the railing. 'Don't worry about it. I get it. He's annoying. He sounds like if a robot was made by Fulham bros who work at a tech start-up for the purpose of infiltrating the black community.'

Hot T-Shirt Guy snorts. 'And failing. I might report him for a hate crime.'

I choke on my sip of wine and he smiles again. Damn. He really is fine as fuck. His hair is in short twists and a fade, looking simultaneously soft and crisp, and his eyes are brimming with a brilliance that activates a long dormant warmth in my stomach, arising from embers that I had thought were long desiccated. When he smiles, I start to feel them glow.

'My man has no idea what he's talking about, anyway. Trash opinions. Rosé is great,' he says, gesturing to my glass. 'I just can't handle it. It makes me slutty.'

I shoot him a wry look. 'Huh, well I would hate to see that, considering the make-out session that I witnessed earlier. Pretty sure you violated a public health code. Where is your future Beyoncé, by the way?'

Hot T-Shirt Guy shakes his head and suppresses a smile. 'That's rude, man. I think of her more as a future Ariana Grande.' He pauses, and scratches his cheek. 'Uh, she actually left. She asked me what I thought about her performance.'

I nod soberly. 'Oh, right. And you, of course, said the truth. That it was beautiful, soul-stirring—'

Hot T-Shirt Guy bites on his lip in a clear, increased effort to repress his grin. 'I said that it was unique and powerful.'

'Powerful like it could wake the dead?'

His grin spills out. 'Wow. You're mean.'

My smile widens. 'Well, you just chased what could have been the love of my life away.'

'I can't take all the credit. I think it was a team effort. Clearly we work well together.'

The air between us draws tight, and it is only then that I am acutely aware that it is only us on the balcony. The interval is over and everyone else has gone back in for the rest of the show. Neither of us make any move to return. From the din of the bar, the muted melodies of a neo-soul song floats through the fire-escape doors and weaves itself through the chaotic symphony of the streets below. Hot T-Shirt Guy clears his throat and says, 'Do you wanna go back in?'

My belly dives in apprehension. 'Do you?'

'No.'

'Me neither.'

His face relaxes further, and the corner of his lip flicks up and pulls my pulse up with it. 'Uh, so anyway, she took it as the compliment that it was, and then she said, "Well, why don't you introduce me to the guys at your work?" Oh, I work in A&R at a record label by the way—'

'Wait, really? Where?'

He looks wary. 'Synergy Records.'

I smile. 'Oh wow, cool. I'm a photographer, specialising in music. I've toured with some of your artists.'

He visibly relaxes and steps closer to me, eyes lighting up, 'Seriously? That's dope.'

'Mmm. You thought I was gonna try and send you my Soundcloud link, didn't you?'

'I definitely, did, yes. I've been through a lot. I'm Deji, by the way.' He holds his hand out, which seems like an oddly formal thing to do, considering we've live-witnessed each other's romantic failings

258

intimately. Nevertheless, I take his hand to shake. His wraps around mine firmly and my heartbeat jounces.

'Um, nice to meet you. I'm Orin.'

His eyes widen and he steps back, as if to take me in. 'Shit, are you Orin Adu?'

'Yeah . . . how do you—'

'I love your work. Seriously, it's stunning. This may be a super nerdy thing to say, but I don't give a fuck— I follow your photography account on Instagram. I've actually got one of your prints on my wall, Burna Boy in Paris? Incredible. Your stuff is real art. Am I fanboying? I'm fanboying, innit. I'm gonna stop talking now.'

His calm urbanity fractures further and gives way to something genuine and wholesome. He holds both warm and cool in his palm, easy-going without being nonchalant, affable without being corny. The sparking embers in my belly birth a beam that I feel spreading across my face, filling up my cheeks, spilling into my eyes. I feel like I'm shining with it.

'Thank you. Seriously, I really appreciate that. Kind of makes me feel like my mum's not-so-secret perpetual disappointment in me quitting law is worth it.'

Deji nods deeply. 'Ah. I feel you. My Nigerian-Parent-Appeasement-Degree was Economics.'

'Classic. Shit— Sorry! I interrupted! Look at me getting all Raphael Akin on you.'

He shakes his head. 'Nah, not at all. That was a monologue. This is a great conversation. So, right, she tells me to tell the guys at work that I have discovered the next Rihanna, and I say, "I'm not so sure I can do that", so she says, "Well, why the fuck not?"' He does what is quite an eerie impression of her voice and holds a sassy finger up. 'And I go "I just don't think you're ready for that kind of career development."'

I nod. 'Very good.'

'Thank you. Anyway, she goes "Well maybe you're not ready for all of *this*!", to which she gestures to herself. She calls me a fuckboi and then leaves. So that's how I figured out that she was pretty much using me for my connects. Disappointing. If I'm used by a woman, I prefer it be for my body.'

I suck in some breath after I recover from my laughing fit. 'I'm sorry. I'm sorry, it's not funny.'

'It kind of is. It's fine, this was only the third date. We had nothing in common. That's the last time I DM slide on Instagram.'

I look at him incredulously. 'Are you sure?'

Deji shakes his head. 'Nope. I mean, realistically, how is anyone meant to meet anyone? I'm working all the time and dating apps make me want to shoot myself in the head. How did you meet Carlton Banks? Excuse me if I'm wrong, but he doesn't exactly seem like your type.'

I laugh. 'Ugh. Yeah, he is essentially the antithesis of what I usually go for. Which is why I went for him. My job means that I'm on the road a lot with musicians, so my type tends to be guitarists, bassists, drummers, you get the drift, right? And it pretty much always ends up the same way: heartbreak. I was complaining about my lack of luck with guys at my friend's baby shower, and one of her friends suggests that maybe it's because I date the same type of guy.

She works in finance and she's like, "You know what? I think I have someone. He's the only black guy in the office." And while corporate racism is a very real thing, now I think he's the only black guy in the office because he killed the rest. Anyway, I figure that maybe a change is good, and maybe my mother is right, and I should go for someone who wears a tie to work. Like, maybe my idea of romance is bullshit and finding someone who gets me completely is a fantasy and maybe I can put up with someone who is entirely the opposite of what I want if they treat me right. Like who needs excitement, right? Maybe it's impossible to have excitement and stability at the same time. But even my attempt to settle didn't work out. Maybe I'll just resign myself to being an extremely glamorous perpetually single artist who owns birds.'

I pause and turn to the blinking lights of the night and I taste the lie in my words. They don't fit in my mouth right; they leave a tang my palate rejects. I shake my head. 'Except I don't really want that. I want to be an extremely glamorous artist who owns a dog with a man who dotes on her. There's nothing wrong with that, right?'

Deji shoots me a small, gentle smile with eyes so soft I feel myself slowly sinking into them. I feel no need to be hoisted up.

'There's nothing wrong with that. I feel you. Dating is the fucking worst. First of all, there's so much pretence involved, right? Like, the first few dates you're basically performing a polished, cooler version of yourself. And that's even if you find someone you want to go on a date with. Then there's the pressure, you know? Both of you are on a date and you know it's for one purpose. You want it to work out. Then, when it doesn't, you're disappointed, and somehow, within that disappointment, you gotta find it in you to build yourself up to do it all over again.'

I click my fingers in the air in affirmation. 'This. Is. It! I just wish you could skip the awkward clumsy beginning part and get to the fun part. Meeting someone who just gets you. Feeling that alchemy of time and circumstance. Right place and right time with someone who isn't so emotionally unavailable that they can commit to a pet guinea pig they take on a world tour but not you having a sock drawer in their apartment.'

'That came from a deep place, huh?'

'The bassist.' My dry chuckle rolls into a groan and I splay a hand over my face. 'Shit, why do I keep putting myself through this?'

Through my fingers I see Deji shrug. 'Hope, innit. That's not a bad thing. It's not a character failing.'

My hand slips from my face and it rests on the balcony railing, next to his. We're standing so close together that our legs are bumping and grazing each other. Deji's gaze glitters with an overflow of something roiling within him and it fastens me to the spot. A comforting warmth spreads and settles itself within me.

'By the way,' he says, breaking the silence, 'stripper and thug is an excellent combo, and if this is it, you pull it off well. You look like somebody's crush off of a nineties sitcom.'

I smile. 'Thank you. That's super sweet and super specific.'

'I had a huge crush on Ashley Banks.'

Heat soars up to my cheeks. 'I see you're a big fan of Fresh Prince.'

'It was my favourite show.'

I laugh. 'Imagine if all dates were as easy as this? Learning each other's favourite childhood shows, witnessing each other's romantic fuck-ups close-up, seeing how terrible the other is at kissing—'

Deji holds up a hand in censure, face dead serious. 'You're crossing a line. That was all her. There was no saving it. I'll have you know, Orin Adu, that I am a badman lipser.'

'Bold claim.'

'I don't talk shit I can't back up.'

His voice dips in tenor and its bass reverberates through me as his eyes pin breath to the back of my throat, slowing time. The muted thumping of the Erykah Badu song playing in the bar slows and inverts in my ear, as if we're rupturing through temporal and physical confines, because I have no idea how much time has passed now and the ground beneath my feet feels immaterial compared to the knowledge that I'm coming into. I can feel the weight of what this is pressing up against my chest, I can feel the heady fullness of what this could be making my heart giddy. There have been very few moments in my life where I have been staunchly confident, but at this very second, I have the unwavering assurance that not only is Deji a badman lipser, I will also not have to take his word for it.

He smiles with those plush-looking lips that look like they're fashioned from marble and cloud. 'You know, in theory, if we go somewhere else, get another drink and maybe a bite to eat, this can count as a first date. Technically, it's kind of perfect, because we don't have each other's numbers. If we have a shit time, we can both go home and forget about it. If one person asks for the other's number and the other isn't feeling it, they are under no obligation to say yes.'

'I'm sorry, is this your way of asking me out?'

'If you're about to say no, then no.'

I grin. 'As long as you promise not to play me like a toy . . . peng boy,' I say, paraphrasing the profound words of Lissa Underscore Loves.

Deji laughs and nods, the bright in his gaze dancing. 'You're terrible.'

'And yet, you want to take me out.'

'Yes, because you're also, clearly, a really funny, smart, interesting and hot terrible person and I would like to get to know you more to truly understand the depth of your meanness.'

I press a hand to my chest and tilt my head. 'That's one of the sweetest things anyone has ever said to me. I guess now's the time to tell you that I think that you're a dick. Honestly, when I first saw you, I thought, "Ew, what an asshole". Imagine my delight when I discovered I was right.'

'Careful, or I'll fall in love with you and it will be embarrassing for the both of us.'

At the restaurant, he orders a bottle of rosé and winks at me.

I am on what is possibly the best date of my life.

Alagomeji

OUR PRINCESS GREW UP ON NOBLE STREET. A road on a slight incline in the heart of Lagos, hidden within a dense metropolis-within-a-metropolis known as Yaba. In the seventies, it is a heaving, cosmopolitan hub that's beginning to shirk the shackles of colonialism. The old red-slate roofs and roman columns that murmur a staid 'properness' sit beside new concrete concoctions; modern, rambunctious and geometrically staggering. They hollered the rise of a new Nigeria. These concrete buildings are patriotic, loyal to their blood. They are re-setting the tone and realigning the country back to its roots, because, if there is anything Nigerians like to do, it is to shout. Eko oni baje. In the swaggering Lagosian way, *that*, of course, is all that matters – that 'Lagos will never spoil'. This mantra is concentrated in Yaba, for here we are in the nucleus of the nucleus, the heart of the heart. And in the heart of the heart, love is rich and in abundance.

This love is overwhelmingly present in an apartment at the top of a block of flats on Noble Street where our princess dwells. This is her tower, her castle. Our princess's name, translated from Yoruba, unfurls into an iteration of 'God Loves Me'; and, indeed, she is cherished with a pure affection. She lives with six family members: a doting, slightly overbearing father, whose firmness is undercut with a sure and tender fondness; a sweet, soft mother, who extends her care to lost children in the neighbourhood; and four siblings, two sisters and two brothers. She is the fourth born and love is poured into her. Love gives our princess space to be herself. Her tongue is fast and sharp and holds a gravitas far beyond her years. It exposes injustice and shames her elders. Throughout her life, she will stand up for what's right and leave indelible marks of good on the world. For it is not that she is a princess who happens to live on Noble Street; she is the person whom it is named for. Somehow, twenty or thirty years before her birth, God placed into the hearts of the town-planners, who set about to construct that street, a *knowledge* that this particular street should be noble. Their self-proclaimed and ignorant colonialist superiority might have induced them to think that they were naming the road after some English commander or civil servant, but they were wrong. The street was named after our princess. It was named after her heart, one that is both strong with integrity and soft with kindness. Noble Street was named in honour of her tender fierceness.

At ten years old, our Noble princess is sent away to secondary in a boarding school in Abeokuta, a two-hour drive from Lagos. From afar it seems this is a draconian punishment, a *banishment* – and from her tears and kicks, it would seem so. However, the truth is much more banal, and somewhat disappointing for the purposes of this dramatic tale. She was sent away because that is what those who purported to love their children did in those days. Love was seen as something that should be slightly fearsome, love was Old Testament, forty years in the desert. Love was seen as force that should merely *push* not pull. So off she went, a little gangly-legged girl, technically a year too young for her new adventure, because she had skipped a grade. Yes, she is smart too.

A poet would describe Abeokuta as a hilly, rustic town of powdery red earth and trees so thickly and richly green it is as if they would have provided a plush rug for the gods. A tourism officer might call Abeokuta a 'shabby idyll', and refer to the goats meandering through traffic as 'pastoral appeal seamlessly blending into the urban'. To a city girl like our princess, it is a dingy, glorified village where people stare too much. What is *green* when you could have the grey of concrete? Soil when you could have pavement? Blue skies when you could have smog? Lagos is a complicated handshake and a jig, it is a warm, teasing insult meant to denote familiarity. Abeokuta is a yawn and a stretch, a bulge of the belly after eating pounded yam. Languid, it is an embrace that can make you feel overheated, suffocated. This feeling is compounded by the fact that the town is underneath rocks, huge rocks, so much so that the town is called Under The Rock (the Yoruba people are naturally literary). The huge mountainous boulders both surround the town and serve as its higgledy-piggledy foundations. Our princess swears to shine through the shadows of the rocks, to not become slow and lazy from the heat.

★　　★　　★

Herbert McCaulay Street is a stone's throw from Noble Street. It is on this street that our prince lives in the seventies. The street is named after the great Nigerian nationalist statesman, who, in response to the British colonial government's statement that they had the 'true interests of the natives at heart', once retorted, 'as the dimensions of "the true interests of the natives at heart" are algebraically equal to the length, breadth and depth of the white man's pocket'. When our prince got older, he decided he would only wear traditional Yoruba attire when travelling for work internationally. 'Let them know who I am,' he would say. He was the son of a man who changed his surname from a white man's 'Cole', which had been assigned to his ancestors, to his father's first name, *Babalola*, which means 'Father is honour'. In a freshly free Nigeria, his new surname also lives freshly free, heralding a reclamation of rightful ownership, a repossession of the ancestral. Father is honour, motherland is honour.

Our young prince would grow to be one of the most honourable men among men. His first name, translated, is a version of 'God loves me' and, just like our princess, he is kept and protected by God's love. He lives with seven family members: a quiet, gentle, peace-loving father; a powerful, firm, formidable mother, who also extends her care to lost children in the neighbourhood; and five siblings – four brothers and a sister. He is the fourth born (two of his brothers are twins) and love staggers through to him, eked out through the gaps between troublemaking, bullying brothers, who soak up attention and emotion. Yet, our boy does not starve – God loves him, after all. So, where our prince's brothers lack, he fulfils; in their brutality, he finds in himself gentleness, in their attacks, he cultivates a firm protectiveness. It is an earthy, organic love, thick as honey straight from the comb. You may risk being stung, but it is all the sweeter once accessed.

Our prince loves to play. He is rough-and-tumble and skinny and scrawny and quick with the quips. One day after school, when he is ten years old, our prince is outside in the neighbourhood kicking a football around with his friends, all elbows and knees and crumpled shirts. He kicks the ball and it lands squarely on the head of a girl who is walking along the street. It thuds against her long, thick black plaits. She is holding hands with someone older with a similar face to her – her older sister. The girl drops her sister's hand, rubs her head and gives our prince the most eviscerating look he has ever seen in his young life. The girl looks his age, maybe a little younger, but she has an imposing air, one of authority and regality. Before he can release a stuttered 'sorry', she throws the ball at him and shouts, 'Watch where you are going. Ah, ah. Are you blind? With that your big eyes!' She picks up her elder's hand and storms off, as if *she* is the one in charge. The prince is impressed, despite himself. He kicks the ball to his friend.

At eleven years old, our scruffy prince is sent away to secondary in a boarding school in Abeokuta. It is a place with an abundance of space, far from the pressures his brothers create, and where his muscles can flex. It is a place he can be himself and grow unimpeded. He reckons it will be an adventure.

Noble Street and Herbert McCaulay Street are situated in a subsection of Yaba known as Alagomeji – two clocks – named after the two clock towers that punctuate the area. It is a place marked by time and, for love, the time has to be *right*. If you ask our princess what she thought when she first properly met the prince, she will probably shrug and release a somewhat coy smile, and say she doesn't know and why are you asking her that? She's busy. If you ask the prince, he will laugh and say, 'She's bluffing. Of course she noticed me. Afro like mine? Cool dude like me?' If our princess is near him when he says this – which will most likely be the case, because most things he says, he says for her amusement – she will laugh hard, scoff and retort: 'What afro? You were already losing your hair, my friend.'

For the first two years in secondary school, he was the playful and benevolently mischievous boy who she rolled her eyes at often. In her third year in school, his desk was next to hers. By the fourth year, they were best friends. They talked for hours and hours about everything, anything, and there was laughing, so much laughing. Their sentences would run into and roll around each other, their spirits compounded into their words, each conversation pulling them closer and closer together. This was to remain years later, with their conversational layers and loops running so deep into the night that their eldest child would stomp downstairs to the living room and command them to 'Keep! It ! Down! You are laughing too loud!' Not knowing that it was a blessing to be kept up by her parents' giggling rather than fighting, not knowing that she was witnessing a unique trick of the combination of love and time; the ability to keep one young. You will mature and your relationship will develop, but love has the habit of keeping a part of you evergreen, retaining within you an adolescent flirtatious giddiness. Ten, twenty, thirty, forty years after meeting, she will still blush when he compliments her or when he playfully chucks her chin. He will still seek to impress her, make it his mission to put a smile on her face, and he will still feel staggered that he is the one she chose.

At school, the young prince and princess spend all their time together and even share a keyholder for their locker-keys; the kind of nonsensical thing that happens when you want to create a reason to be around someone. When you ask either of them how their friendship came about, they will shrug. It just happened. They just happened to be two Alagomeji kids with different versions of the same name sent to the same boarding school in Abeokuta. Their desks just happened to be next to each other. They just happened to want to talk to each other all the time, to balance each other out; his humour, her grace and their integrity matching up and melding.

Their feelings mature faster than their ability to recognise them for what they are. When someone is so woven into your life, you take that warmth and that presence for granted, and the prince felt the chill when the princess started casually courting a friend of his. His tropical island was suddenly overtaken by a cool breeze when, one day at lunch, he saw his friend buy her a Fan Ice. From afar, an iced dairy product probably does not have the same romantic gravitas as a dozen roses or the ability to sweep the princess off her feet, but the prince knew his friend well. He knew it was a statement. It was a statement that made his stomach turn, as if he was the one who had ingested a Fan Ice that had been out in the sun too long, bought from a sweating man with a rusty cart. That particular friend was a known miser. If you borrowed a kobo from him, he would demand it back as soon as you gave it to a seller. If a gust from his window blew on you on a hot day, he'd blame you for his sweat.

The miser was around an inch taller than the prince, and the prince had begun to wonder if he'd missed a trick in not wearing those new heeled loafers that were in vogue then. He hated them, but suddenly he wondered if this was a necessary addition to his wardrobe. It may have afforded him some advantage over the miser. The prince liked the miser, despite his ways, as they had fun together and he was a good laugh, but now? Oh, he hated him. It was a particularly warm day, but our prince felt cold. He almost shivered. The princess smiled at the miser, and though the prince recognised the smile as a thin replica of what was usually reserved for him, he could have sworn the cool breeze had turned into a Baltic blast. It felt as if he might contract hypothermia. His pulse staggered.

That night he couldn't sleep. He tossed and turned as the image of the princess and the Fan Ice churned around in his head as if in his own internal picturehouse, dedicated only to the worst of films. The next day, during a free period, while they were sitting on a crumbling wall somewhere on the school campus, the prince, unable to keep his disconcertion in, interrupted their usually easy, aimless rambling.

'Why did miser buy you Fan Ice?'

Princess blinked at him, and then laughed. 'What do you mean? Because he wanted to, na.'

The prince tried to make his voice sound like he wasn't grumbling. He had a feeling he'd failed. 'He doesn't want to buy anything for anyone.'

Princess shrugged. 'Eh. Maybe he was feeling generous. You know he got three lashes the other day for insubordination. Maybe he had a concussion.'

'They didn't lash his head.'

'Why are you acting like somebody lashed your head?'

'Forget it.'

Silence.

Princess cleared her throat. 'He said he wants to take me to the picturehouse next week. You know he is thinking of going to university in England? Like me.'

The prince felt faint. He did not feel like eating at lunch. He *always* felt like eating. And though the beans the canteen served up tasted like stewed soil at the best of times, it was better than the taste of putrefied Fan Ice that somehow took over his tongue whenever he tried to consume something. He felt as if he was going to topple off the wall. The truth was, he always felt like a frog perched by a flower next to her. This was more a comment on her than him, because he *liked* himself . . . but her? She made everything feel light and bright. He liked to be around her light and bright. She saw him, directly, clearly, and he'd never felt like he'd been seen before, not really. At home there were too many people for eyes to take in and so, by the time they got to him, they were tired. But she saw him breezily and he bloomed under it, grew taller, like a sunflower stretching for the sky. And she was smart, as we know. Our prince was also smart, but she was *smart*, life-smart, wise-smart. She saw a problem and immediately knew how to fix it; she saw his bad mood and would make a list of the reasons why he should haul himself out of the pit. She didn't know it yet, but she was at the top of that list for him. She was the beam of light shining into an abyss of a well.

Our prince blinked, and though there were many things he wanted to say to her, all that came out of his mouth was, 'Why didn't you tell me you wanted Fan Ice? I would have bought it for you.'

Our princess raised a brow. 'I didn't know you cared if I wanted a Fan Ice or not.'

'Of course I care. I care about everything you want.'

The princess looked at him for what felt like months. The prince felt sure he felt the season shift from Rainy to Harmattan. Then she looked out, to the deep, green hills and rocks, as if seeking their aged wisdom. Eventually, she turned back to him. He freed the air he hadn't realised had been held captive in his mouth.

She shrugged. 'The Fan Ice even gave me a stomach-ache. I think he bought one that was expiring to save money.'

At seventeen and eighteen, the prince and princess both set out for university. She boards a plane for the first time in her life and heads to England, while he loads his rickety car and drives the three hours it takes to get to the town of Ifé. There is a tacit agreement that they will stay in touch, but there is also a concealed fear from both that the other will grow numb and forget.

At university they both explore new universes. The prince melds into his new world easily, for though it is a new world, it is really the old world, for Ifé is the root of his people, the heart of Yorubaland. At the University of Ifé, he thrives like a trueborn on his own turf.

Charismatic, smart, likeable, with a strong sense of right and wrong, it's as if all he is destined to be is honed here; he belongs.

The princess, on the other hand, is hurtled into a foreign land with cold air and cold faces. She works gruelling, thankless jobs to put herself through university for people who look through her or stare at her too much. Though love was poured into her, by the time it was her turn to attend university, her family's money had run out. She makes it her duty to replenish it. In the first two months, she stays with friends of friends, family of family, or in tiny hostel rooms with thin blankets and thinner smiles and tells herself it will be worth it. That, in this sunless land, she could still shine. This does not stop the chill of lonely from setting in or the dark from descending. Then, on one particularly bleak morning, she receives a letter. She recognises the handwriting, elegant yet sturdy, deliberate yet breezy, and slightly rotund, like a hearty chuckle. From the stamp she notes that it must have been sent around two months ago, with the Nigerian postal system plus the international fees delaying receipt. She sits on her narrow, slim bed and rips the envelope open.

I bet you don't need Fan Ice where you are, she reads.

In the dull, she glows.

The letters build. Within six months, she has stacks. They are more than enough to insulate her from the lonely. They are thick and sturdy enough to form the foundation of a home, they form a kind of insulation between the walls so that she is warmed with love, and somehow, somehow, both of them sourced the only paper in the world that doesn't turn to dust, the only ink that doesn't fade, so their words remain today as fresh as the moment they wrote them. What they say to each other on these ancient parchments is between them, a sacred scripture, and, in reverence, we shall keep it unarticulated. However, its sentiments live and flow through them, in the world they build, coating the walls of their city, on a hill, so that, from afar, visitors see a great palace with beautiful, decadent, flowered vines twining through the gates, spilling over its fences.

Of course, by now they realise that they are in love. It has been an immutable fact for a while, but the recognition of it is encouraged by the miles between them. Distance draws them closer. It wasn't so much that they tripped and fell in love, it was more that it was always their reality and in their atmosphere. A fish does not recognise its need for water until it is gasping for it.

Our prince graduates and moves to England. In their time apart they have honed themselves and discovered more of their individual power. Their self-awareness only makes their love richer, and they feel that, together, they have enough to build a kingdom together. And so they do. Their marriage is officiated back in Yaba, in the area with the two clocks, two lifetimes marrying together. Our prince and princess become king and queen.

They plant their love into their kingdom, and it grows, abundantly, into a thick forest with trees so plush and green they could be woven together to form a blanket for the angels. The fruit it bears is delicious, full and sweet, and anyone who bites into it is blessed, because God loves them. They have so much love that the fruits can feed surrounding towns and villages. The king and queen invite people in, feed them, and the people often find themselves fortified, replenished and indulged with enough good health and good spirits to go and start their own kingdoms. They start a family, three girls who grow up underneath the warm light of their affections, who understand laughter as a language and friendship as an active ingredient in true romance. The natural arguments that occur can be fierce, but the foundations of the house are built on years-old mystic paper, and so they are strong and the walls do not crumble, though they may tremble.

The eldest of their daughters is so inspired by the king and queen that it forms how she sees the world. She recognises the mundane mystique of romantic love that is ubiquitous at a glance, but, when you look closer, you notice the tessellation of understanding, patience, friendship and attraction. She sees both the miracle of the spark igniting and also the working, because it takes work, and for the work to work, you have to respect each other, like each other. She is fascinated by how much romantic love can soften a hard life, highlight the best of you, not condemn the worst of you. It is a gift she cherished witnessing with the king and queen, and so she made it her mission to capture a little of it and gift it to others; the hope of it all, the light of it all. The king and queen brought love to life for her. She saw it up close, in vivid, bold, bright strokes of pigment. She saw the nobility, its integrity, its rock-like stolidity in rich, illuminating colour. In sharing it, she hopes to make the world a little brighter.

Time was constructed with love in mind. It is why the moments before a desired kiss stretch, why when your lips are finally introduced with another pair, it feels as if they have wanted to meet for some time, and why a day with your loved one can feel like an eternity on turbo-speed. Achingly, deliciously slow, but too fast, over too quick, melting between too-hot fingers. Time and love are intertwined, they are both measures of life, they are the two clocks. And, for love to operate as it should, it is imperative that the timing should be right. Just as it is in this story.

Author's Note

WHEN CHOOSING WHICH TALES would form a basis for my stories, I was careful to select those with themes that I could draw out and weave upon. As many of the original folktales and myths are so ancient, they're impossible to date, and, naturally, they were rife with misogyny and violence and were created within heavily patriarchal contexts. With this book I was able to re-imagine these stories in a manner that meant that the women were centred; it was less about being chosen and more about their agency in allowing themselves to love and be loved.

Naleli's story, for instance, was originally from a tale entitled 'How Khosi Chose His Wife', within which the heroine is a woman whose extreme beauty was hidden by her parents with a cloak of crocodile skin to protect her from roving eyes. While hidden in a bush (extremely creepy!), Khosi spies on her washing in her pool, disrobed of her crocodile skin, and proceeds to 'fall in love' with her and selects her as his bride. In the original story, the woman has little consent, and the prince is predatory. However, with the crocodile skin, I saw the potential to write a story about a woman who is judged and treated differently throughout her life because of her external looks, but eventually she learns to love the skin she's in, without having to shed anything. Another example is Yaa's original story; she was a shallow, ditzy young woman damned to the land of the dead for choosing to marry a rich, glamorous and handsome stranger, instead of the noble prince from her village that her parents had chosen for her. The moral of the story was essentially 'parents know best'. I decided to invert the tale to make it one about agency and resistance against parental expectations, which can sometimes suppress our essence. It's about not being punished for exercising autonomy but rather being empowered by it, a theme evident in many of the tales.

This book provided me the wonderful opportunity to play with myths, stretching them into newer versions and worlds far removed from where they began, while still ensuring they remained tethered to their roots. Psyche and Eros had me trying to cram Olympus into a sleek office building, imagining what Cupid would be like if he was a charming media bro. The original story of Zhinu is called 'The Cowherd and the Weaver Girl', in which both characters represent stars (and, incidentally, is another story in which a man walks in on a woman bathing naked in a pool). It was so fun asking questions such as: what if she wove songs? What if I consolidate myth and reality and make her a star on earth; a popstar who doesn't know her worth? Also, how do I bring a cow into this new story alongside bridges formed from magpies?

With others I got to delve into and twist history. In Nefertiti, I got to meld fact with fantasy in a way that was thrilling for a casual history nerd like me. The mystery surrounding the specifics of the life of Nefertiti gave me so much ambit to play with. I turned Ancient Egypt (Kemet) into a dystopian metropolis where the gods were mortal. I distilled Ancient Egyptian philosophy and built a world from it. Ma'at was a goddess of justice, harmony and balance, and Isfet was a philosophic concept of chaos, injustice and evil. I wanted to raise questions of justice: where does it lie, and what does it mean in a world that *is* evil? Can justice exist in a universe where that which is dark is posited as light? Ultimately, in the story, we see justice side with Nefertiti, a woman who fights to end oppression through morally questionable acts. Though a romance, it was such a privilege to have the room to tease out complexities like these, even in a short story.

In Siya, I had the opportunity to explore a lesser known Ancient African civilisation: the Soninke people of Wagadou. Here, I remixed legend so Siya was no longer a helpless 'virgin' damsel who was to be sacrificed to a snake-god and saved by her betrothed – an army officer named Maadi. In our story, she leads an army and is far from helpless. In our story, they seek to save each other.

Though some stories are more closely tied to their original inspirations than others, it was so exciting to find ways to retain themes and homages while re-shaping them with my imagination, being adventurous with genre and tone. I had the privilege of reading a swathe of folktales from so many different cultures when curating which to work with for this book, and the ones I left out (with much reluctance) are because I feared I would not be able to de-tangle themes without totally robbing them of the rich cultures they were sourced from, and thus doing them an injustice.

Ultimately, all my stories are so very precious to me, and the ten stories inspired by myth and folktales are made all the more special by the research I got to do to make them, discovering and learning about worlds that weren't my own, and challenging myself to relate and meld them to what I know. Though they are my stories – poured from the heart – I owe so much to the cultures that provided the seeds and inspiration. They wouldn't be mine without their existence. It was such an honour and privilege to have the opportunity to breathe a new sort of life into them: I hope I did them justice.

Sources of Inspiration

Ọṣun: Yoruba myth and religion, Nigeria

Scheherazade: 1,001 Nights, Persia

Psyche: Eros and Psyche, Ancient Greece

Attem: Ituen and the King's Wife, Calabar peoples, Nigeria

Yaa: The Princess' Wedding, Asante Tribe, Ghana

Siya: Ancient Soninke Legend, Soninke People, modern Mali, Senegal, Guinea, The Gambia and Southern Mauritania

Naleli: How Khosi Chose a Wife, Lesotho

Nefertiti: Ancient Egyptian fact and myth

Zhinu: The Cowherd and the Weaver Girl, China

Thisbe: Pyramus and Thisbe, Mesopotamia

Acknowledgements

Firstly, I would like to acknowledge that I am writing the acknowledgements for this book. That's a big deal, right? Let's take a moment to imbibe that. There were times (in front of my computer, in tears) when I struggled to picture that happening. In those times, though, I reached for the things that would pull me through the mire of insecurity, doubt and fear. This is, really, a list of these things.

My faith in God. I am strengthened through Him.

The fact that my dear editor, Katie Packer, somehow believed in me enough to carry this idea to fruition. Katie, you are a bad bitch, so smart, so savvy, so emotionally intuitive, and always there to assuage my rambled hysterical rants and bring me forth with a fortifying Beyoncé quote and to giggle over a shared celebrity crush. Somehow you saw me so thoroughly that you were able to bring out the best of me, trigger me to excavate my potential, and therefore making me grow as an artist. I could not have done this without your technical and professional support, sure, but I also couldn't have done this without having you as a teammate, pulling me up when I felt as if I was stuck, and reminding me why I do what I do, and what I *can* do. You are such a force and I cannot wait till you are running this industry. You are so crucial and so powerful. One of the best parts about this process is gaining you as a friend for life.

That my literary agent, Juliet Pickering, read a short story four years ago and somehow believed in it enough to catapult me into a literary career and sign me. I was in the middle of fixing up my manuscript for public consumption when she said, 'F*** it, I'm going to sign you'. Obviously I am paraphrasing (barely), but this is what it felt like – a pure and potent *faith* in me. I am so grateful that it was you that helped breathe life into my dreams. Thank you so much for responding to my typo-ridden, anxious, 2 a.m. emails with such steady calm and patience. Thank you for very sweetly, very gently kicking my ass when I needed it to be done. Thank you so much for being a beacon of support emotionally and professionally. Your guidance is forever appreciated.

That my TV agent, Jessica Stewart, was waiting on me to finish this book! Ha! I would like to thank you for your patience and encouragement and allowing me the space and time to write this. So glad to have you on my team.

That my mum and dad did not emigrate to the UK for me to be a flop! Mummy and Daddy, Olukemi and Olufemi Babalola, I adore you so much. As I write this, I'm crying a little, and I am glad I am not writing it in front of you, Mother, because I am sure you would roll your eyes. You are both everything to me. I would not have my career without your support. Since I was little, you have always told me I could do whatever I set my mind to. Thank you both for seeing the whole of me, and not trying to confine me to prescriptive notions of success – thank you for knowing that success is being able to be myself totally, and to do so with kindness, honesty and integrity. You are the best cheer team a girl could ever ask for. Every ounce of confidence that I have in myself is substantiated by your love and faith in me. Thank you, Daddy, for insisting on sending a WhatsApp blast to everyone on my phone with a link to my book. Thank you for talking everyone's ear off about 'your daughter, the writer', ever since my very first newspaper article. Thank you, Mummy, for fortifying my backbone and for being there for every late night, for every frustrated cry, for every meltdown, with firm softness – telling me to cry it out and get over it, because I am destined for greatness and what was the alternative? *Not* achieve everything I've dreamt of? Ko possible. E se, ma. E se, sir. Everything I do is empowered by your love.

The faith and support of my friends.

Amna Khan – you know me almost better than anyone else, and your pep talks are second to none. Your encouragement is spiritual and deep and fortifying, and when I speak to you, I always feel renewed, well fed. We have been friends since we were fifteen years old, and you have seen me grow, seen me talk about this very moment. Thank you for never seeing my talk of my dreams as anything other than an assured prediction of the future. I am certain that going through this journey with you has made me a better, more positive person. I love you.

Folarin Akinmade, who proofread my first short story, 'Netflix & Chill', and has been the best brother a girl could ask for.

Sase Aimiuwu, my ride or die, whose humour literally carries me through and embraces me. You are sunlight.

My delightful Hannah Williams, who saw me crouching in front of my laptop secretly writing while working at [redacted]; Gena-Mour Barrett (the yacht girl, the yacht!); Kechi Nwagou (your random texts of support lifted me up at times I needed it the most); Asha Mohamed, the first reader of my novels EVER, you are my sister and I know you know how I feel, so let's cut out the mushy crap; Oyinlola Agboola: sis, I am so grateful for the laughter you bring into my life; my fairy godmuva, Camilla Blackett, who literally let me run to her in LA when London was just too much (I needed the clarity in order to write, and I will be forever indebted to your generosity and love. You are truly an angel); other members of my LA family: Tanya Fear (LOL. Love you, Zim queen) and Alanna Bennett (fellow romcom lover and hopeful romantic); Obioma Ugoala, for messages of support when I needed it the most; Charlet Wilson, for a brilliant, generous heart and light that constantly inspires me. For the bants, the belief and the relief from the darkness of the world. To the spice rack, Kieran Yates, Jo Fuertes and Kirby Partington – thank you for all the encouragement and the laughs!

I am so grateful to Nikesh Shukla for his constant support over the years, from being a key voice in encouraging me to apply to the short competition that would catapult my career, to his unwavering belief in me. You're the best and the industry is lucky to have you.

Acknowledgements

The elite PPE!! Emma, Bridge, Dani and Can. The laughter, the memes, the unconditional support of each other, has truly made me feel safe and secure in an industry I am still trying to find myself in. It is so comforting to know that, after a hard day I can come to you and be held. You are a group of truly extraordinary women and I am so blessed to know you.

My big sister, Daniellé Scott-Haughton. Don't start crying on me when you read this. My pastor, my sis, my rock. Thank you for prayers, thank you for your belief, thank you for letting me cry to you on the phone during the hardest, toughest periods of my life. Through heartache and trials, you have been there steadfastly to hold me, as you have been there to celebrate my successes and joys. I hope you know that you are an angel, and so special, and I am so blessed that God brought you into my life.

Candice Carty-Williams! Literary baddie! Do you know what a flex it is to say that I can ring you up and just say, 'Can, I'm losing my mind', and for you to say, 'It's okay, babe. You're allowed to, it's normal.' You have quite literally been there from the beginning. You started the literary competition that launched my career, and your penchant for bringing people in is incredible. Thank you for your grace, kindness, for being my sister and for being my friend.

If I mentioned all the friends who supported me, this part would be as long as the book, but I want you to know that every message, every comment, every boost has been so monumentally important to me. I cherish you all, and I feel so privileged to count you all as part of my life. I hope I can bless you as you have blessed me.

My (blood) sisters, Bomi Babalola and Demi Babalola. I love you.

Let's not be corny about it. It is what it is. Same genes and that. You both inspire me in so many ways. Bomi, you have the sweetest, softest heart that belies a strong core. Demi, you have a strong exterior that belies the softest soul. You are both extraordinary women and I am so proud to be your big sister.

My cousins, the Magbagbeolas, the Adedirans and our Abiona baby. I love you all and I am so grateful to count you as my extended siblings. Shout out to Ore and Ibukun. Gang gang.

My followers on Twitter, who have seen me grow over the years. You are some of the sweetest, kindest, funniest and most supportive people. Writing is often a solitary job, and I needed Twitter to let off some steam, have a laugh, talk shit. You all have allowed me that space to be myself, and you *embraced* me. You amplified my voice. You may not even know, but your messages of support and encouragement, the funny memes or references, have dried tears, have bolstered me through depression, have picked me up from a mire of self-pity. I am so grateful to have you on my team. Love you guys, truly.

To the young black women who sent me messages telling me what this book means to them, who saw themselves in me and made the time to encourage me. Your kindness inspires me from the soul. Thank you. This is for you.

Without the aforementioned, this book would not exist. This is what I clung to and this is what propelled me. I am grateful for all of it. Thank you for being part of my journey.

If you loved *Love in Colour*, why not try *Honey & Spice*?

The sharp-tongued (and secretly soft-hearted) Kiki Banjo is an expert in relationship-evasion and likes to keep her feelings close to her chest. As the host of the popular student radio show, *Brown Sugar*, it is her mission to make sure the women who make up the Afro-Caribbean Society at Whitewell University also do not fall into the mess of 'situationships', players and heartbreak.

But when Kiki meets the distressingly handsome and charming newcomer Malakai Korede – who she has publicly denounced as 'The Wasteman of Whitewell' – her defences are weakened, and her heart is compromised. A clash embroils them in a fake relationship to salvage both their reputations and save their futures, and soon she finds herself in danger of falling for the very man she warned her girls about.

A funny and sparkling debut, *Honey & Spice* is full of delicious tension and romantic intrigue that will make you weak at the knees.

Available from Waterstones, Amazon and all other good retailers